RAVE REVIEWS

" Oy vey. Be prepared for the wild ride that is *Our Jewish Robot Future*. With author Leonard Borman acting as chief carney, you will be tossed and turned, amused and edified, and in the end, left slightly dizzy.*"*

—LORNA LANDVIK,
AUTHOR OF ANGRY HOUSEWIVES EATING BON BONS

" In *Our Jewish Robot Future*, Leonard Borman has woven an instant classic with venues ranging from the Garden of Eden to the fields of modern fertility science. Not only has Borman written a brilliantly entertaining, smart, and mindful allegory of faith and existence, he has found that eleventh commandment most of us didn't know was missing: "Thou shall not nosh thy brother." Readers won't nosh on this inspired novel, but wolf it down in one or two helpings.*"*

—NEAL KARLEN, AUTHOR OF THE STORY OF YIDDISH

" So Nu! Sit, relax, bite into this genre-bending, spicy stew of a novel. First-timer Borman skillfully blends space travel, bible studies, robotics, and senior citizen sex into a delicious and thought-provoking tsimmes. Elements of Asimov, Michael Chabon's *Yiddish Policeman's Union*, the Coen Brothers *Serious Man* and Dr. Ruth, add fragrance and nuance to the dish. Enjoy, bubbeleh.*"*

—DAVID UNOWSKY,
FORMER HUNGRY MIND/RUMINATOR BOOKSTORE OWNER

" Leonard Borman's first novel is a hilarious blend of history, theology, science fiction and satire that would equally make both Mel Brooks and Monty Python proud. His debut novel *Our Jewish Robot Future* is uniquely funny, thought provoking and just plain fun to read. Readers will be drawn in by his keen sense of humor and his excellent and engaging sense of narrative style. I truly suspect we will be reading many more good books from this author in our coming *Robot Future*.*"*

—M.L. LIEBLER, AUTHOR OF WIDE AWAKE IN SOMEONE ELSE'S DREAM
(WAYNE STATE UNIVERSITY PRESS), AND EDITOR OF WORKING WORDS:
PUNCHING THE CLOCK & KICKING OUT THE JAMS (COFFEE HOUSE PRESS)

" Entertaining, creative and unusual, Leonard Borman's *Our Jewish Robot Future* is not only a refreshing spiritual take on the story of human creation, but a cautionary tale for nice Jewish boys and girls: give your nice Jewish parents the grandchildren they deserve … or else. "

—WENDY SHANKER, AUTHOR OF ARE YOU MY GURU?

" Leonard Borman has created that rarest of beings: a madcap sci-fi novel that will appeal equally to talmudic scholars and to what my grandparents would refer to as the goyim. What can I say, it's the definitive Jewish robot novel of our time! There are robots. There are Jews. There are Jewish robots. What more could you possibly want, you yold? "

—MICHAEL RUBENS, AUTHOR OF THE SHERIFF OF YRNAMEER

" A brilliant merging of Sci-Fi comedy and Midwestern charm. A real reason for Detroit to smile again. "

—LAURA C. MCGOWAN, PH.D, SENIOR HELP FORUM

B

" For anyone wishing to take a flight of sci-fi adventure, Leonard Borman's *Our Jewish Robot Future* will meet the need. It falls into that literary genre that seeks out the ideal and wished-for land of promise—Shangrila, Never Never Land, Narnia. Here, our hero Alex Haralson seeks and finds the Garden of Eden—and what a surprise he gets! This novel is not suited for pragmatists but for readers eager to suspend their unbelief. "

—REGINALD KEITH, AUTHOR OF THE MALCONTENTS

" Watch out Woody Allen, Leonard Borman is taking over a piece of your Jewish funny guy territory. But instead of a schlemiel, Margaretta, the Italian-born narrator in Borman's page-turning novel is a fire-breathing Jewish mother, plotting to marry off her self-centered kids and reap some grandchildren—like any Jewish mother—except she's bawdy, lusty and witty, and Borman gets her right on. Wow, what a woman. Alex, her husband is no schlemiel, either, he's an accountant, who proves heroic in the face of abduction by extra terrestrial robots (well, they're Jewish relatives, after-all), cannibals on the planet Airets, the great god Yahweh, and most important of all, his wife. The reader will enjoy a romp though the universe, which covers the gamut of marital and existential questions, ones we all want to confront but just haven't dared. The glossary, alone, is worth the price of the book. "

—GAY RUBIN, EDITOR AND FOUNDER OF MICHIGAN HOT APPLES

OUR JEWISH ROBOT FUTURE

our jewish robot future

A NOVEL ABOUT THE GARDEN OF EDEN
AND THE CYBORGIAN TRANSFORMATION
OF THE HUMAN RACE

::

leonard borman

Fourth edition published December 2022

Calumet Editions, 6800 France Avenue South, Suite 370, Edina, MN 55435.
ISBN — 978-1-960250-00-1

Book design by Mighty Media Inc., Minneapolis, MN
Cover and Interior: Chris Long

10 9 8 7 6 5 4

dedicated to

Abraham and Molly Borman. Pioneers to America.

acknowledgements

My wife, Bobbie, my 7 children, my 14 grandchildren, my family, my editor and publisher, and everyone who encouraged me to write. Thank you.

GLOSSARY

Abeshter—A fatherly God. When an ignorant comment is heard, look heavenward with a pleading hand and say, *Abeshter, Heirst.*

Antenata—Ancestor.

Arroganza—Arrogance.

Baalebusteh—Head of a household who rules swinging an iron fist.

Beemah—An elevated part of the synagogue from where services are lead.

Beth NeeSaw Emet—House or Cong. Lofty Truth.

Bubbe Meinsah—A story of dubious truth. Literally a grandmother's story.

Bubbelah—An affectionate way to call close family members or friends.

Caballero—A Gentleman.

Chazzerei—Mental garbage (literally pig's feed).

Chutzpah—Unmitigated gall. A millionaire asking for money to pay utility bills.

Divar Torah—A talk by a leader on the Torah incorporating a life lesson.

Draykop—Literally a head spinning. The person causing the spinning.

Drek—Literally garbage.

Dumkopf—In hillbilly speak, a dumb butt.

Eusthenopteron—Fish, 385 million years ago that emerged onto land.

Farbisseneh—A sour or bitter person. Frau Farbisseneh was a character in the *Austin Powers* movies.

Fardrayt—Confused, mixed-up, or distracted.

Farmidsht—Confused to a point when you don't know the day of the week.

Farputst—Dressed to the nines. Wearing a tuxedo to a grandchild's first birthday party.

Farshtunkener—Figuratively a rotten and smelly person.

Fayggela—Literally a bird. Used by some referring to a gay man.

Futura moglie o marito—Future husband or wife.

Gansa megillah—The entire story you must hear, no matter how long or boring.

Gaon—A righteous, knowledgeable, and wise person towering above whoever is in second place.

Gefilte fish—A dish of chopped fish with spices served on Sabbath and Holidays.

* *Gelt*—Literally money. Used in conversation about high net worths and significant earning power.

* *Genug*—Enough. Said when trying to end an argument.

Goy—A non-Jewish person. See Goyim.

Goyasha—Anything not connected with Jewish thought. Jews believe because of history's poor treatment, every worst-case scenario must be anticipated, such as walking into the next room.

Goyim—Non- Jewish people consisting of 99+% of the world, but considered miscellaneous.

Goylem—In Jewish folklore, a rescuer from anti-Semitic attacks. Mary Shelley may have based Frankenstein on the legend.

Grauber—A person who is coarse, crude, ill-mannered, vulgar, uncouth.

Grosse k'nocker—Big shot, top guy.

Hadassah—Women's Zionist Organization of America.

Hortus conclusus—An enclosed pleasure garden with paths leading to nowhere.

Il sapore e buono—The taste is superb.

Kibitzer—One who offers unwanted advice or commentary.

Kinderlach—Children or grandchildren.

Kishkehs—Literally one's intestines. Also a sausage shaped comestible guaranteed to significantly raise cholesterol rates.

* *Klop*—A whack or smack. Also referred to as a *Zetz*.

Koom aherst—Literally come here. If heard, run in the opposite direction.

Kopp—Head.

Kvell—Burst with pride, especially with successful children.

Kvetch—Complaining about anything, no matter how trivial.

La Sfogliutella—Literally a lobster shaped pastry filled with yellow custard.

Longa lokshes—Literally long noodles. The reference is to persons a head taller than yourself.

Machatunim—Relatives, in-laws.

Maiale—Pig.

Mamma Nu—Said after receiving overwhelming news. It means Wow.

Marito—Husband.

Marito Mio/Mio marito—My husband.

Maven—An expert. No professional credentials required.

Mazel—Luck.

* *Mazltov*—Congratulations.

Mensch—A decent human being, always taking the highroad.

Meshugga—Literally meaning crazy. A daredevil act.

Mi vuoi sposare—Will you marry me?

Mia bambina—My baby. The direct object of the novel.

Mio figlio—My son.

Mishegaas—Literally craziness. Blood relative to *Meshugga*.

Mumzarum—Untrustworthy persons.

Nafka—A slut. For men, a woman you know, but can't recall her name, as she's fully dressed.

* *Narishkeit*—Foolish or stupid.

Nogoodnik—Troublemaker; someone without good morals.

O Bellissima Donna—Most beautiful woman.

Oy—A pang causing discomfort. A reaction to hearing news.

Oy vey—Woe is me.

Paskudnik—A nasty, contemptible low-life.

Pasticcini—Pastries.

Pazzo—Crazy.

Pishach—Crying.

Pishers—Referenced to children capable of seeking a restroom, when needed, but still in diapers relating to life's big pictures, such as marriage.

Plotz—To faint or collapse from excitement.

Pushka—Little box (charity box).

Rabbi—A spiritual leader subject to the same life vicissitudes as his congregants: adultery, stealing, and lying.

Saychel—Using one's brain to think. A person using brain power is considered smart and respected by peers.

Schloyma—The Yiddish word for the name Solomon.

Schlump—An unkept person who walks stoop-shouldered due to depression.

Schmahta—Literally a rag. A schmata salesman is a clothing rep. Also used in reference to an overworked housewife: a mule.

Schmarital—The *sch* is a prefix meant to mock the English word it precedes.

Schmeck—Literally smell. Most times referring to garbage.

Schmuck—An evil person wheedling great power. Also a penis.

Schnorr—A taker of money, usually relatives, willing to give back nothing in return; not even a phone call to wish you a happy birthday.

Schtup—Literally to push. Used in reference to sex acts, instead of the f-word.

Shabbat—A holy day that begins Friday evening.

Shalom Aleichem—A greeting meaning *peace unto you*. Reverse the words to reply.

Shedim—Demons or spirits.

Sheytl—A wig worn by religious women.

Shiddach—An arranged marriage. Word evolved into the term *shot-gun wedding.*

Shikker—A person consuming a fifth of liquor a day thinking himself a social drinker.

Shiksa—A non-Jewish woman. The quintessential type being Marilyn Monroe: drop dead gorgeous, speaks in a dopey voice, and loves sex.

Shlemiel—bungler, inept person, dolt.

Shlepp—To drag anything, including your ass. A *shlepper* is a person who purposely dresses like a homeless person.

Shmaltz—Chicken fat or cooking fat. Also, embellishment of a story.

Shmateh—Clothing.

Shmegegi—buffoon, idiot, disorganized one.

Shmendrik—Fool, nincompoop, inept person.

Shmooze—To shoot the breeze or network.

Shnell—Quickly.

Shpilkes—Ants in the pants. Impatience.

Shtarkeh—Strong/brave person.

Shtik—A gimmick often done to draw attention to one's self.

Shtunks—People with permeating body odor. Usually accompanied by smelly disposition.

Shusking—A whispering conversation.

Sotto voce—Literally *under voice*; intentionally lowering one's voice.

Su fuoco—On fire.

Torah—Five Books of Moses.

Trayph—Forbidden food by Mosaic Law.

Tsedrayt—Nutty, crazy or screwy.

Tusch—When seated, your backside. Doubles as a cushion when overweight.

Ungabluzen—A person with an inflated self worth leading to impassive behavior.

Vay's meer—The same as *Oy Vey.* Woe is me.

Yenta—Busybody, gossipmonger (female).

Yold—A simpleton. Derived from the Hebrew word *child.*

* Most words are Yinglish and Italian. Words marked with an asterisk are regular Yiddish.

meeting
rabbi merton

Bella bambina, light of my life, luck of my loins, you coo inside your cradle, your little eyes shifting from one raised arm to the other. You are the future, the alfa Robota, Roberta for short. Stretched in a hammock beside you, I swing gently, charmed by the fascination you have with your arms. "Holy transformers," your eyes seem to say. "What the hell are these for?" My line of sight takes you in, the rich colors of the backyard flowerbed and the clear blue sky beyond. The afternoon sunshine feels fantastico. Who would think the world could ever end? Sometimes the rhythm of the cradle and the hammock aligns us, enabling me to give your cradle a gentle shove.

You were programmed to carry forward the Haralson family history one thousand generations. I was determined our family lineage be remembered as more than just entries in a genealogical record. I've inserted a little pink computer chip in you, just to be sure.

Future Haralson generations can research us and, if they fancy, add chapters of their own escapades. In a million years, our descendants will know that my fierce husband, Alex, was an accountant, a rather impatient one; an intellectual explorer, a rather pedantic one; and an enthusiastic golfer, truth-be-known, a rather poor one. They would know I was born in Roma, Italia, was a good cook and a homemaker who ran a tight ship. I was good at languages because my papa was a wandering Jew who met my lovely mother in the Quarter and settled down *shnell* into the baking trade so he could keep her. In the bakery I heard every language, and one day the language of love, when my Alex came to claim me and bring me to America. I imagine our future kin saying, "Weren't they wonderful." Cain and Abel became well-known because they fought. If they hadn't, I doubt the Biblical names would have raised an eyebrow. The Haralsons are different. We get on fine as long as Alex acknowledges that I'm always right and gives me what I want. Thus, *bambina*, we have peace and longevity.

You and I sway over the exact spot where the scene of the crime occurred. Well, it wasn't exactly a crime. Your father and I, on occasion, had intimate relations in this hammock, usually under cover of night, but not always. The entire city of Birming-ham, Michigan, heard us, or, to be more accurate, heard me, because for days after our last, rather extreme encounter, my hus-band received strange and knowing looks from our neighbors. In fact, the city Animal Control Department called once, asking if we were keeping coyotes in our yard. *Schmucks!* They know noth-ing of passion!

On another occasion, I was relaxing in this spot when a rel-ative showed up unannounced at the front door. Retired, with nothing to do, Alex embraced him, finding him intellectually stimulating. I concluded he was attempting to *schnorr* money from a rich relative. I said to his face, "Go back home. Mingle among your own kind, the lazy lay-abouts." Besides, his after-shave nauseated me. We didn't know he was one of Danziger's spies.

If I'm talking too much, Babybot, you'll just have to put up with me. I'm postpartum and postmenopausal. You don't have anything better to do except gurgle and poop. Just think, one day you'll grow up and marry a loudmouth just like me. I may be madder than a hatter—whatever that means—but this spot is now my perch, a place to express myself, to pontificate, to spill the beans. I hope you're listening. At what point in time do I start? Do I start from now and work backwards? Do I start at the beginning? Do I start in the middle and go in both directions? Yes, that seems most reasonable and the simplest. Listen, Baby, to the story of your conception.

Once upon a time your father and I waited in the reception area outside Rabbi Merton Freyburg's study. Besides our agendas, I planned to mention that the couch needed replacing. Sitting on it made my tusch itch. I leafed through a *Hadassah Magazine*, while across the rattan coffee table your father folded his arms and raised his round chin, fixing his gaze at the ceiling. He made me nervous. I wasn't sure what he pondered, but knew the wheels in his brain were grinding overtime.

I suggested picking up a magazine to read. He scowled at me, nostrils flaring. He glanced down at his wrist watch; slowly his eyes rose and telescoped, taking direct aim at me. I knew what that meant: Merton was late and Alex was having *shpilkes*. He was measuring Merton's tardiness. My Alex timed everything: wait time at doctor's offices, wait time for waitresses to take an order, telephone wait time on hold, and now wait time for Merton Freyburg.

Alex muttered that friends don't make friends wait. That when Merton came to his office, his secretary escorted him in immediately. God forbid he should keep his Rabbi waiting. And that was equally true for Merton. To be exact, *never* keep your accountant, congregant, best friend, supporter, or protector waiting.

I said, "*Bubbelah*, what's your complaint? You're retired." His eyes shot daggers at me. I suggested we go home. "Merton can work on more important matters. He doesn't want to hear *mishegaas*." I knew Alex couldn't wait to tell Merton his story. Alex squinted, sat back in his seat, and kept silent. He realized he was beaten, for now anyway. I too was eager to speak to the Rabbi.

Before his recent adventure, a golf game would have been fore-most on your father's mind. But the night before, when I walked into the living room to tell him supper was ready, he was standing in front of the fireplace lecturing to empty sofas, using sweeping gestures. He looked up, and, seeing me, relaxed. He knew Merton would *plotz* when told about the robots.

I said, "You've rehearsed your story umpteen times. I'm sick of it. Anyway, we're meeting Merton to discuss our unmarried children, not your nonsense."

That got Alex's dander up. "Those *pishers*," he said, "have *chutzpah*, getting in the way of my agenda. Their behavior gives me heartburn."

I said, "Those *pishers*, as you say, are your children. They aren't some watermelons I shit out."

Your father fumed. "Excuse me. Let me qualify my remark. They became educated mental *pishers*." He ranted that our son, a doctor, a grown man with a beard, should be looking after his parents, not living in the basement smoking weed while totally immersed in Playstation 2. And our Master of Social Work of a daughter ought to return home to Michigan and quit counseling immigrant *shtunks*.

I gave a knowing look and said, "Are you including Italian immigrants?" He backed down with a sheepish shrug.

Alex clasped his hands, pleading, "What are they waiting for? Do they think they are Sarah and Abraham, to get married and have children in their dotage?"

I dared not say out loud that I thought our daughter having a child out of wedlock, even with a *shtunk*, would be better than no grandchild at all.

I said, "Alex, why do I love you? Because you're direct, because you leave no wiggle room, or because your patience is zero?"

Alex's punctuality found its way into our family life. Many years ago, when my pregnancy reached nine months, he asked if I was ready to go to the hospital. Forget that labor pains might be a better indicator of readiness. Babies shouldn't keep fathers waiting!

Despite his rant, Alex insisted we open our conversation with Merton by telling him about his trip to the Garden of Eden.

I retorted, "How about a closer: Shut up! The children come first. Before we aggravate ourselves to death fighting about whose agenda should be first, let's keep some distance between us. What I put up with from you should earn me sainthood."

"Jews in America don't become Saints."

"Italian ones do."

"What are you, a comedienne? Jews can't be saints, woman!"

"Pedantic wretch," I snarled.

I wasn't sure if I was better off with your father sitting on the other side of the table or next to me. Since his return from Airets, my libido had been calling at weird times. My friend Annabel, Merton's wife, found that unusual. She said sex drive slowed after menopause. I knew better. If my husband sat next to me, I might have made a scene. I might have uncontrollably combed my fingers through his flowing gray hair. We sat apart—otherwise ear nibbling might ensue.

I secretly wanted to confuse Rabbi Freyburg's secretary, Edith Smith, whom I detest. Let her think we're there for marriage counseling. What other conclusion could she reach when couples sit separately? Edith must have witnessed the same scenario a thousand times: couples sitting separately in the waiting room, muffled drama with the Rabbi, and exiting in tears.

Edith worked in a glass cubicle. Her profile was in my direct line of sight. I noticed she occasionally peered at us. She closed the glass window and continued to type on her computer. Then the unthinkable happened: I saw that her lips were moving. That sneaky bitch wore a telephone headset and she positioned the microphone so I couldn't lip-read her gossip. Everyone associated with the synagogue knew Edith. She worked with a calm demeanor. That was a front.

I could just hear her: "Alex Haralson is finally having trouble with that crazy Italian wife of his. I said it would happen years ago, didn't I?" She relished the troubles of others. Why had we decided to split up? Was it money? Or was it an affair? *She's mad, that woman, mad! Divorce, divorce, divorce—Oh, I can't wait.*

She knew me from prior visits to Merton. She'd heard the scoop when Merton verbally spanked me because I was too flirtatious at Sabbath services. She broadcasted it to her friends. The gossip got back to me. I retaliated. I told a Women's Club Meeting, "Edith'll be looking high and low for a second husband. Her shopworn Salvation Army outfits are a fright. It's no wonder. She has no *saychel* to go to a Hadassah Thrift Shop and buy donated designer clothes. Her haggard appearance reminds me of Mrs. Frankenstein. Her lipstick reminds me of a fire engine. And I can't decide whether she's wearing a black *sheytl* or if she covered up her gray hair with shoe polish."

She'd want revenge, so I knew her heart pounded for details. Calls to all her friends with the news couldn't wait until we left the building. But the most she would hear through the Rabbi's walls would be strident remarks about our progeny.

Edith opened the glass partition and said Merton should be coming in the door at any minute.

Alex folded his arms and gazed at me.

I stood and walked to him, sat on his lap, licked his ear, and whispered, "Relax! She's watching."

I turned my head and saw Edith gazing at us; her expression mechanical—the sack of vipers was trying to contain her disappointment.

Her husband died of a heart attack. Married to her, I completely understood. How else could he escape the marriage? She was a pain. As to her secretarial skills, the Rabbi only had to look at his calendar to know where he was supposed to be. She set times for funerals, weddings, and office consultations. Note cards with Shabbat sermons went home with the Rabbi on Friday afternoons for review. Credit where credit's due: she was a damn good lackey.

Alex mumbled that Merton's tardiness was probably due to his working overtime rewriting sermons. Alex had complained before his voyage to the Garden of Eden that Merton's sermons sounded overworked, too balanced; in other words, tentative. I suggested, "Don't bitch about Merton's sermons. Lie and say you love them. Remember, one day you'll die and you don't want a two-word funeral service: Heave Ho."

My poor *marito* was a lost soul. He loved his work, but was forced to retire after a successful forty-year accounting career. His accounting firm's policy mandated retirement at sixty-five. He went into mourning, stopping short of tearing his clothes and pouring ashes on his head. I suffered too. I had attended many dinners when he wined and dined clients on a company credit card. Clients loved him and reciprocated by inviting him to dinner or to play golf at their lavish country clubs. That was the only time he was patient. Alex didn't mind at all if clients took eight or ten strokes per hole. What's the hurry?

All these perks stopped when the senior partner, Carter Benoni, went into Alex's office and asked impassively if he'd forgotten that the firm had a mandatory retirement age policy. Alex told him he still had a spring in his step and mentally had both oars in the water. Carter dismissed Alex's claims, saying "being able" didn't matter. Carter's obduracy didn't surprise Alex. Alex had teased Carter many times for his feminine mannerisms. He once informed Carter, "A real man looks at his fingernails with his fingers pointed inward." Alex once, seeing Carter in the hallway, pirouetted past him. Now, with Carter lording it over him, Alex tried to ameliorate the situation by saying how sorry he was for all the nasty ribbings of the past. Carter lifted his nose in the air. With seemingly no other choice, Alex groveled. He fell on his knees and grabbed one of Carter's legs. He bawled while asking Carter what he was supposed to do for the rest of his life. Machine-like, Carter suggested Alex do pro bono tax returns for a while, and then maybe drop dead. Alex retorted that Carter was cruel. Poor people don't earn enough to pay taxes and therefore don't need a tax preparer. Carter's parting shot was a cold-hearted "Oh well. Then it'll have to be an early eternal nap." He shook his leg free from Alex's grasp and left the soon-to-be-vacated office.

Your father retired to teach accounting part-time at a local college. At other times he clipped coupons. He was handy when I had to do grocery shopping. He held the shopping list, brought the coupons, picked the freshest produce, and carried the groceries to the car. The shopping trips created a time and place for female admirers to mingle with him. It didn't matter what he wore or how he looked; they awaited his arrival. They teased with toothy smiles or knowing rubs on his back or arm. It infuriated my Roman blood, but what could I do? We had to eat.

I'll never forget what one admirer, Prissy Gum, said to my husband. She wanted a kiss, so she could stick her tongue down his throat. She didn't consider the embarrassment of leaving fiery red lipstick all over his face. I quickly stepped between them, but this bitch refused to back off. She put firm fingertips against my solar plexus saying, "Stand aside, you Italian hussy." She bent her head to look past me, saying to Alex, "Come over to my place anytime with a bottle of Viagra." She looked me in the eye. "You could never match my sexual prowess." With his looks and money, my husband could, in a heartbeat, run off with anyone.

Thank God he stood by his woman. He told me I shouldn't worry. Their huge rear ends and drooping breasts belonged on a used car lot. When I asked what about women with enhanced breasts, he said he preferred my swinging fun bags to volleyballs.

He met some of my male admirers: bald, gray, and overweight. He teased me about whether or not they could drive at night or perform the hubba-hubba. I had no firsthand knowledge, nor did I have a rebuttal. He knew he had no competition.

My story was different. Homemaking to me was a numbers game: cleaning, cooking, and washing. When the children were young, there were four of us living at home. The number reduced to two as they left for college. With Roman returning home, the number upped to three. I, a normal Jewish mother, albeit an Italian one, wanted something more: grandchildren! Hello! But my son and daughter lived modern lifestyles—selfish hedonists! A crazy idea swam into my head. If my children refused to cooperate, I would take matters into my own hands and have my own baby, making sure the new addition understood me, married, and had children—third time lucky. That's you, precious *bambina*, but *mamma mia*, you did not come easy. The task required hurdling a big barrier. I was sixty-two years old. *Oy vey*, time passes like a wind from the mountains, our asses expand, then we're forgotten like fallen leaves!

Prenatal encouragement arrived when I viewed a Wolf Winslow TV talk show. On it, several women told about conceiving and giving birth in their late fifties. Ah, I thought, here we go. One fifty-eight-year-old woman detailed her life after giving birth to a girl just two months earlier. She said, "No planning. It just happened." I felt violently jealous as she described her happiness. Resolving my feelings would be difficult. I had to conceive first. I could get past the no planning part with my Latin libido. But how did I get past the "it-just-happened" part? Get an ovary transplant? Adopt a child? Right, like a Puerto Rican? *Oy*, My daughter was currently dating one. I was ready to collapse.

Another child was a pipe dream. The best I could reasonably hope for was a dog. I would name it Michelangelo Haralson. And would I ever lavish it with love! Many women my age do. They get *farputst*. The dog gets *farputst*. And they go out and strut together, either shopping or stopping off for a bite to eat. It sounded like a very practical here-and-now solution. But the future looked obscure. The Haralson ability to speak would degenerate to being unable to carry a conversation past saying "Woof."

Hurrying down the hall, Rabbi Freyburg approached, saying, "Margarita and Alexander, a thousand apologies."

Attached to Merton's six-foot-two-inch frame was a portion of flab. His suit jacket clinched around his shoulders and to button it required sucking in his stomach. He invariably wore this dark blue suit, sprinkled with dandruff, and black brogues, worn at the heel. He wore this outfit to weddings, funerals, and Sabbath services. Edith might have helped by sending Merton home on

Friday with a note to Annabelle: Buy new *shmateh*; visit cobbler.

What am I thinking? Edith dressed like a *schlump* too. I was holding back on telling Merton how shabby he looked. His blue yarmulke with a Star of David banded around the perimeter covered another problem: "Deconstruction Zone. Balding in Progress."

He hugged me—a little too squishy for a dandruff-dusted, asexual spiritual advisor, but attention is always good. "*Come stai, Margherita?* How's my Roman Lucille Ball?" He said, showing off his miniscule Italian. He held me way too long and I felt wood developing.

Miffed, I said, "*Bene, grazie.*"

He released me so that I could breathe again and hugged Alex as if he had the flu. "*Mazl-tov!* How's it feel to be married to Sophia Loren?"

Alex lifted one side of his face, raised the opposite hand and shoulder, and limply said, "Expensive, expensive."

I speak three languages and they equate me to a bimbo. You, baby, are going to know languages! Not like these *narishkeit* Americans.

His arms thrown over our shoulders, Merton ushered us toward his study. I glanced at Edith. The luckless *shmegegi* now knew for sure that we didn't need marriage counseling. I imagined the *yenta*'s vocal chords going temporarily limp. No juicy gossip today, bitch.

I remembered waiting in this study a month before Alex and I married. We were to meet with a very late Rabbi Simirenko, a man whose gaberdine always smelled a little of urine, and who, when he finally arrived, counseled us about the importance of maintaining religion in our new roles as husband and wife. I didn't understand much at the time, having just arrived from Italy. We were young and had averred our wedding vows in bed. The official ceremony in the sanctuary tied up loose ends.

We entered Merton's study and I became giddy with its succulent atmosphere. Alex warned me beforehand that Merton had redecorated it with a faux biblical theme. Potted cacti and date palms littered the floor—a Garden of Eden replica, sans fruit trees. We needed to push aside shiny green branches bursting with leaves to find the seats. The Rabbi convinced the synagogue board that a new and unusual look would impress potential donors; they fumed more at the remodeling cost of $250,000 than at the decor. Alex, always in Merton's corner, told them it was worth every penny. Alex must have had a say in the design since the pile carpeting felt like a putting green underfoot. I wasn't so impressed, I thought parrot and monkey calls would have added a little ambiance.

On one side were picture windows looking out onto an atrium; on the other stood rows of bookshelves. My husband judges people by their libraries. "A house without books on display," he says at least once a week, "is no better than a dog's kennel." I waded through the foliage to get a look at Merton's bedtime reading. It comprised the usual rabbinical snore zone: Psychology, mythology, and self-help; biographies [about rabbis by rabbis]; instruction manuals on how to practice sex after marriage. Get real already! The rate of abstention before marriage is about zero.

Significantly absent were a memoir about a visit to the Garden of Eden and a book on diseases robots might carry. Your clever father planned to write a book on each of those subjects. Merton's *Playboy* collection, I presumed, was hidden behind a secret panel. And for myself I sought a medical text about having children after menopause. No such luck.

I noted a title, *Divorce from a Jewish Perspective.* How fitting for Edith. She could contribute a section on waiting room manners. She'd recommend telling the gossip to the secretary first and then the news to the Rabbi. I approached my seat. Behind Merton's desk hung various diplomas. Merton earned a master's degree in psychology. That was in addition to his rabbinical ordination diploma. I squinted to read his marriage counselor diploma. How can a rabbi with dandruff counsel anyone?

I sat in a cushioned chair and blew a palm frond away from my mouth. Your father, always ready to get down to business, was already seated. It certainly didn't mean I would allow him to talk about his agenda first.

Edith, who had been waiting by the door, walked in and handed the Rabbi his mail. As Merton went behind his desk, he asked us where we had been. He was right to ask. We hadn't been to Shabbat services recently. Alex had taken an extended trip while I flogged myself every day because my children and I had a different view of *it's about time you got married.* He nodded to Edith who stormed out with a *farbisseneh* expression and shut the door with a diploma-rattling din.

I thought, ah wonderful, she's left. The gladiators have entered the arena, ready for action. Places everyone! Engage!

chapter

TWO

dueling agendas

Your father and I sat holding hands, waiting for Rabbi Freyburg to finish flipping through his mail. Alex, ever the accountant, told me that important mail arriving at home was always bills, and important mail arriving at synagogues was always checks. Merton looked cheerful as he examined the letters, probably noting the contributors' names on the return addresses, and tossed the special ones in a separate pile on his desk. Your father did fundraising for the synagogue and I believed many of the letters in the special pile contained contributions due to his efforts. Oblivious to time, Merton kept flipping. Often, he stopped to write a note on an incoming letter. Did he forget about the overanxious congregants waiting in his study? Under my breath, I said, "Christ, Merton, will you finish?" Alex shifted in his seat, sucking in deep breaths. I noted him looking at his watch. *Oy*, letter flipping joined the list of wait time irritants.

Alex, chomping at the bit, couldn't wait any longer. He broke the silence, uttering to a preoccupied Merton that he had visited the Garden of Eden. I expected Merton to stop immediately and look up surprised. He kept on shuffling letters and writing notes. I cringed. Since he didn't react, my impression was Merton knew about Alex's trip. Still playing mailroom clerk, Merton finally commented he'd heard Alex left unexpectedly for a couple of days. He chuckled and inquired about Adam and Eve's health. I wondered if Merton was trying to start a war.

Alex replied, "They're fine." His tone, though louder than rabbis like, remained calm and devoid of sarcasm. Merton said he'd heard the expedition went to a site in the Caucasus. He teased Alex, asking if he went there to do Adam and Eve's tax return. Under my breath, I told Merton to watch his step, but the *dumkopf* kept up his sarcasm. "Did they file jointly or separately?"

Alex's body stiffened like an animal ready to leap. His eyes blazed and his pent up wish to rip our Rabbi's nose off was only recognizable to me. It made me shudder. Alex, nostrils flaring, replied that he'd be writing a book about his experience. Merton without missing a beat said, "*Mazltov*," He laughed, "Will it be a thriller?"

Alex, about to pop, said he wasn't writing a story about a deformed reindeer with a red nose for a headlight that saved Santa's ass on a foggy Christmas Eve. It would be a serious book. He suggested that if Merton knew what was good for him, he'd better ease up on the sarcasm. Alex unclasped our hands and placed my arm in my lap like it was a drumstick he was done with but might gnaw on later. Like a fire-and-brimstone preacher, he unleashed a tirade complete with a shaking fist, saying that Merton should take a good look at his dusty old bookshelves. When his book came out, all Merton's theology and wisdom-for-Jews could be sold for scrap. He claimed with clenched fists that his book about the Garden of Eden would replace all the others, and would be the only one ever needed. Ah, how sweet, I thought, my little Mussolini.

The Rabbi placed the mail on his desk and surveyed us. He said, seeing Alex's blazing face, that a restful vacation was in order. Merton thought we had come to talk about synagogue business. But if Alex was looking for a fight, he could recommend the name of a nearby gym with resident sparring partners. Alex continued his attack. His outdoor adventure, he emphasized in expressive diction, wasn't a powder-puff archeological dig for wealthy old farts. Merton spoke in a pained voice, asking Alex to ease up, saying his demeanor failed to radiate wisdom.

I interrupted, telling them to stop bickering and calm down. I blurted, "Edith's probably got her ear against the door. Do you want her to hear what we're saying?" The room went quiet. Merton scowled and said Edith kept things confidential. I reminded him that he wasn't out there watching her every move. He hit back saying he knew that many conversations between his wife and me were quite, shall we say, newsy. What is the Italian word for *gossip*, Margarita? I fumed and said that Annabelle wasn't here to defend herself. Smugly, Merton lifted his phone's receiver, asking would I like him to set up a conference call? I asked him if he could tell me the Hebrew word for *bastard*.

Flushed with his temporary triumph, Merton turned to Alex, saying he understood his story embodied great importance, suggesting they should speak and listen to each other with concern. Merton offered himself as a mentor. A calmer Alex said to Merton that he felt Yahweh's divine presence lighting the room. I crossed myself like a nun and prayed in Italian, "God, thank you for joining the meeting," Merton's nose flared, but Alex tapped the desktop and said what he wanted was to inform an old friend about where he'd been and what he'd been doing.

Merton threw up his hands and came around to the front of his desk and thumped down into a visitor's chair, saying, "Okay, Alex you win."

I said, "Alex rehearsed his story like a crazy man every hour."

Merton's eyes switched between us.

I told Merton we came to tell our stories to our respected Rabbi; Alex's about his trip to the Garden of Eden, and mine about our children, adding that Alex's story was bizarre and mine was practical. I explained to Merton that since *mio marito* retired he'd been ill at ease, craving a purpose.

Merton turned to Alex, suggesting that abandoning his charitable work had been unwise. I stood and pointed a finger at Merton. In a strong voice I said, "Charitable work, *schmaritable* work." Every committee he worked for made him Treasurer.

Since being forced to retire from accounting, I wanted my husband to retire from charitable work also—that included raising money for the synagogue and Merton's personal projects. Merton looked wounded, and asked what a man like Alex would do with his time.

I explained, "I've repeatedly suggested we travel more. Hawaii for a month—with a side trip to Capri. Scuba diving in Kho Phi Phi, a hike up to Machu Pichu. 'Yeah, yeah, yeah,' Alex says, bending like a Christmas tree, but nothing happens until he disappears and I find out he went on a trip without me—to an ancestral homeland inhabited by lunatics."

Merton said dryly, "Don't tell me, the Garden of Eden."

I smiled and nodded. Then I looked heavenward, "Thank you God. Your guidance spared me the trauma of meeting more crazy people. My cup overflows with the nutcakes I've already met." Alex growled and curled into himself like a hedgehog in a huff. Merton grinned like a crocodile.

I said I wanted to bring to Merton's attention the problem with our children. "Roman and Caroline are single with no *futura moglie o marito*." I pulled a tissue from my purse and wiped my tears. On the verge of breakdown, I sighed that my part in life was to be a devoted wife and doting mother. Merton interjected glowingly that I had been such a person.

I admitted I was now being forced to use a heavy hand on my children to see that they married. Everything had changed since the robots from outer space contacted us. Merton's mouth dropped open. He inquired whether he had heard me correctly, asking if I said *robots*. I replied yes. Merton looked at Alex to confirm that what I said was true. Alex, eyes closed, arms folded, nodded.

Merton pressed on, asking what robots I was talking about and where they came from. I said the ones from the future. I was about to continue when a reddening Merton broke in saying that if he didn't know us so well, he'd have us thrown out. He stressed he did marriage counseling and consulting on religious matters—not psychotherapy on cybotronic obsession.

My blood pressure exploded. I screeched in Italian that I wasn't done, that I'd never be done until I had a grandchild, that they were no better than beasts if they couldn't give a mother what was due her.

They got the point, *bambina*. My native language is the best in the world for throwing shit-fits. I will teach you. Your father tried to calm me. I told him to back off or I'd bite his nose. Merton and Alex made eye contact and sat still.

I calmed down and began again. Alex tried to speak but I told him to shut up. I am the storyteller. A robot named Jonathan Chapman cunningly kidnapped Alex and took him to the Garden of Eden on a distant planet. Meanwhile, at home a robot that looked just like Alex was a stand-in while my Alex was away. At first I didn't notice anything different since my dear husband often goes through periods of having a somewhat metallic personality. One day, all was revealed when Robot Alex sat next to me on the couch and started crying like a baby, literally—he hadn't been programmed to cry like an elderly Jewish American. "Waa, waa, waa! *Antenata* Margarita, we need your help."

Astonished, I asked what was the matter. Holding my hand, he confessed the robot ruse and explained that I was an ancestor to him as were my children, and that he wasn't really my husband but an artificial version of him. I thought Alex must be going mad. Amid spurting tears, he said that the future existence of humanized robots like him depended on the continuation of the Haralson lineage. He insisted that our children get married immediately and have offspring. He pleaded on his knees for the entire race of robots, who were likewise desperate all over the galaxy. Otherwise, he said, the future for them would never happen.

I thought my husband was engaging in some kind of metaphorical game to get my attention. "Give them time," I said, not really believing my own words. "They'll get married and have children eventually."

He burbled between sobs, "Do you think I'm an idiot? You have a pothead for a son, singing through his ass all day alone in the basement. I see no offspring in that loser's future. And your daughter is being escorted about New York City by her gay *caballero*! *Oy vey*, what is the girl thinking?"

I challenged him by saying, "How dare you say that! My children are wonderful. I'm not listening to you anymore."

"I'm telling the truth," he shouted.

"Okay, so prove you aren't the real Alex."

He said to touch his shoulder. When I did, he morphed into an exact duplicate of my Uncle Ernesto, who had been dead for several decades, sang a Puccini aria, and then evaporated. I had hysterics for a few seconds, but when I realized no one was coming to pay attention to me, I stopped.

Rabbi Merton, understandably bemused at my story, rubbed his forehead. He asked if he heard correctly that robots wouldn't come into existence unless my children got married and had children themselves.

I choked out a yes. "Merton, I hurt badly enough because I might never have grandchildren without those outer space assholes reminding me."

Alex interjected that time was of the essence. Transformation of humans into robots needed to happen within one hundred and fifty years.

Merton looked at Alex and asked, "Because?"

"Disease mainly, but pollution, famine, and war will do everybody in. We're headed the way of the frog."

I explained how the Garden of Eden my Alex was taken to was also one million years in the future. He learned that all the robots would be our progeny. Our future children would rule the universe. I, an Italian peasant, will be an iconic ancestor to future world rulers. I *kvelled* when I heard this news about our family's glorious future. At the same time, I died on the vine thinking about our family's present precarious situation. "Help us."

Merton looked skeptically at Alex. He said that our story was quite a *Bubbe Meinsah*. I wondered what else poor Merton was expected to believe? He mused aloud whether our son had spiked our food with LSD.

Alex replied, "No, this is all real. The trip happened." Robots took him on a spaceship into the wild blue yonder. On the way, they told him all about the family connection being a generational line of robots and about the ominous crisis awaiting humankind.

Merton shook his head and said Alex should have earned a degree in fortune-telling, not accounting.

I said, "Alex's biblical education was what they wanted. They found out he earned a master's degree in biblical history." I explained that the robots started life as normal human babies, diapers and all. They grew to adulthood in a time when only technical and mathematical knowledge was taught, the humanities being considered superfluous, and therefore had nothing in their data about the origins of sentient intelligence. The search for origins became a fad in robot culture and once they understood the workings of dimensionality they realized that their jumping around had caused a rift in time and that they needed to confirm their own existence. You work it out, I don't get it. They sought out Alex, since he could impart knowledge of religion to them. The fools didn't even know they were Jews until we explained matrilineal descent. Once they knew they were supposed to be Jews they started stooping and using expansive gesticulations. Jewishness completely explained their excessive fatalism. They were whole at last, but all was lost without our little link to their future.

So, to sort of restart the human engine, our robotic relatives took Alex to a Garden of Eden they discovered on the planet Airets. The joke was on them. They could have found all the answers they wanted just by looking and using their brains. My Alex, on the other hand, returned with a mound of information. He learned the length and width of the Garden of Eden story by observing it.

Merton was still skeptical. Alex had been a friend for many years. His tax and financial advice had made Merton rich. Alex defended him from the synagogue board, which wanted to fire him. He asked Alex how he could become so *farmidsht?*

Alex chuckled a chattering teeth laugh, and claimed in a high-pitched tone that he wasn't insane.

I gripped his arm, saying, "Relax." Then I turned to Merton and said, "Alex's outbursts sometimes ape the robots."

Merton blushed. Alex brought his voice down a couple of octaves and said that Merton would be impacted by what he'd learned. His rabbinical calling was *kaput*, defunct. Merton inquired who was after his hide. Alex tried to reassure Merton that it wasn't about him specifically. It was the bigger picture. Evolution would make the rabbinate obsolete. Merton retorted he thought synagogue boards had the exclusive right to terminate. Alex pleaded for Merton to believe him. His story was no fairy tale. Alex said, "Let it sink in."

Merton's stare was incredulous. He turned pale, claiming he was suffering an attack of heart palpitations. He groaned because it appeared Alex wasn't kidding, was he? He heard silence. He said he had listened to us long enough, hoping we would shake the bullshit from our heads. When we failed to do so, he became totally *tsedrayt*. He asked Alex if he went to Turkey or if he went to Planet X? Smiling at the joke, Alex corrected that Planet X was named Airets. "Ay, ay, ay," said Merton. "I thought I heard that earlier. You mean *Airets*, as in the Hebrew word meaning *Earth*, don't you? Alex nodded.

Merton asked who initiated the name Airets? Alex said that the robots did. Merton slapped his palm to his forehead, "*Oy.*" Exhausted, he shook his head in disbelief.

Merton said he'd heard from synagogue chitchat that Alex left town and at the same time that he didn't leave town. "Which one was it?" I said the reason no one was aware of his leaving town was because Robot Alex moved into our house and stayed until my husband returned. The public couldn't tell the difference from the real Alex. At home behind locked doors, I couldn't tell the difference either. He acted like any hot-blooded man: no foreplay, all business.

Alex turned to me and screeched, "You had sex with him?"

I said, "Darling, I didn't know at first, and then you were gone a long time."

"What about after you knew?"

"Was I not entitled once in a while to a good pump with my electro buddy? Lots of women have them."

Merton slipped down into his chair and undid his collar. Alex stood and asked if he should get himself a robotic *shiksa*-whore. I replied he could if he wanted to risk surgery while sleeping. Alex pointed a finger at the end of my nose but Merton told us to cool down. He took a deep breath. Suddenly, he sat up straight in his chair, saying that a lightbulb went off in his head. He claimed he now understood. He related a story that had happened about a week earlier.

He was schmoozing with Stewart Stine. Stewart mentioned that Alex acted a little funny playing golf. One day, Alex played like a beginner, scattering the ball all over the place. The very next day, Alex was hitting 350-yard drives straight as an arrow, hitting approach shots inches from the pin and sinking every putt.

Merton asked me if that was Robot Alex. I answered with an affirmative shrug. Alex glared at me. "You let Robot Alex play golf at our club and use my brand new golf clubs? Did the hero come home afterwards and cool off with a massage and some afternoon delight?" I timidly remarked that the Haralson genes were responsible. He screamed, "Where did you learn about robots having genes? Did that cock-hound robot tell you that bullshit?" I averred he was a custom-made robot: an alter ego, nothing but a sex toy. Your father fell back, beaten.

Merton flailed his arms. *Genug!* He told Alex to remove the boxing gloves. He said there had been enough fighting for one day. Merton accused Alex of starting the ruckus with him when the meeting began and of now starting to swing at me. Alex reproached Merton by saying, "You have a lot of nerve siding with her, after all I did for you." Merton flopped back in his chair and rubbed his temples. He asked if we came to discuss grandchildren or fidelity? We sat quietly.

Merton's expression grew thoughtful. I judged him to be trying to understand the connection between the grandchildren and the robots. He requested that Alex tell him more about the robotic grandchildren. He needed to make a connection in his mind from the children to the robots. But first Merton asked what he could do to help. Could he talk to Roman and Caroline about what their faith expected of them? Alex harrumphed. Merton admitted that he now clearly saw them as the linchpins to our Jewish robot future. What can we do but our best? I chimed in that failure would be over my dead body. Alex said the robots that took him to Airets were electronic humanoids, our great-grandchildren thousands of generations into the future. Failure destroys history.

Merton leaned toward me. He asked if I had heard all the details of Alex's trip. I replied yes. After Robot Alex finally told me where my Alex had been taken, I was aware of everything that happened day by day. Robot Alex was linked to all the other robots. I started to cry, saying I agreed with Merton's assessment about Roman and Caroline being the linchpins. I pleaded, "Help me marry them off. In Caroline's case, find a secret stud."

Alex told Merton all he wanted for his sanity was grandchildren, grandchildren, and more grandchildren. He said he needed more diversion than spending his golden years going every week to see an urologist because he couldn't take a leak. Our poor Rabbi sank back in his chair, looking a hundred years older. You could see five millennia of responsibility rising in him like acid reflux.

At last Merton suggested we were imagining this robotic world because of being under non-grandparent stress. I said, "Not true, Merton. My Alex felt stress, when he was on the spaceship and couldn't hug and kiss his grandchildren. They were cores of electronic clusters housed in synthetic material."

Merton nodded he understood. He changed subjects asking, "Other than the obvious physical changes what else changed? For instance, what changed for our religion?"

As an example, Alex mentioned the blessing of *Gomale*. As Merton knew, it is a prayer of thanksgiving recited under four conditions: A successful journey across a desert or ocean, recovery from illness, escape from danger, and release from captivity. Alex said that computers traverse across great distances without incident. They don't suffer illness, don't have accidents, and don't go to prison. They are above all harm. Why would they need religion? Merton said Alex made them sound as if they're harmless angels. Alex said angels, no, harmless, hardly. Their universe ran on science: physics and chemistry. If threatened, they would punch your lights out.

Merton asked if the robots believed in God. Alex replied that in the robotic world, consciousness about God was nonexistent. Merton asked if they were atheists. Alex replied you have to know about God in order to be an atheist. The robots were Jewish only because of their maternal lineage.

Merton concluded that the rest of the world was in trouble. "If the robots don't have illness or unhappiness, the righteous *goyim* will have to permanently close their churches. They'll scapegoat the Jews for their problems." He bellowed an *Oy vey*, "Here come the pogroms! I am going *meshugga*. The thought of robotic great-grandchildren is insane!" With his eyes skyward he cried, "*Abeshter*, help! Give me understanding. Find me a new job."

Merton looked at me, wanting to escape back to the more normal discussion of our children. Roman, he remembered worked as a doctor in a remote part of Canada. And Caroline worked as a social worker in a New York City Family Service program. "Bring me up-to-date."

I responded that Caroline still lived in New York and hung with bums. I related that she once visited us, bringing home a Puerto Rican who worked in a warehouse rolling garment racks onto trucks. All he did was look around the house to see what he could steal. And to top it off, he was a *fayggela*. My Alex cut in saying he suggested to Caroline that when she returned home with her honcho, she should drop him and find instead a rich Wall Street investment banker. My Alex could relate to such a man as a son-in-law. He told her our family was not a social experiment. She informed us that she was searching her inner self about her sexual orientation. "Where did I go wrong?"

Merton, jowls shaking, piped up that that was no way to think about a daughter. He strongly suggested we curb our intolerant expressions.

He asked about Roman. Tears obscured my vision. I said, "After Alex returned home and Robot Alex moved out, Roman came back home to live with us. Why? He's broke. All his medical services in the wild were paid for with chickens and milk." Merton asked if he had secured a medical position in Michigan. Of course not. All he does is smoke dope, check his Facebook account, and play video games—so he says. For Roman, Merton suggested a Jewish singles group, J-date, Internet dating. "Why didn't I think of that?" Merton said he would ask Roman to lunch and have a quiet talk. As to Caroline, he'd call her. He wanted to learn more. I said, "She might tell you to mind your own business." Merton replied that he'd taken punches on the chin before. He wanted to digest and think about what he'd heard in this meeting. Then he'd decide if we should check into a mental hospital. He dismissed us by saying we should have Edith set another appointment.

THREE

i'm in heat

I lounged in bed with a sexy novel, eating chocolates. I heard the shower running while my Alex *boom-ba-dee-boomed* a beat he must have learned from a tribal drummer on Airets. I preferred something romantic like Sinatra or Mathis, either of whom could sing to me under the sheets anytime.

I felt rejuvenated, enjoying the pleasantries of my bedroom since its renovation. The work began after your father retired from accounting. Removed were the bulky and confining dressers, replaced with walk-in his-and-hers closets. The new bedroom design allowed me enough space to act out fantasies. I placed my book on the dresser, leaped from my bed, and twirled about. Enlarged windows allowed in more daylight, which energized me. I danced close to the window, as if for a camera, allowing the neighborhood to peer through the viewfinder. I peered out, hoping someone might be watching. I didn't care that I was naked. I broadcasted, "Hey everyone, I'm naughty." I stood still and treasured a cloudless sky. "Alex, it's a glorious morning." I jumped back into bed, covered myself, and giggled.

The extra space also allowed us to buy a king-sized bed and a cabinet for a high-definition television and DVD player. My husband and I on many occasions cuddled on our new soft mattress while we watched science fiction movies about robots gone wild. They shot everyone and crashed trucks into everything. I placed my chin on Alex's chest and said, "That's our progeny." One night Alex played *Terminator II*. The robot was Schwarzenegger, the hero, saving Earth from a doomed future by shooting everyone and crashing trucks into everything. "See, our progeny grew into caring robots."

Yesterday, I felt relieved when we left the meeting with Rabbi Freyburg, resolved to work with Alex for the benefit of our children. Merton was feeling bushwhacked, learning he would soon join the unemployed ranks. I felt sorry for him. Knowing his fate, it was a mystery how he endured listening to a sneak preview of Alex's adventure to the Garden of Eden and the link from our children to the future generation of robots. And he even agreed to meet our children and hear from them progress on matrimonial prospects. What a *mensch*. He put aside the burden of eventually losing his job and he concerned himself with the here and now of why aren't our children married? He heard our plight and agreed to intervene. Annabelle should feel fortunate to have such a great husband. Even so, a few names of eligible candidates from rich families would definitely help resolve matters quickly.

An added dimension to the meeting was Merton being the first person whom we told about the robots or about my Alex traveling to Airets. Our Rabbi teetered in a difficult position, having to balance a friendship with a story reaching lunatic proportions. Zooming around in outer space was hardly believable. We needed to produce something tangible to keep his relationship with my husband cordial.

I believed every word your father said about his trip. I know Australia exists, even though I've never traveled there. In the same way, the Garden of Eden in outer space exists. How could I dispute it? I knew two eyewitnesses. A direct pipeline through Robot Alex reported all the news to me. A monitor attached to his stomach showed where Alex was located, whom he was with, and what action occurred. Who would believe the adventure besides me? The outer space story however needed more meat on the bone for the outside world.

Hearing my husband say he planned to write a new interpretation of the Garden of Eden legend might have been seen by Rabbi Freyburg as a ploy to grab his attention and put down the mail. I knew otherwise. My Alex intended to chronicle his voyage. I was happy. By writing, he found a path of sensible and meaningful pursuit. Your father wasn't afraid to move into an unfamiliar field. He seemed motivated and at times spoke with exhilaration. Rabbi Freyburg, who had completed a couple of books about marriage counseling, told Alex writing a book was no easy pursuit. Merton warned that preventing embarrassment was the hard part.

My only real complaint was some recent restless nights, when I awoke sweating. Hot flashes! My menopause began about ten years ago. Its effect was a significant drop-off in sexual activity, maybe to three or four times a month. That didn't mean I didn't love my husband. On the contrary, I loved my Alex to death. But now, the effect accompanying the hot flashes was reversed: my sexual excitement was heightened. And the frequency increased to five times a week, sometimes twice a day. This change began soon after my Alex returned from Airets. At first, I took no notice. Then each day the signs escalated, in number of episodes and in their strength. I needed to do something to control my anomalous symptoms. The way I felt, Robot Alex might not have been my last indiscretion. Poor Alex can't always keep up. Oh dear, in my state of mind, I'll need to be strapped down for a doctor's examination!

I sprang out of bed and headed to the closet. I opened the door and looked closely at the attached full-length mirror. My face was sultry. I ran my hand down my cheeks and felt a moist residue. Suddenly craving privacy, I walked inside the closet, turned on the light, and closed the door. The air smelled musty. I stood back from the mirror and stared at myself. My body shone with moisture. The hot flashes explained the sweat. What explained the sexual arousal? I moved my hips in a strip tease gyration. I liked what I saw. My body cast a lustful glow. I turned to observe my backside. My buttocks were in decent shape: a touch plump and a little lower, but definitely not saggy. I faced front. My breasts drooped, but were desirable, with picture-perfect dampness. My body was lean, with sexy curves for a woman in her sixties. I imagined dancing for a platoon of Italian soldiers.

My body burned with desire. Sweat glistened and my nipples hardened. Immediately a sensuous odor overtook my mind, not the earlier musty smell. It made every body part tingle. I concluded that the outbreak was an obsession, not a menopausal hot flash. I flung open the door and ran around the room to track down the source. I climbed on the bed and stalked in feline fashion. I lowered my face and sniffed the sheets and blanket. My excitement heightened. I snarled. Water flowed from my pores, a veritable wellspring. My mouth salivated, a wolf's jaw, dripping, ready to strike its prey. I rolled on my back.

A minute later, I heard the shower turn off. My Alex walked out of the bathroom with a towel wrapped around his waist. He stopped still when he saw me. I waited with my legs spread, one arm poised over my head with my hand bent in coquettish fashion and the other hand gently stroking my pudenda. My tongue rolled in a circle, licking my lips.

Breathily, I told him to cancel his golf game. I strutted toward him and said he wasn't going anywhere. The bed may be king-sized but once we start making love, we might roll off. I put my arms around his neck and looked into him. I flung aside the towel at his waist. No Viagra needed yet, but it might be soon. I said for now, I'd take good care of him. I kissed my husband passionately and we backpedaled onto the bed. We were going to make a baby.

After our morning delight, Alex and I went downstairs. Carefree, we laughed and teased each other all the way to the kitchen. We looked at each other feverishly. I planned, after some breakfast, to return upstairs with Alex and continue where we left off. Roman stood by the sink, shoving a fistful of cold pizza into his mouth. He reeked of pot.

I looked at Alex significantly, while my hand rested firmly on his shoulder. In a whisper, I asked Alex to be nice. He grimaced.

I walked toward Roman. I said, "Hello, dear." He turned towards me and kissed both cheeks. He had a sliver of cheese on his lip, which stuck to my face. Alex asked Roman if he was trying out for a part in *Animal House II?*

Roman tried to answer Alex with a witty reply. Instead, he lost his footing and fell onto the floor, breaking into hysterical laughter. Acting as if he were drowning, the kitchen counter being the gunwale of a boat, he pulled himself up. After Roman stood, Alex said to me, "We don't need a dog to eat the scraps. We have Roman." Roman giggled and then started to gag. He sprayed the remainder of the food in his mouth in Alex's direction. Alex remained calm, as I had requested, and dusted the gobs of pizza off his clothes. Roman wobbled and asked what all that yipping was earlier. Are you and Mom trying out for geriatric Internet porn? I grimaced: I mean "yipping" for crying out loud! Roman grabbed and shook his potbelly. Alex chuckled and said, "Our grandchild problem is solved. Roman, are you pregnant?" I gave Alex a significant stare.

Roman looked like a shoeless homeless man. His black hair was uncombed and his face unshaven. He wore shabby jeans and a stained T-shirt. He picked up and held a wedge of coffee cake, then buried his face in it.

Alex said he was glad Roman had the munchies. He saved us the trouble of throwing any leftovers in the garbage. I accompanied Roman to the breakfast table saying that he was covered with the smell of pot. "Please take a shower and wash off that odor."

Roman sat down at the breakfast table bleating, "Yeah, yeah, yeah." His eyes were half open and he sported a dumb grin. Alex chimed in, asking if Roman flunked the course in medical school where they taught hygiene.

I could sense an ugly scene developing. Roman countered with, "Dad, you're funny. Was there anything else?" Alex said he was never short of words. He suggested that Roman grow up and get married, unless he was planning to make a grand announcement that he was gay.

I blurted, "Alex!"

He continued, "Margarita my dear, how is it possible for an intelligent person to leave home, serve mankind doing noble work for underprivileged people in Canada for three years, and return home a pot-headed doofus?" Alex was right. Roman's behavior wasn't from anything we taught.

What was the catalyst that changed Roman? He was fine when he came home from Canada. I wondered if Alex's trip to Airets might be a possible reason. Why not? It wasn't just my libido that had increased on Alex's return, but my sense of smell had increased too. Now Roman's pot smoking was out of control, and it began around the same time. Then I remembered. Roman looked disorientated before I detected him smoking. On many occasions, he made dinner for himself when Alex and I went out. Oh my, there were a couple of leftover brownies he once made that Alex and I ate. We were in bed afterwards absorbed in foreplay, giggling with delight. We were high on marijuana. I concluded Roman acquired a sensitive sense of taste. It set him off to become a food addict. Marijuana encouraged him to stuff his face with food. Forgive a mother's justification of her boy's bad behavior.

Meanwhile, Roman foolishly egged Alex on. "Dad, are you worried that I'm overdoing it with my video games?"

Alex said sarcastically, "No, never! I'm waiting for your wife to tell you to stop." With sweeping gestures, Alex painted her as a duplicate of me, an Italian *pasticcino*. Her complexion will be dark, her hair jet black. She'll be about five feet six inches, with makeup applied to perfection. Her fingernails and toenails will be well-trimmed and painted with red nail polish. The crowd will murmur, "She is drop-dead gorgeous."

How long did Roman think his princess would put up with being married to a doctor who is acting infantile? Roman shielded himself with his medical diploma, saying, "She wouldn't divorce me—I'm a doctor!"

Alex said, "That depends. If you were married to a *shiksa* bimbo, she'd say, 'whatever Roman wants.' Married to a Jewish wife, you'll be taking a cold shower regularly."

Being zonked, Roman stupidly asked Alex what he meant. Alex attacked, saying, "Add a medical diagnosis to your repertoire. Symptom: wife upset by husband's behavior. Cure: no pussy until further notice."

I screamed, "Alex! Behave!"

Roman, dumbfounded, changed his expression back into a dumb grin.

I told Roman it would help if he pulled his act together and sought a job. Alex piped up that in Roman's condition, he'd spill the patients' bedpans onto the floor before a nurse could empty them in the toilet. I gave Alex a stare. He smiled. I turned to Roman. I told him I would enjoy going to lunch. I asked if we could have lunch the next day. He nodded. I said he should go to his room so his father and I could talk. Roman stood to leave, saying, "Ciao." He licked his fingers on the way. I asked if he could *please* open his bedroom window. We watched every step of his blasé exit.

Upset with Alex at the way he treated Roman, I was about to launch a verbal barrage. Alex caught me and remarked he would say nothing about Caroline. I said, "How smart of you. We'll keep it to one fight a day."

After a few moments in silence, I said we were skirting the issue. The children must be told about the robots and the importance of them getting married and having children. Your father said I had a luncheon date with Roman, so broach the subject with him then. I said I was afraid of how he'd react. Alex said, "What is he going to say? In fact, it might help. Once he hears the story, he'll sober up fast. It woke up Merton Freyburg."

I agreed. Breaking the news to him would be difficult for me, but it had to be done. Alex suggested I tell him that the characters in the video game were real robots that are his progeny. I shook my head and said, "Not cute, Alex."

In addition to the bedroom, the kitchen was also modernized, making cooking fun again. New cabinetry was installed, as was an island counter with gas burners. The old breakfast-room furniture remained, having once belonged to Alex's parents. Alex insisted on keeping it for sentimental reasons. I wasn't convinced. Hoarding everything was another of his compulsions. He kept accounting records stored in a warehouse from the inception of Adam and Eve. When I asked why he didn't throw them away, his reply was they were buried treasure.

The breakfast room was special. We loved to eat and watch the sunrise. We had an arm around each other's waist, and looked through the window where we could see our backyard. Your father called it our *hortus conclusus*. To the right was the patio with a hammock. Abutting that was a row of low-cut evergreens with a Japanese maple growing in the center. Past the evergreens was lawn and beyond that a stand of oak and a line of maples.

Jokingly, I said, "Would you like to spend a week with Prissy Gum?"

Alex smiled and replied, "Sure. I can't wait to shack up with her." Alex asked what I would do while he was whoring with her.

I was in heat and said, "Maybe Robot Alex could come back."

Alex growled at me and said, "You've become a robotic sex machine. Have your pinch hitter plant a marijuana patch for Roman between innings."

I countered, "I'd pit his prowess against yours. I'll insist he alter himself to look like a handsome and strapping *Italiano*."

Alex said, "That will look good for the neighborhood to see: a foreigner tilling the bushes outside and tilling your bush inside." He asked if I wanted Robot Alex back. He sounded as if all he had to do was make a phone call.

I said, "No thanks. I have you."

I made breakfast. I took out the frying pan and kitchen utensils from a drawer. Alex had already placed some eggs, onions, mushrooms, and tomatoes on the counter next to the burners. I made omelets and Alex made coffee.

We sat in the breakfast room and ate staring at each other. I said I would eat him when I finished my food. I wanted us to be Aida and Radames locked up in a tomb forever. Alex said I was over-the-top, but I couldn't help myself. Alex was saturated with a primal scent acquired from Airets. I couldn't explain why, but my libido had exploded because of it. Every aroma emanating from his body excited me. My sense of smell was so keen that if I opened the refrigerator, I could detect every fruit, vegetable, or cold cut with my eyes closed. Its effect on me was unending sexual desire. I'd turned into a slut and I couldn't get enough of him. I put my arm around my Alex's neck and said that my holy of holies was all his. He said I must have been constantly doing Kegel exercises. I suggested buying some sex toys. He asked if that would help cool me down—I was wearing him out. Even so, he admitted we were better in bed than we've ever been. He especially loved the way I teased him by saying we were going to make a baby; it activated something ancient in him—made him tumescent.

I longed for it to be true and the longing set fire to my insides. When I heard Robot Alex pleading, and the possibility of extinction, I thought, why did childbearing have to stop at Roman and Caroline? I imagined my eggs dropping. Your father said we shared the same values and longed for the same things in life. For now, he wanted to relate to the world the importance of the Garden of Eden. He had credibility. He needed people to trust him that robots really did exist.

I said, "Let's go back to bed. I'll rub you down and the dilemma will disappear." He asked if that was an Italian home-spun remedy. I snickered. I said, "I have an idea. Write your story as a poem and put it to music. Whether it's true or not won't matter. It'll be entertaining and everybody will listen. A joint could be included with every album sold. Isn't that a nice idea?" Alex laughed, saying Roman would be our first customer.

I said one more thing before we went back upstairs to make a baby. I said one thing to thank Jonathan Chapman for is taking you to Airets. How else could he have brought back those pre-historic aromas? I pushed him ahead of me, spanking his *tusch* to hurry him up the stairs.

we are family

Alex plopped back onto the pillow and wanted to know why I was so concerned about the future. He said, "If robots happen, then they'll happen. Stop worrying. You'll see. I have confidence our lineage will be carried forward by our children. Stay calm. Worry about the here and now."

I admitted the new familial trend of adopting a dog had some worth. The here and now of loving and caring for a dog, compared to living with a pothead for a son, won by a mile. I said waiting for our children to start families was unacceptable. My anxiety couldn't wait for Jonathan Chapman's boss, the head honcho robot Danziger, to anoint me the queen bee of the robots. That's why I yearn for the future. Maybe Danziger will reincarnate me as a robot.

I took my husband's remarks as his agreement to be a participant in creating the future generation. I didn't like my Alex saying the robots behaved like a bunch of jerks and dictators, just like the present world's jerks and dictators. Under my tutelage, they'll morph into lovable creatures. I planned to brag about the robots to my friends and anyone who would listen. I didn't feel I had to wait all those years. The world belonged to me now.

Alex said, "Getting pregnant is a pipe dream. You're too old." I suggested he wait and see. "If Abraham's main squeeze could do it, and if there are robots coming back to talk to us from the future, then anything's possible. Stop being so rational, I hate rationality. The robots will be family." Alex backed off and said he felt a connection with them even if they were lapsed Jews. He quoted Gandhi, I have no idea why, but it sounded knowledgable: "I love your Christ, but your Christians frighten me ..." He continued saying our ideals were akin to that: we loved strong family ties, but hated our relatives. Being an unqualified and non-degreed sociologist he spouted that family wavered intellectually from dumb to smart, and politically democratic to autocratic.

I said, "You mean all robots were not created equal?" He laughed. Some were warriors; some were dumb butts. *Mia bambina*, your father loved them. He praised them, saying they arranged for him to see the original Garden of Eden. What could he say to them but "thank you" one thousand times?

I asked Alex why they would connect and bond with us. He said, "Oh, my dear. Look at it from their position. They'd formed a link with our ancestral generations." Alex asked if I remembered when Chapman conned him into traveling to Turkey by saying artifacts from the original Garden of Eden were found there with sophisticated underground detectors. I said yes. Alex said when Chapman and he were headed to the airport, Chapman gave him a packet with maps, layouts, and reports. Alex thought he would review the material and they would begin to discuss the Garden of Eden project. Instead, Chapman started talking about Alex's Uncle Harry.

Ah, *mia bambina*. Uncle Harry, a relative you have not met: a *shikker*. I lapsed into a daydream. Your father described his family's personal history to me many times. He portrayed them as a Russian gang, riding around on horses, drunk. The main figurehead, Uncle Harry, died about forty years ago. Alex's most unforgettable childhood memory of him was on a visit to his house. He delivered a doctoral dissertation to the family on the best blends of whiskey, pausing every so often for a taste. Behind the drunken lecturing professor was a photograph, which sat on the mantel-piece. In it, Uncle Harry wore a Cossack tunic and kalpak. He stood about five feet ten inches, wide in the shoulders: a Taras Bulba type. His expression sported a menacing air, ready to lead his troops into battle. Alex guessed his age to be about twenty years old. In the background was a building bearing a Russian language inscription over the entrance. Alex heard sordid family stories that as a youngster, Uncle Harry lived a reckless life. Fight-ing with Russian peasants and knocking over carts in the market square were common. Alex believed the picture on his mantle matched the stories.

Alex said, "While inside the limo, Chapman elaborated glee-fully on a story about when Uncle Harry, dressed in his Cossack outfit, galloped a horse through a Gypsy encampment, slashing at people with a saber. He knocked over tents and campfires, stabbed farm animals and yelled that he was going to kill every-one. 'No one scares my sister. Get out of here by tomorrow.'"

Alex continued that he'd heard a lot of old stories about the family in Russia. Alex knew his father and his brothers were wild. He didn't know why no one ever told him about his aunt being menaced. Chapman, the robot, got the credit by telling it first.

I said, "Whom could you ask to verify the story? Our parents' generations have died." Alex had only Chapman, and was Chap-man a reliable witness?

Alex said there were times when you heard a strange story from a pretty straight shooter; like when he said he was kid-napped by robots for a month.

I interjected, "Like Merton Freyburg hearing your story?

Alex looked hurt. I said Merton hadn't abandoned him yet.

Alex said he told a strange story and Merton considered it a *Bubbe Meinsah*. Discouraging, since he knew anything unveri-fiable would be labeled as myth by perfectly reasonable people. Alex considered Chapman's story a myth since it couldn't be veri-fied. At the point in time when Chapman told him the anecdote, Alex didn't know Chapman came from the future. Chapman's response when Alex asked who told him about Uncle Harry was that no one told him. He saw Harry in action.

Alex was nonplussed. He looked at Chapman like he was crazy. Chapman kept on talking. He said, "Oh Alex, you of little faith. Trust me, you'll find out what I've said is true."

Alex told me, "I am familiar with many other facts about the family in Russia, but so was Chapman. He had a wealth of information." He told Alex the name of the village in Ukraine where his father's family lived: Pischunka. Alex had learned that name from his father. Chapman said Bershad was a nearby city. The trails leading out from the village ended after a mile in a no-man's-land, making travel dangerous. What Chapman related to him, Alex said he heard from his family. But, who told Chapman the specifics? Your father asked Chapman where he learned so much about Alex's familial home. Chapman responded that he saw Pischunka firsthand and his father as a young boy. Alex thought robots had to be either the dumbest or the smartest persons in the universe.

I suggested to Alex that if the robots could time travel to us, of course they could have hung out with his uncle. We were both shocked at the implications—no privacy for anyone anywhere in history; think of all the abnormal things humans do in private that they would not want obnoxious robots from the future looking in on and snickering. The only normalcy in my life was I married an unflappable accountant and a robust and sturdy stud. My biggest heartache and worry is our unmarried *bambini*. I said we surely couldn't save the world by ourselves. We need fresh blood, like a baby. Alex groaned. He said he felt confident Merton was thinking about us and would come up with a solution.

I curled up next to Alex. I said we were scheduled to see Merton tomorrow and I couldn't wait.

Hmmmmmmm! I loved to hold tight onto my Alex when he talked in a serious tone of voice. Then I could tease him. Not that teasing was a trait I showed exclusively with Alex. I did however use it as an amusement when we first met. My family owned a confectionary located in the old Jewish quarter in Rome. Our family business, a quaint shop that attracted the after-dinner crowd, was in a tourist area with many restaurants, jewelers, bookstores, and historic sites nearby. Mezzaluna, a marzipan, was our signature delight.

I worked late afternoons and evenings with my sister behind the counter. My father manned the cash register and every so often yelled orders to my mother to bring more stock to the front. My sister and I were visible through the front window; we brought in the crowds, even if it was only for directions to Il Tempio, which was in plain sight. I rebuffed many men who asked me out by saying the Portico d'Ottavia was on the next block.

One day a man walked into the store and smote me. It was Alex. He looked Italian with dark hair and a touch of olive skin coloring. He stood out as American: jeans and a sport shirt with a mechanical pencil inside his shirt pocket. He stood about six foot one. He browsed the pastry cases, while I browsed his body. I turned to my sister, Roma, who was filling a box with a customer's order, and said in a low voice, "Cover for me. Tell father I'll be working on a big order."

She looked at Alex and then at me. She smiled and said, "A bit square, but not bad."

Alex strolled about the store looking at the various offerings.

At the right moment, I spoke in my limited English, but used my sexiest voice, "May I help you?"

Alex looked up and said he was interested in some Cannoli.

I cut a Cannoli into sample-sized bites. I offered one to him. He wanted to take the piece from my hand, but I shook my head. I opened my mouth. He took the hint and I fed him.

My father walked over and stood between us, facing Alex. He said, "May I help you, sir?"

Alex replied that he was browsing and enjoying a sample.

My father turned to face me. With a scowl, he said, "What did I tell you? I said stay away from Americans. They're trouble. They only want women for the hubba-hubba." Alex smiled. He didn't need a translator.

I left to help another customer. Alex bought a few items from my father. After he left the store, my father glanced in my direction and wagged his finger. He upset me by guarding me so close. I wanted to meet Alex again.

I asked my father why he was so protective about Alex, when he knows many young men come into the store to strike up a conversation and he leaves them alone.

He said he saw Alex's leering look when he came in. Besides, he saw him earlier at a cappuccino bar. He was sipping from his demitasse wearing his suit coat over his shoulders. That American learned well, how to be an Italian gigolo. His eyes were romantically focused on the breasts of the girl he was with.

I was upset there was competition, but glad Alex frequented the neighborhood. The next day, before going to work, I stuck my head in nearby cappuccino bars. There he was standing sideways against the bar, waiting for the next conquest to enter. I didn't disappoint. I walked up to the bar where Alex saw me and said, "Ciao, bella."

As I blushed, he said, "You work at the bakery down the block."

"Yes. You came in yesterday."

Alex said, "Your father made sure we didn't have a chance to talk privately."

"He thinks you are a flirt."

Alex said he'd come to the store later and talk to him about taking me out for a date.

I was surprised and said, "You will?"

Alex nodded. "I will tell him you are Italia, which translated from Hebrew means the Island of the dew of God."

My heart fluttered and I felt warm. I said it might be better to meet away from my family. I told him I worked in the morning at La Rinascente, located at the Piazza Colonna. I said, "Come by tomorrow. You'll find me in the young people department."

He said he had nephews who would be thrilled to receive Italian clothes as presents. I added he could use some clothes. I commented what he was wearing looked drab. He asked for a personal shopping tour. I said I would oblige.

Alex came to my department the next day. He bought clothes for his nephews. I took him to the men's department and showed him what to purchase. He asked if my father would like him with the new clothes.

I said, "Unlikely. For one, you didn't speak Italian."

"How about Yiddish?"

"It's not normal around here, but he speaks it, and if you do too he won't think you're a complete *grauber*."

"We can tell him in any language you like that I want to marry you."

"It is normal, I believe, to ask me first."

"A formality, surely—since you came to find me." I punched his arm, the first of many beatings he has received from me. "Will you marry me, beautiful girl?"

It was madness, but I found my mouth saying, "I will."

The next morning, Alex and I took a solitary walk through Birmingham. When we go for such walks, we always pass Greenwood Cemetery, a fenced-in city pasture. The headstones are etched with names of veterans who served in the Civil War and the War of 1812. As we approached the cemetery, Alex said, "I wish I could bring back Uncle Harry. Then we'd know for sure if Chapman's story about him riding through the Gypsy camp was true. It's been forty years since he died. I wish I could hit the rewind button and reverse time. I'd sit on a wall near Uncle Harry's grave and wait for the gravediggers to appear. The hearse would arrive and carry Uncle Harry back to the funeral home. He would be removed from his casket and taken to the hospital, where he would reawaken. I'd ask him, 'Uncle Harry, in the old country, did you threaten Gypsies by riding through their camp on a horse, swinging a saber?'"

I didn't understand why it mattered whether the stories were true or not.

FIVE

the robot rings the doorbell

I looked in the den and saw Alex bent over his computer key-board, typing feverishly. His fingers moved like those of a pianist. He being the computer *maven*, I asked what interesting web sites he surfed. Alex said he was researching the topic of pregnancy over fifty. I walked up to him while he typed and wrapped my arms around his neck. His odor intoxicated me. As I nibbled his ear I asked if he had found the answer to our problem. He answered, "Besides Sarah giving birth to Isaac at ninety, Margaret Krasiowa of Poland married at ninety-four and had three children."

I whispered, "We can do it then."

Trying to ignore me, Alex said Rosanna Della Corte of Italy had a son at sixty-two through assisted reproductive technology. I thought, at my next gynecological visit, I will request a pamphlet. ART works wonders for others, why not me? I encouraged him to keep up the good work while I went grocery shopping. Knowing my libido was in overdrive, he played me, the swine, "Yes, yes, get outta my hair for a while, woman." I didn't really want to go shopping, I wanted him to throw me on the floor, but he was in a hermeneutical mood, so no chance.

As I turned to leave, Alex reminded me of our appointment with Merton that afternoon. I nodded sulkily and walked to the garage, glad that at least he was fulfilled. My revenge would be to hit Tiffany's before the grocery store. I hoped to clear my mind, which nagged at me about my children's marital status. The question was, what did I have to do to focus their minds on marriage: lick their spoiled feet, twist nipples, what? However, the *Wolf Winslow Show* inspired a new possibility: the prospect of a newborn. What would Roman and Caroline say if they were to find out a new sibling was being cooked up to replace them? With relish, I envisioned announcing my state to them. This child will follow my instructions. It will marry and deliver grandchildren. "You two losers are fired as procreators." That'll spring them into action, because they'd be thinking about Alex's will and their grandfather's properties in Rome.

Usually I got *farputst* to go shopping at upscale stores, maybe wearing designer jeans and a white blouse with a turned-up collar. Wearing open-toed pumps with polished toenails completed the "look at me" statement. Today, I wore gardening clothes: a pair of grungy jeans and an old sweatshirt from an accounting convention with "Expo 1997" on it. I wanted my clothes to disguise me. My husband's female admirers who'd recognize me otherwise might approach and ask his whereabouts. They were shameless and swarmed him in every store. The infectious sexually arousing odor he brought back from Airets could be the only explanation.

As I pulled into the mall parking lot, my cell phone rang. It was Annabelle Freyburg, Merton's wife. "Hello, Annabelle. How are you?"

"Fine. I've missed you, M."

I said I'd been preoccupied with family matters. She replied she'd heard. I snickered to myself, well, well, well, Annabelle was in the loop after all. Merton's office definitely needed repairs to plug the leaky walls. Why should I be surprised? In the past, Annabelle related to me the story *du jour* about extramarital affairs she'd learned of from Merton. Contrary to his claims, confidentiality is not guaranteed within synagogue walls. I thought about the upcoming appointment with Merton. Why keep Annabelle in the dark? I invited her to sit in on the meeting.

It was an operational one-two punch. Edith, Merton's secretary must have tipped off Annabelle that we met with her husband. Since it wasn't marriage counseling, Edith concluded something big was brewing and called her. After hearing about our meeting, I believed Annabelle waited for Merton to arrive home. She no doubt yanked hard on Merton's privates for details.

Somewhat breathlessly, Annabelle asked if there was anything she could do to help. I enjoyed declining her offer, saying, "Annabelle, you know I love and cherish you, but the subject matter is rather sensitive."

"Merton told me," she admitted, "that your offspring act as if marriage is outmoded. Since Merton can't handle all the family issues that come across his desk, I may be of some assistance."

Loving this, I retorted, "Trust me, Annabelle, no human on this planet can help."

She backed off, saying, "Well, all right." Then she said brightly that the other reason she called was personal. It seemed a strange problem had arisen since our visit. Merton's sense of hearing had gained strength and intensified to a point where he could hear conversations from a far distance. I held my breath, trying to prevent blurting, "*Oy*, I don't believe it!"

Apparently, during morning services, while Merton delivered his sermon, a couple of old geezers in the back row whispered to each other. Normally, Merton couldn't hear them and *shusking* didn't bother him. This time it was different: he heard them *kvetching* over our useless Detroit Lions. Incensed, Merton shouted at Annabelle afterward, as if it were her fault. How dare they think a stupid sport like football is more important than a spiritual message?

Annabelle sniffled a little, "Merton never shouts at me." I assured her I would tell him to use a calmer tone of voice with my best friend. Of course, Annabelle was missing something. Merton could now hear every piece of synagogue gossip while sitting in his office. Merton didn't have to wait for marriage counseling to know which congregants slept about town.

I returned to the main subject with Annabelle. Merton was partly right. My children avoided marriage. "It's killing us," I sobbed. "Grandchildren are missing!"

Annabelle there-there'd me, "Poor thing, we're both concerned and worried."

Gloating, she was. I couldn't let it stand. So I asked if Merton told her about Alex's trip to the Garden of Eden.

"No, should he have?"

In a delicious conspiratorial hush I said, "Annabelle, dear, swear on your life that he didn't mention anything about the robots."

She replied meekly, "Well, yes, sort of. It's a little far-fetched."

Satisfied, I let that rest, thinking, this is not the sharpest pin in the hatbox.

I said, "You mentioned Merton's sense of hearing is now way beyond the norm. Something similar has happened to me. Except it is my sense of smell. Alex brought back a lingering odor from his visit to the Garden of Eden that's driving me nuts. Its effect brings about a craving to boink every man in the world. I dream about being a hooker working for a charity."

Annabelle said, "Oh my God. You and Alex must be very busy. I wish Merton's improved hearing had the same effect. Instead it's encouraged him to render more pontifical opinions." Merton told her that after services ended, he went up to the elderly gentlemen and told them the owner of the Lions should fire the coach. Their mouths dropped open.

I interrupted Annabelle, saying I had to rush home. "I drove Alex's car to the mall. His lingering odor in the car has made me hot. Good-bye, dear!" I immediately dialed home. Alex answered. Panting, I said, "Get ready big boy, I'm hot and wet. I'll be home in five minutes. Good-bye!" In recent weeks, my private area never saw so much sunlight. I made it home in four minutes.

We returned to Merton's study as planned, and sat in the same seats as last time. Feeling quite sore, I held onto the chair's side arms and lowered myself down. Alex looked exhausted. When I got home, sans jewelry or groceries, we went at each other like animals. Somehow I had the presence of mind to set an alarm clock; otherwise we would have missed the appointment.

I noticed that Merton wore the same suit and shoes as before. If my earlier phone conversation with Annabelle had lasted longer, I would have told Annabelle to buy new clothes for him. I didn't need Edith as a messenger. Anyway, why wasn't Annabelle here? I thought I'd invited her.

Merton said we looked tired. My Alex and I glanced at each other, clasped our hands and smiled. "Stress," said my husband. Merton rolled his eyes. He told us he had called Caroline. She didn't answer, so he left a message. "While we're here together," he said, "I told Edith to put through another call to your daughter. Maybe we'll get lucky and get her on the speaker-phone." Ah-ha, I reflected, so Edith's pretending to do secretarial work ... calling Caroline. That old nosey wants in on all this.

Merton reflected that he remembered Caroline from religious school. "She was one of our brightest students, a nice kid. Boys were always interested in trying to get better acquainted with her. She rebuffed them. School came first ..."

I interrupted, sniffling, "And now she's ... she's dating a bum. Why couldn't she be interested in dating one of those boys from school?" Merton squinted at me. I bawled. "I'll bet some are still unmarried. She could have her pick."

A buzzer rang. Merton sat and looked at me with exasperation. He reached and answered his intercom. It was Edith on the conference speaker. She informed Merton that Caroline was unavailable. Merton said, "In the meantime, Edith, please call Cantor Hames and tell him to stop rehearsing. I'm in conference and can hear him from the other end of the building." My Alex looked dismayed. I forgot to mention Merton's newfound aural sensitivity.

Merton turned to me and spoke a bit sharply. "M, be thankful she's working at a profession she loves, which earns her enough money to support herself. Be glad bodybuilding or being a motor-cycle gang bitch plastered with tattoos isn't her thing. Enough said?" A brief silence thickened the air. I thought Annabelle was right. He'd become louder.

Merton opened the discussion about the robots, saying he felt baffled. The subject had obsessed him since our visit. "How did you meet them, Alex?"

Alex stretched out and grinned. I was still sniffling; he looked at me with a sarcastic air, and asked when I would finish *pishach-ing*. Let the children tear your heart later. I thought, why didn't I bring a baseball bat? Mr. Stud Service is ready to speak so the planet has to suspend all activities.

Your father said it began innocently enough about six months earlier. He was stretched out in our bedroom reading *Accounting Digest* and about to take a nap. I had left earlier to go to Macy's. The doorbell rang. Alex refused to answer at first. He was drowsy. The doorbell rang again. And again. He kept ignoring the door-bell until the ringing changed to pounding. Enough already! He suspected it to be a proselytizer. They thump bibles and thump the doors of adulteresses. He paused in his tale to look at me. He knew I was between a rock and a hard place. For his insolence, any wife would have cut off marital relations immediately. Not me.

When the pounding on the door continued, Alex rushed downstairs in a hot fury. On the landing, he looked out the front window and saw a black limousine parked in the street. It wasn't a livery service—no side logo or decal. Puzzled, he continued downstairs to the side door and walked around to the front to see a well-dressed man facing the door at attention, with his arms at his sides and large fingers gripping the handle of a briefcase.

The man turned to him. His vapid eyes, dazzling Steinway teeth and phony grin looked familiar. His expression reminded Alex of that character Bob on male enhancement commercials. Alex grinned back, assessing the guest to be about forty-five, with his blondish hair tinged with gray. He wore a light brown suit, a yellow foulard tie and lizard skin shoes. Other than his shoes being a bit out of style, he was expensively dressed and rode in an expensive automobile.

"Are you Alexander Haralson," the man asked. Alex replied that he was. The man then made a couple of exaggerated shoulder jerks and introduced himself as John Chapman. Alex, by comparison was unshaven, and wore jeans and a Beethoven T-shirt. When Alex shook hands he found the man's skin clammy, with metal parts churning beneath fingers and palm, and he was glad to retrieve his hand without injury. Chapman claimed to have a gift for Alex.

"I suppose I'll win a million bucks if I buy your magazines," scoffed Alex. Chapman replied that he had something even more valuable. Alex pressed on, saying, "You have a check for two million dollars for me? Give it over already."

Chapman started to unravel. He repeated himself, saying, "I have something even more valuable." Alex thought *who is this guy? What's wrong with him?* His expression stayed the same—that Steinway smile. The shoulders jerked again. Alex said he seemed to be trying to shift into second gear. Chapman finally blurted that he knew Alex was retired and looking for meaningful work. Alex countered, asking if John was from the CIA. Chapman looked puzzled, then complimented Alex on his beautiful home. He hoped he hadn't interfered by visiting unannounced.

Merton cut in, hitting his intercom button. In a sharp voice he said, "Edith I can hear you speaking with Annabelle. Please restrain yourself." He looked at me and then Alex. "Please continue."

My Alex continued, saying that Chapman claimed to work for a publisher. They needed a working relationship with a researcher and writer. The subject was the Garden of Eden. Chapman then dropped the plum. He said they did a personnel search for possible candidates and Alex was chosen. Chapman related that his organization had made discreet inquiries and found that Alex was an intelligent man of passion. My Alex was dumbfounded: him a researcher and writer. He didn't apply for any job, but Alex told Chapman how interesting the job sounded.

I thought, here's a man who makes a living dissecting people's private information. Alex didn't know what a *yold* he could be—a box of spare parts shows up at the door, posing as Max Headroom, and Alex is tempted by a job as a retread. I was grateful Chapman didn't offer him swampland in Florida or sacks of old apple seed.

"Crazy, crazy, crazy," whined Merton. Was he hearing right that Chapman laid on the table a plate of pork and beans and the star accountant ate it up? Alex replied that Chapman jumped right to the point: a serious job offer for a brilliant man testicletied by premature retirement. Flattery gets Alex every time.

Alex said Chapman would share his findings, which was all about the exact location of the Garden of Eden—a subject close to your father's romantic old heart. He could spend as much time as needed. With the information he gleaned, Alex could write a book. Merton broke in and asked Alex if he realized at this point that Chapman was a robot. "No," Alex replied, "but, if Bernie Madoff was substituted for John Chapman, would the story sound more plausible?" Merton deferred, being a great fan of everyone's friend, Bernard.

Alex invited Chapman to the cedar deck in back of the house to tell him more. They sat down at the patio table.

Chapman claimed that his employer, Malus Enterprises, had reserved $25 million to finance the Garden of Eden project. Its director, Danziger Kantaphel, was personally committed. Alex told Chapman to set a meeting time with the director.

Chapman continued as if he hadn't heard. Knowing the exact location of the Garden of Eden, Mr. Kantaphel committed the money, believing a need for a new interpretation of the story existed, one which would be factual. Chapman suggested Alex could be the next *gaon* of biblical analogies. Alex swooned, thanking Chapman for putting him in the heavyweight division of biblical thinkers.

Then my rational Alex worried that he wasn't the right person for the job. Archeologists would be the ones most interested. "Why didn't you get in touch with a University? Throw money at them. You'll get plenty of attention. In fact," Alex continued, "I imagine a testimonial dinner in your honor. You'll receive a plaque of commendation."

Chapman said working with academics was a bore, same with spiritual leaders. Chapman winked, saying, "I know you can do it." It didn't take long for Alex's ego to assert itself, and he soon put himself back on center stage and accepted the position.

"It has been rumored," Alex stated, "that the Garden of Eden's location was in the West Caucasus Mountain range. Is that true?"

Chapman waffled. "It's in a location where nobody thought to look. We'll travel together to Turkey and I'll show you what's there."

I broke in saying it was at this point that I returned home. When I walked into the house, I heard Alex call me out to the patio. I saw what I thought was a well-dressed mannequin, grinning like a game show host. Alex introduced us, saying, "Margarita, meet John Chapman." Chapman extended his hand. Alex dove at me and restrained my arm. He said, "Watch it, M— bionic hand." Chapman withdrew his hand and broke into a tooth-chattering laugh, half monkey, half alarm clock. I looked at Alex in disbelief.

Alex explained Chapman's proposal. His organization had found the location of the Garden of Eden. "They want to take me to the site."

Chapman nodded said, "We must hire your husband to write a book about the findings." I asked Chapman the whereabouts. He mumbled the word Turkey, then started whirring—not a very good liar, obviously—but the whirring stopped after he banged his head with his fist.

I looked at Alex with disgust. I turned to Chapman and said, "Are there any spare burial sites? I'd like to buy one for my husband."

Chapman replied, "I'm sure we can find him one." In a fury, I turned and stalked into the house. While inside, I heard Alex tell Chapman that my remark was a joke.

I said, "Merton, let me explain something. Chapman had not yet disclosed any plans to shuttle Alex to planet Airets. Alex thought the Garden of Eden location was a site in Turkey. I misunderstood, thinking Chapman meant Tour Key, some island near Florida, or the Torquay in England."

Earlier, Alex asked Chapman why anyone hadn't found the location before. Plenty of people had searched the Caucasus Mountains. Chapman replied it was well-hidden. Chapman said he was so sure of his find, not wanting to waste Alex's time, he'd advance a $50,000 retainer. Alex called me out and said Chapman raised the ante. With that enticing statement on the table, the idea of not considering Chapman's offer was dumb. Although Alex wasn't qualified to do research and write on such an esoteric subject, he demonstrated great ability and versatility in completing complex tasks—like fooling the IRS. I looked directly at Chapman: "How about an extra kicker of $25,000 to close the deal?" He said, "Yes. Mr. and Mrs. Haralson, you won't be sorry. With two of your three children married, Alex, you'll have plenty of time to focus on work."

My Alex and I looked at each other aghast. I said, "None of our children are married. And we have only two. Who told you otherwise?"

Chapman replied he had observed it. "Your oldest children, are they in their forties?"

I said, "No, Roman is thirty-five and Caroline is thirty-two."

Chapman said he knew he wasn't mistaken, claiming his information was reliable. "Part of our search included learning all about you: your family history, your career, and your interests. Alex, you left footprints everywhere. Biblical subjects are your most visited sites on the Internet. You earned a master's degree. Golf is your passion. Your business credentials are impeccable. You're a devoted husband and father." Chapman said, "Did I miss anything?"

Alex burst out, "You're a regular Peeping Tom, Chapman."

My mind was riveted on the part when he said our children were married. I thought, *when did he observe them*? My heart pounded, my resistance weakening.

Chapman had a request. He wanted to see a picture of our parents. Alex went indoors and returned to the patio with our wedding album. Chapman flipped to a picture of Alex and me with our parents. He pointed, said, "Oh yes, I recognize your parents. Alex, your parents immigrated from the Ukraine, and Margarita, you came from Italy, *o bellissima donna*."

We couldn't believe what he said. We were drained. Into the silence, Chapman said quietly, "I want us to work together."

Chapman handed Alex a business card, which bore a company name and a street address on Apple Lane in the town of Spitzenberg, Spitzbergen, telephone 277-53. "Peculiar address for a corporate office," commented Alex. He asked where Chapman was staying and was told downtown Birmingham at the Townsend.

Alex and Chapman shook hands. I was about to offer mine, but remembered what Alex said earlier; I clasped my hands behind my back like an Orthodox Jew. Chapman looked at me, his expression the same as when I met him: a crazed, petrified grin. "Good-bye Mrs. Haralson." Euro-style, he kissed both my cheeks with his playdough lips. We walked him to the edge of the driveway and waved good-bye. I watched his swaying gait as he walked to his car. An unusual specimen, he was.

Deep in thought, Merton slouched in his chair. Finally, he said, "The part that got my attention today was that he disclosed some relevant part of the future. He knew all about your children: three instead of two, and that the older ones were married. M, are you pregnant?"

Taken aback, I said, "Of course not."

Merton continued, "You're obviously still having active marital relations."

I replied, "You heard that from Annabelle."

Merton said, "I swear I did not. In my business, people around your age tell me that things have slowed down or are non-existent. I know having a child sounds preposterous. But it's starting to make sense. M, you said that Chapman's or Robot Alex's existence wouldn't happen until grandchildren were born." I concurred. Merton continued, "I'll bet he's counting on you to have another child. *Oy vey*, Roman and Caroline, no longer the center of attention! Ha!"

Alex blurted, "Merton, you're crazy. Haven't you ever heard of menopause?"

I screamed, "What do we name the child, Houdini? *Schloyma?*"

Merton held up a hand, "Please, I'm only expressing an opinion. How about Isaac? Damn that Cantor Hames. He's started again. Excuse me, I've got to tell that bastard his rehearsals are interfering with my work." Merton stormed out.

I said, "We didn't tell poor Merton about my sensitivity to odors. Chapman returned you home with that infectious scent. God bless John Chapman. Let's go home, I think I'm ovulating."

chapter

SIX

should we tell
roman?

Spread-eagled, feet in the stirrups, I breathed deeply as Dr. Lewis Green administered a pelvic exam. He was a bit of an old fart and grunted as he poked around inside me. When he completed the exam, he said all appeared normal. I said, "I forgot to abstain from sex the usual twenty-four hours before the appointment. My husband the biblical researcher being in tip-top shape, was insistent, sorry." Green replied that he noted evidence of intercourse.

My ideal, I revealed, was to mother another child and to go forward with ART treatments. I hoped to sound well-informed. He tilted his head and squinted when I used the medical acronym. He looked down at my chart and asked if my age was sixty-two. I responded yes. He lapsed into contemplation. I imagined him searching for an appropriate response. He might ask himself, Who is she kidding? How do I let her down gently? Or, Why do all nutty women make appointments to see me? Would he say, "I see you've researched fertility procedures?" Or, "Why don't you consider adopting a pet?" I coaxed him, "Well, Doctor?"

He finally said he wasn't sure if I would be a good candidate. Dr. Green had boyish looks, despite his age. I sat up on the examination table and wrapped my arms around his neck. I pressed my lips to his ear and said he had done a magnificent job examining me. I told him about my overheated sex drive and that his fingers tantalized me. "Can't you see, doctor, I'm desperate to conceive?" His neck tightened. I held him tight and said, "I'll bet you could deliver into a test tube a high sperm count specimen."

He shouted, "Mrs. Haralson, please!"

I said, "If you don't like that plan then, as an alternative, I've got a daughter named Caroline who's ready for a man like you. You could be the father of the grandchild I need."

He groaned and ordered me to get dressed. "I'll meet you in my office to discuss ART treatments. Bring your husband in for testing."

I said, "Why, thank you, Lewis."

Later that afternoon, Alex entered the kitchen and went straight to the lower part of the pullout freezer. Everything was kept neatly stacked by my husband. Open the freezer and rock-hard bagels, hamburger patties, ice cream, and three-year-old *shmaltz* is at your fingertips in alphabetical order. Alex removed two steaks and placed them on a tray. I loathe accountants.

Alex ignored me. He knew my sense of smell might ignite, forcing me to grab him and start us toward the bedroom. He lifted the tray and said, "I'll be in our *hortus conclusus*."

I came around the kitchen counter and wrapped my arms around him. We nuzzled about a minute. I said, "I love it so, when you use dirty words."

He replied, "A garden locked is my own, my bride, A fountain locked, A sealed-up spring."

I said, "After dinner I'm unlocking your fountain." I squeezed his *tusch* and said, "Don't get lost."

With my extraordinary sense of smell, I was having all the fun: sex, sex, and more sex. Merton was dealing with his problem of extraordinary hearing. I called Annabelle and learned that

Merton was disgusted with everyone. He told her it's bad enough to hear everyone's pettiness and mendacity. Now he heard what congregants thought of him. General consensus: boring sermons, pompous ass. They didn't give a shit what he had to say. Merton heard no one discussing charity, human kindness, or tolerance. The poor dear grew quite depressed.

To add to his troubles, Annabelle wanted what I had. Of course she'd told him everything. They were both sick with envy, but she believed that God decreed it and they accepted His will. She asked if by any chance Alex had brought back an aphrodisiac from outer space. I sadly shook my head, "Just his smell, Annabelle, just his smell."

I asked if Edith filled her in on our meeting with Merton. She said no. Edith had called me after our meeting, but only spoke about the preparation for the kosher cooking classes I'd be conducting next fall. I was taken aback. This was not the Edith I knew.

Annabelle said eagerly, "Don't be shy, tell me about the meeting." I told her we talked a bit about how we came into contact with a robot named John Chapman, but our meeting was cut short. I told her that Merton suddenly became irritated, claiming he had to silence Cantor Hames's off-key rehearsal. "I couldn't hear anything, but he stormed out of our meeting. Trust me Annabelle, Merton will never need a hearing aid."

I told her we met up with Merton a few minutes later in the parking lot, and it was another installment about the robots. I said, "We were walking to our car and saw Merton speeding toward the exit. He looked in our direction, drove over to us, stopped, and rolled down his window. He apologized for leaving so abruptly. The cantor kept disrupting him. He swore he'd had it up to his eyeballs with Hames's histrionics. They'd just had a heated argument. Merton said he and the Cantor agreed to fight it out at the Fitness Center. Alex said he knew a golfing Rabbi, now a boxing Rabbi. We laughed."

Merton said, "Anyway, enough of me. Let's continue. I have ten minutes before battle. Alex, I'm curious about something you mentioned earlier. When you concluded your meeting with

Chapman, you were skeptical, but took Chapman's proposal seriously. Eventually, you got on board a spaceship. Obviously you shook hands on a deal."

Alex laughed and said that Merton had formulated in his head an aboveboard agreement between Chapman and himself. "Did you also believe logistics would flow smoothly afterwards? Think again." Alex continued, asking Merton if he knew where Shain Park was. Merton said he did. Alex said there was a thirty-foot sculpture by Marshall M. Fredericks named *The Freedom of the Human Spirit*.

Merton interjected, saying, "Yes, it's a soaring depiction of a mythological hero and heroine, a bit modern for my taste."

Alex said, "Okay then, the spaceship I was forced to embark launched about a hundred feet away from that site."

Merton slapped his forehead and said, "*Gevalt*, why didn't I just go straight to getting my face punched?"

I cut in, saying, "Merton, *caro mio*, Chapman's first visit occurred on the Friday the Shain Park Fair opened. On Sunday, Alex and I always put down whatever we're doing to attend. My interest is to say hello to old friends, while Alex roams around the rides, walking like James Dean."

I couldn't read what lay behind Merton's eyes, so I continued to tell him that the fair was packed and we strolled around the park, looking fabulous. The rides were always the same, old and rickety, with teenagers screaming. Then we neared the space rocket ride. Alex noted it was new. It didn't move or shake, but hissed smoke from its bottom.

Merton asked if the rocket ship was the ride that launched. Alex said yes and I continued the story. We stood at the space rocket ride towards the end of a ride cycle. Alex commented on the rocket's realistic design. It was about twenty-five feet tall and fourteen feet around, with steam dissipating. The teenagers who finished the ride were laughing and yelling to their waiting friends that it was the best ride at the fair. The kids said the ticket taker told them they were going to the moon. "It sure felt like it." Others screeched, "It was awesome, dude."

Mia bambina, don't ever call your father dude. He hates it.

I told Merton the exterior of the rocket ride was a silvery metal housing shaped in the form of a 1950s Buck Rogers spaceship.

Merton interjected, "Go on."

I said that Alex noticed the rocket's personnel. A woman was inside a booth selling tickets and at the ride's entrance a man was ripping them. He was an atypical fair worker, dressed in khaki pants and a collared shirt. The man turned and looked up towards us. Alex said he couldn't believe his eyes. He nudged me to look at the ticket taker. I said, "*Marito mio*, what is the matter?"

Alex said, "Do you see the blondish man?"

I looked and replied, "Yes."

"It's John Chapman. Can't you see his smile, that mouthful of teeth?"

I looked in the direction of the space ride, trying to focus. It was difficult without my glasses. I turned to Alex and said, "Yes, he's Chapman." But that was impossible. How could he be a ticket taker at a fair; he worked for a large company. Alex felt bamboozled, started fuming. I thought how it was actually quite possible for a well-dressed businessman to convert into a ticket taker at a fair. I put my hand on Alex's shoulder and said, "Calm down, we're just being silly old snobs." He shrugged my hand away. Bruised ego—big baby—avoid like the plague. I said to go over and say hello. "You'll find out who he really is." I said I'd known him to confront people he'd had difficulty with in the past. Alex quipped that was brave talk on my part. I locked arms with him and we approached the ticket taker.

Merton, leaning now against his car, admitted that the story was getting exciting. Alex said, "Then shut up and listen."

I resumed the story by explaining how Alex addressed the ticket taker, saying, "Hello, young man, I'm Alexander Haralson. Is the owner of the ride here?"

He responded, "No sir."

Alex looked at the young man's identification badge on his shirt, which said, "My Name is John." His face still wore that shit-eating Viagra smile, but it was a younger face—a spooky younger version of the John Chapman we'd met earlier. I wondered if perhaps they were a family of Mormons. Alex and the kid shook hands. Alex looked at me and said, "Just as I suspected—a bone crusher."

Alex inquired what time the owner would return. The ticket taker said 6 a.m. He also said the fair closed in a couple of hours and that early the next morning they planned to pack up and leave.

Alex asked the name of the owner. "John Chapman" was the response. Alex looked at me and then back at young John saying, "Please tell Mr. Chapman I stopped by." The ticket taker John nodded.

Rabbi Merton, mouth agape, said he wished he could have been with Alex at that particular moment. Chapman's duplicity sounded demonic. Merton was writing a book on duplicity and would have found the direct observation useful. Chapman's stone-faced expression at the fair sounded like it was worth a chapter.

Alex folded his arms and unloaded a cannonade. He said, "When it comes to duplicity, Merton, you're the expert. Put a video camera in front of your desk so it captures you."

To stop a row, I chimed in, "Merton, don't you have to go and fight the cantor?"

Merton looked at his watch. "Yes, I've got to get going."

After Merton drove away, I told Alex he had a week before the next appointment to calm down. "You'll apologize, of course."

"Never," he said.

Annabelle, who had been listening patiently, said she was sure Merton would forgive Alex. Anyway, she said, "That was an incredible story. It seemed everything went out of perspective: you with a heightened sex drive, Merton with extended hearing powers, and Alex with his robot relatives. And now an added feature: the boxing Rabbi. I need to help Merton. If he keeps this up he'll look like Mickey Rourke. His hearing causes stress. He and Cantor Hames argued over the phone late last night. Merton accused him of upstaging his sermon with overdramatic chants. Another fight was arranged. It's enough work just to make sure he changes his underwear and keeps his butt-crack clean."

I said, "Annabelle, dearest, I hate to interject a testy subject, but encourage Merton to wear a different suit the next time he sees Alex."

I heard a deep breath at the other end of the phone. Annabelle said, "M, I hear you." She started to cry and said good-bye.

I thought, poor Annabelle. Being a Rabbi's wife is a pain in the *kishkehs*. She was expected by congregants to be as knowledgeable about traditions as her husband. At least I had an outlet: sex and more sex. When Merton was called as Rabbi of our synagogue, all he did was talk, talk, talk: sermons, eulogies, advice, and public relations. His words carried him to being a successful spiritual leader. But when it came to listening to directives by the synagogue board, Merton was totally deaf. He sidestepped orders and the board grew furious.

I knew my Alex was coaching Merton. I'd overheard a telephone conversation when Alex said to Merton, "Don't listen to those windbags." Merton courted disaster, but it didn't prove to be detrimental. Membership improved. Collected dues boomed, resulting in a healthy financial picture. Now that Merton's hearing was supercharged, he could no longer avoid or ignore any board member speaking to him. He was in prison, forced to hear every word of every opinion and directive. Would membership now decline?

Alex brought the barbecued steaks to the dinner table. I said he seemed a bit quiet. Alex said it was Roman. He said we had to tell him about the robots. I had broken an earlier luncheon date with Roman, unable to face the robot topic. I said Roman was attending a rock concert. With Roman gone, I really wanted to talk to Alex about my gynecological visit. But Alex had raised an important issue. I replied, "What can we do? He won't be able to understand, since he's in a continual stupor. Hearing about the robots while in this state might make him laugh himself to death."

Alex said a man-to-man talk seemed best. But how would he broach the subject with a pothead? And how could he explain the link between himself and the robots? He said, "Could you imagine us talking? 'Roman, I've never told you this, but there's a distant relative, Danziger Kantaphel, in our family tree. He is a bit strange … being a robot.' Roman would say, 'Dad! Did you find my stash?'"

I said, "Your point is, how are we ever going to explain the robots to anyone's satisfaction? You're writing a book to explain the Garden of Eden because you were there. Under normal circumstances no one is required to believe you. When you introduce the robots, you'll take away any hint of believability. Don't forget that your good friend Merton heard the story. Did he believe? Maybe. With his new hearing powers, he'll listen to you much closer. Once he has bought into your story, he'll link his hearing to your trip."

Alex said that when Chapman made his proposal he was invoking Saul Bellow's *Henderson the Rain King*. The fictional character Eugene Henderson divorced his past life and traveled to Africa. He came home a changed and happy man; everything came together. He had a purpose. Alex Haralson started off on his journey a stable person with a loving family, thinking he was bound for Turkey. There was no chance of discarding his relationships. He returned home and found his wife had turned into a nymphomaniac and a good friend turned into a *yold*. He was writing a book that was so bizarre it might well turn into a comedic bestseller: this from a person known about town as the antithesis of Henny Youngman. Since his return, he tried to stay his collected self. What he saw was everything around him transforming into the action more associated with very annoying dreams.

Alex was right. He and everyone who came into contact with him changed into madcap jesters or ill-mannered clowns. From my schooling I recalled that the court jester was a favorite buffoon in literature given the power, due to a physical abnormality, to say or do things frowned on by societal norms. This role fell mostly onto Chapman who took honors. His antics added to the confusion. And the guinea pigs were the people near and dear to Alex.

It all played out when Roman and I went to lunch a few days later. We sat down in Salvatore Scaloppini, a favorite restaurant in Birmingham. I said, "Roman, what are you going to order?"

He replied, "One of each."

"*Figlio mio*, you must regain your self-respect." Roman was dressed in his new formal wear: a dirty and torn T-shirt and jeans. It was bad enough that he smelled awful, competing with the kitchen odors of garlic and tomato sauce. His uncombed hair made it appear to the other patrons that I brought a hairy wild beast in order to make an animal rights statement.

The waiter arrived. "May I take your order?" I said I'd have the vermicelli with the palomino sauce. The waiter turned to Roman with caution. Roman said he'd have the same. Make it a double. Roman then ripped a loud belch.

I turned to the waiter and said, "He'll have a dish of spaghetti with garlic butter."

Roman complained, "Why did you change my order?

I said, "I hope the garlic will work as a disinfectant. Listerine is not listed as a spaghetti topping." Roman laughed hysterically. Heads turned. Embarrassed, I said, "Roman, is there any chance you could behave yourself? I need your attention to discuss a delicate subject."

He put his elbow on the table and rested his head in his hand. He said, "All right, Mom. I've heard the 'You're a loser part.' What's next?"

I said, "Your level of patience and your father's are zero. There's a saying, as to patience, that wise men use it."

Roman said, "Oooo, I'm dining with Sappho."

My Italian instincts were deciding what action I should use to resolve my son's insolence. Hitting him over the head with a frying pan from the kitchen was reserved for husbands. Acting the part of a lunatic, yelling at him while pulling out my hair and threatening to kill myself, was a recommended home exploit. All was resolved when Tracy Newton approached the table.

She said, "Hello, Margarita dear." She gave a double kiss about a foot from my face. She looked at my glassy-eyed son. She said she could not tell if it was Roman or Caroline without lipstick.

My blood pressure went ballistic. Roman was whacked out and fell out of his chair onto the floor. The water glasses tipped and spilled onto his head and T-shirt. It saved the embarrassment of a cleaning person with a mop. I said, "Tracy, it's Roman. Since he has come home, he's been having a difficult time getting reoriented to life in Birmingham."

Tracy said, "Oh. Well, if you say so. Roman, why don't you give my Shirley a call? She's home for a week's visit before she returns to London."

This was news to me. I said I'd thought she was married. Tracy said the engagement broke off at the last minute. Her fiancé was intimidated, as she was earning more money as a financial advisor. Something was going on: she looked desperate. She said that shouldn't be a problem with Roman, who's a physician, amply salaried. I could not tell her about his collection of goats and chickens on the tundra.

Even so, I smiled with delight. I remembered Shirley, a good-looking girl, personable and intelligent. Finding out she was single was a godsend. I sensed a match—with children. When Chapman showed up, Alex would be able to tell him that his worries were over: the marital problem had been solved. Alex would have called me a *dumkopf*—counting chickens before they're hatched, but I knew that potential offspring could plan on coming into existence. Roman will be getting married. I thought, *Oy*, the *gelt* she must make. It sounded as if she earned a six-figure income. Alex and I have hit the jackpot. And my immediate problem of telling Roman about the robots was solved. I don't have to say a word. If Tracy hadn't come along, I'd be telling Roman about his robot relatives while he's stoned. I couldn't imagine the scene he'd make.

I said, "Tracy darling, I'll have Roman call Shirley. When he picks her up, you won't recognize him." *Sotto voce*, I added with a wink, "I'll see to that."

Smiling discreetly, Tracy said, "Margarita, I can't thank you enough. I know Roman and Shirley would make a perfect couple. Though I'm worried Shirley's sometimes standoffish."

I said, "Darling, don't worry. I will have Alex pay her a visit. Recently, he's having a strange effect on people. Everything will, how do you say, loosen up." Tracy looked befuddled. I said we should do lunch sometime.

She replied, "Yes." My mind soared that our conversation would be about wedding plans. Roman, eyes boggled, mouth slack, looked like he might be having an asthma attack. I patted his hand to calm him down like when he was child and didn't want to eat his gefilte fish.

Tracy and I said good-bye. I said, "Roman, are you ready to go home?"

He said, "I didn't eat anything."

I said, "Darling, sure you did. You're in a fog. I'll take you home. Video games await." I had to rush home and tell Alex. I grabbed Roman roughly by his elbow to escort him out of the restaurant. When inside the car, I turned to him and said I would personally see to it that he cleaned up his act. I began by saying smoking pot was forbidden. "You will have a clear head when you call Shirley for a date. You haven't yet encountered my boiling Italian blood when something important to me needs to be done. I will kick every *gebuttska* and give orders like Mussolini. Any questions?"

Roman muttered, "Dude, I'm an adult in his thirties".

I positioned my face directly to Roman's, "*Non me ne importa un cavolo.*" Loosely translated it meant I didn't give a damn.

Roman replied, "You're scaring me."

I said, "Good."

He tried to counter with, "Dad will never go along with your dictatorial behavior."

I lied when I said, "Yes, he will—if he ever wants to have sex again during his lifetime."

Roman put his delicate white hands over his ears and shut his eyes tight. I wanted Chapman around to see this. Proud he would have been of the battle waged on his behalf, even though I can't stand that lying *shlemiel.*

Roman sulked all the way home. Alex opened the door for us and without a word said by anyone, Roman scowled at Alex, then at me, those drugged-out eyeballs popping, and went upstairs to his bedroom. We heard a door slam. Alex said, "I take it the luncheon topic didn't play well."

I hugged Alex and said, "Oh, but it did." I told Alex all the particulars. Afterward I asked if he could contact Chapman to have him scatter some sex enhancement potion onto Shirley Newton.

Alex recoiled. "Do you mean Tracy and Arthur's daughter?" He continued, "You'll turn her into a tramp."

I said, "Isn't that a great thought, Alex? Or did you forget that was how babies are made? We want it to happen. All our problems will disappear." And if Caroline could straighten up her act, which Alex would see to, she'd provide the surety that grandchildren were on the way.

Alex collapsed on a sofa. He said I talked too confidently. I sat next to him and put my arms around him. I said all problems were solved. He said he felt faint. I said, "Please don't. I need to tell you about my visit to Dr. Green."

the amusement ride

With Alex promising to apologize, we returned the following week to Merton's office as scheduled. The meetings had assumed a regularity, like attending Sabbath services without a sermon. Hopefully, *mia bambina*, all services will be that way when you grow up. Edith greeted us with a bright smile and, actually wearing an unhideous outfit. Her words tasted like the sweetness you get drinking cough medicine. Hellcatness had dissipated. She said the Rabbi expected us and would be ready shortly.

We sat. Alex leaned over and whispered that Edith's smile was noticeably toothy, reminding him of Chapman. He suspected that her new disposition wasn't bought from a pharmacy. And he said that the *pièces de résistance* were her firm tits and ass protruding under her blouse and skirt. I viewed Alex's remarks as ongoing payback. Robot Alex enjoying my favors gnawed at Alex's insides. I gritted my teeth. Alex didn't stop. He planned to ask Merton what was up with Edith. Her hair flowed like a ski slope. I elbowed Alex and told him to behave. To the mindless male eye, she had clearly transformed into a sex kitten. I wondered in what ways she might rival my libidinousness?

Don't you just love that word, baby? Doing the business with libidinousness ... ness ...

Was Edith a robot too? The only explanation for such an immediate change was my Alex. On our last visit she must have breathed in Alex's feral microbe from Airets. I've heard about travelers to exotic places bringing back deadly ailments. This one, instead of killing those infected, changed personalities; in my case, an ostensibly respectable housewife transformed into an incorrigible nymphomaniac. Edith's transformation would reveal itself in time.

Merton, eyes bloodshot, face puffy, came out of his study and ushered us into his air-conditioned jungle. As we settled into our chairs, Merton said he had spoken with Caroline. Alex and I leaped to the edge of Merton's desk. I cried, "What did she say?" Merton said to relax.

He said many times family relationships are tested and bring out the worst or the best in people. We shouldn't presume to think we were number one or two on her hit parade of favorite people. "M, Caroline told me that your bigoted attitude was despicable. And that Alex, your heavy-handedness was uncalled for."

I replied, "Did she break up with that bum? That's all I care about." Merton said I was a tough crowd to please. I said if she didn't break up with him, I'd hold my breath forever—that would teach the ingrate.

Merton said, "M, your relationship with her is a problem. To her, marriage is important, yes—but your interference makes personal relationships difficult. She isn't stupid and knows what you want: a suitable husband for a beloved daughter." Merton continued that Caroline respected me. I had been a good mother.

I huffed, saying, "I should say so—she was like a tree trunk coming out of me. It took months to get my figure back."

Merton said Caroline knew Roman acted unstable and was giving us heartaches. "She's called him a couple of times, trying to pinpoint what ails him. So far, no insight into the problem by the social worker. When Roman lived out west, they spoke often. He sounded happy. She concluded that the pot smoking and laziness started when he returned home." I made a mental note to commit Alex to an isolation ward. Unless he was institutionalized, I would need to warn everyone that a worldwide epidemic of insanity loomed. He had sprinkled fairy dust on everyone who came in contact with him. Except for me, the results were disastrous.

Merton said there was another problem that would ruffle our feathers. He related that one day while Caroline was at work, an applicant for social services came into her office for help. When the interview began, a facial feature that struck her as most unusual was his teeth.

Alex screamed, "Please don't tell me it was Chapman!"

Merton said, "They talked and Caroline thought he seemed personable. Then the conversation changed and she was surprised to learn from him that he was a distant relative. Caroline asked him how they were related. He responded that they shared the same ancestral grandparents. Being facetious, Caroline asked if he meant Adam and Eve."

Alex jumped from the chair and yelled, "That's my girl! She didn't fall for that cybernetic spiel of his."

Merton calmly told Alex to sit down. "Chapman broke down in tears and explained she was his ancestor and he needed her to get married so he could come into existence." Alex yelled that Chapman had a lot of nerve feeding Caroline his self-serving agenda. Merton rolled his eyes. "Chapman told her he met *you*: her parents. He even gave her your description. Caroline was baffled. Exactly who and what was this Chapman guy? Rather than call you and get mired in the ongoing stinky family business, she returned my call. I expected to talk with her about her marital status. Instead, she talked about Chapman. She asked if it was true that there was a planet named Airets, that there were robotic humans of the future walking around, and that her parents befriended a human robot. I covered my ass by saying, as to Airets, I wasn't an astronomer, as to robotic humans from the future and her parents befriending a human robot, I hadn't seen any YouTube footage yet. I told her you mentioned meeting a robot named Chapman." Merton finished by telling Caroline he would be a true believer if he encountered a smiling robot named Chapman.

Alex became uncharacteristically apologetic, as opposed to his usual apoplectic. "M, I'm so sorry," he said. "I didn't mean to involve you. Merton, that goes for you too. Forgive me for being short with you last week. This … call it a project, was to be my baby, exclusively. Now we're all in the soup together. Forgive me." A contrite Alex? Not a good sign for the future of humanity.

Speechless, I grabbed my Alex's hand. Finally I babbled something about Caroline having good reason to hate me. Merton told me to call her. She was on my side and he believed Caroline had the strength to learn the truth. With all my remaining vigor I muttered that I would call her.

Merton smiled and said, "Now for some good news." He fumbled for the right words. "Apparently, the boyfriend, the bum you despise, made an overheard remark at a gathering. He said that Jews were money-grubbers. The breakup was immediate."

With my eyes toward heaven, I thanked God. "A miracle! An anti-Semite! What *mazel*. I couldn't have stuck my nose in any better. We have a chance for a Jewish husband."

Merton said, "Not so fast. Chapman suggested to Caroline that the whole family take a trip to a faraway place."

I yelled, "Oh, my God. All of us will come back from Airets and turn into sex maniacs."

Merton sat still, eyes glazing, as if he was hearing his own thoughts. He then looked at us, seemingly unable to restart the conversation. Finally, he said, "Well then, if that happens more babies will solve Chapman's problem." Merton again tried to revive the chitchat saying, "Why don't we go back to where we left off? Alex, you said last week you were going to meet Chapman at 6 a.m. What happened?"

Alex told Merton he didn't have time to think through the mechanics of Chapman's proposal. Chapman's visit was a setup. Here's what happened: Chapman called Alex at home, the Sunday night after the fair closed. He told him how happy he was to learn we stopped by the spaceship ride. Chapman offered to chauffeur Alex the next morning. They would go to a private lounge at the airport to meet Danziger Kantaphel, the head honcho from Spitzbergen, to finalize the discussion of a book deal. Alex agreed. He envisioned meeting the person in charge of the money tree. The next morning, Chapman picked him up in his black limousine and drove to the airport. On the way, he humored Alex, giving him material to read about the Garden of Eden site in the Caucasus Mountains. His company, Malus Industries, pinpointed the location with a deep Earth x-ray machine. Alex would be the only person outside the company privileged to learn and view the exact location. Chapman ridiculed archeologists, who for years, he claimed, conveyed to the world a reason to believe the Garden of Eden was there. They published an oral history from nearby tribes, and artifacts of human habitation. Chapman claimed the evidence was insufficient. Malus Industries' evidence was on a concrete foundation. Chapman's sham would last a couple more hours. Your father would then realize Malus Industries' discovery was a hoax.

Alex tried to picture Danziger. He had to be a man who ate, drank, and slept business. The pamphlet Chapman gave Alex about Malus Industries contained technical information. How disappointing: no picture of Danziger or any biographical sketch. When Alex worked in business, he read a lot of investment information given to clients for consideration. Most were public relations pamphlets containing glossy pictures. They tried to convince you to write a check without getting you 'laid.'

Danziger Kantaphel was not a blue blood. His name spoke of Russian origin. He scared Alex. All Russian businessmen he'd heard about cut off body parts when double-crossed. My Alex said emphatically that his wife considered his genitals most precious.

Alex and Chapman met Danziger at the airport. Sure enough he looked like some sort of Russian, the short and fat kind, with a laugh like surgical instruments being thrown in a tin box. He was a perfect picture of a pudgy fat cat portrayed on TV commercials—with Steinway teeth.

Merton said Danziger sounded like another robot. He added they seemed to be populating the world. Alex continued, saying that after meeting Danziger and having his bones crushed shaking hands, there was no chitchat. Danziger launched into a lecture stressing the importance of the project. Before the meeting concluded, Danziger handed my Alex a contract to take home and review.

After the meeting Chapman drove back toward Birmingham. On the way, Chapman said he needed to make a quick stop by the Shain Park Fair to see that the dismantling of the space ride was progressing properly. Chapman said he'd get Alex home in plenty of time for lunch. On the way, Alex asked Chapman about his company's ownership of amusement park rides. Owning an industrial corporation and amusement park rides seemed odd. Chapman replied, "Mr. Kantaphel owns and operates amusement park rides all over the country."

I assure you, baby, your father had no reason to doubt him.

They arrived at Shain Park and Chapman invited Alex to look around inside the space ride. The walls and ceiling of the room were theater screens, with forty seats arranged in a square. A musty odor gave away the fact that the ride was old. Attached to the armrests of each seat were wrist straps. Each seat tilted backward, allowing the patron to view the wall and ceiling screens. During the ride, movie projectors in the center beamed onto the screens the outside vista of a spaceship traversing space. Underneath each seat was a mechanical device, allowing the seats to shake during the ride. The visuals and motion gave patrons a sense of traveling to the moon.

Chapman invited Alex to sit and relax. He needed to go up to the next level to attend to some business. It would only be a moment. Chapman went to a nook and opened an electrical box. He pushed a button that released a latch in the ceiling. A door dropped open and a mechanical device on the second level lowered a ladder with a whirring sound. Alex looked up while Chapman climbed the ladder. The second level appeared dark. It didn't deter Chapman, who disappeared into the ceiling's opening.

Instead of sitting, Alex strolled about the ride's interior with his hands clasped behind him. His business mind asked, Could any changes be made to the ride to earn more money? Someone should scour the floor. Loose change falling from patrons' pockets was inevitable.

Suddenly, after about a minute of silence, Alex heard a faint digitized voice from the second level say, "He's waiting." Alex stayed quiet and listened closely. He heard nothing for about five minutes.

Then Chapman called to Alex, "Could you please come up and help?" Chapman said he was having trouble releasing a couple of latches. When they were done he'd drive Alex home.

Alex climbed the ladder. When his head passed through the ceiling's opening, the second level was immersed in darkness, but Alex was able to step safely onto the second floor landing. After his eyes adjusted, faint shadows in the distance was all he saw. No more musty odor. Alex said, "Chapman, could you please turn on a light, so I can move about?" No reply. Instead a soft whirring sound began. Alex realized soon enough it was the ladder retracting. When it completed its cycle, the whirring sound stopped, the open door slammed shut, and the latch clicked. The landing was pitch black and totally silent.

Alex asked what was going on. No reply. In a strong voice he asked if Chapman could hear him. Alex's voice sounded deadened, as if he was in a soundproof room. Alex tried yelling for Chapman again. When no answer came, he was so nervous he didn't know what to do, faint or scream. Alex put out his hand to grope for the ladder. Nothing! Where was it? He was near the opening. Taking baby steps, he shuffled about, trying to find it with his feet. He kneeled, searching for the opening with outstretched fingers. No ladder. He pleaded, "Lord, I promise to help the homeless. Please, right now, get me out of here." Alex felt he wasn't alone. He remembered earlier he'd heard a digitized voice from below. Alex yelled if anyone was there could they please help him. Total silence. He decided he would walk to an exterior wall. He could pound on it and hope somebody on the outside might take notice. He stood and advanced using his hands as feelers. After two strides his hand touched something metallic. It was round shaped, like an arm or a shoulder. Light gradually enveloped the area. Alex looked down and saw his hand had come in contact with a metallic ball. It stood on a robot frame about three feet two inches in height. Alex gasped when he saw it and withdrew his hand. "Why me? Help!" He screamed.

A digitized voice said, "Mr. Haralson, welcome aboard the spaceship *Northern Spy*." Alex couldn't believe what was said. He asked if they'd met. The robot said he was Commander Jonathan Chapman.

Alex countered, "Like hell you are. Where is the real Chapman? We drove here together."

Commander Chapman's stout, golden form with his attached blinking lights made some robotic gestures and his body expanded proportionally until he came level with Alex's face. He reminded Alex of a miniature C3PO, from *Star Wars*, beeping and whirring. He grinned, showing his Steinway teeth, and asked Alex if he recognized him. Alex cried yes indeed he was the same Chapman who came to his house and who rode back with him in the limousine. Alex said that was yesterday's news. What was this place? What was going on? He pleaded with Chapman to take him home. His blood pressure had to be over 250.

The room became brighter and in the background there were walls jammed with computers ablaze with blinking yellow, red, and purple laser lights. Alex spun about. It made no sense. Laser lights beaming around the room made more sense at a Wayne Newton show in Las Vegas. Alex asked what all this was about. Chapman replied it was Alex's dream of a lifetime. He would take him to the Garden of Eden. "That *was* what you wanted."

Alex said yes but he thought the Garden of Eden was in Turkey. Chapman said that Garden of Eden was a sand pile in an archeological playground. Chapman said he would take Alex to the existing Garden of Eden; the real one, which Chapman mentioned had all the physical evidence. Chapman said that Alex would soon be standing on sacred ground within its gates. Alex asked how this was possible. Chapman replied he'd arranged for Alex to travel to another period in time. Alex asked if he was in a time machine. Chapman told Alex he was in a rocket ship that could go forward in time. They would land soon.

Alex felt blood rushing to his head. His heart pounded. He muttered, "Forward in time. Impossible." Chapman asked if he remembered the patrons' reaction when they exited the ride?

"They exited the ride thrilled."

Chapman continued, "Those large virtual reality screens I showed you earlier simulated a ride going to the moon." Chapman said he went one step further. "We really took them to the moon."

Alex couldn't believe a Buck Roger's contraption in an amusement park was a spaceship that flew. And forward in time. Alex tried to gain his poise. What was he to do: start a fight? He said, "Chapman, you're crazy. Take me home."

Then an idea hit your father. He thought, Whoa! He hadn't signed any agreement had he? He pulled out the agreement in his pocket and said, "Chapman, the negotiations are over. Please let me leave."

Chapman grabbed it and ripped it into pieces. With a firm voice, Chapman said to Alex, "You weren't planning on leaving?"

Alex thought this was a prelude to a one-way ride. He moaned if Chapman let him leave, he'd promise not to tell anyone what he saw or that they ever met. Chapman was upbeat, saying, "Alex this moment in your life is your great divide. Moses saw slaves mistreated and his life changed forever. You are Moses approaching the burning bush ready to commit to a new destiny." Chapman said he had attended Alex's master's degree graduation. That was Alexander the thinker he'd heard addressing the audience. "You had the spirit and passion. You need to express ideas to get the world's attention. This spaceship will take you to your destiny and you will achieve your goal. You're Alexander the warrior! That's who you are. Enlighten the world. Tell them to throw away their Bibles and Korans. The book you'll write will supercede them. You have the brains to develop and tell the story."

Merton slumped in his chair. He complained of hearing jackhammers. Where was the noise coming from? His ears were popping. Merton, in a dreamy mood, said he'd heard about husbands who wanted to die because of a miserable married life. I asked if Edith's husband was one of them. Merton lifted his head and looked at me with curiosity. He asked how he could escape from all this lunacy. He needed a vacation. He looked upward and said, "Dear God, please let me have a heart attack. Make it quick."

I ran into Merton's private bathroom. I dampened a washcloth and raced back, putting it on his forehead. Merton said, "M, you're a dear." Merton asked us to leave him in peace; he needed time to think.

But then he changed his mind. He asked me how I found out about the spaceship. I told him it started out as an ordinary day. I expected Alex to spend most of the day with Chapman. It all changed around lunchtime. I went to the front door to answer the doorbell. A Birmingham police officer stood facing me with a somber look. His badge read, Officer Jonathon Dougherty. He inquired if I was Mrs. Haralson. I replied that I was. He continued by asking if my husband was Mr. Alexander Haralson. Apprehensively, I answered yes. He asked permission to come inside to speak privately, his expression rigid. I opened the screen door and escorted Officer Dougherty to the living room. I braced myself for bad news.

He said he was inside his patrol car when he saw Alex earlier in the morning in Shain Park. He was walking toward the spaceship ride with another gentleman.

I replied, "It's possible. He was picked up early this morning by Mr. John Chapman. They went to the airport and must have stopped by Shain Park on the way home. Is everything all right?"

Officer Dougherty nodded. He took out a notepad and I saw him jot down Chapman's name. He said, "I was patrolling Shain Park where the space rocket ride was at about 8 a.m. I saw the gentleman, Mr. Chapman, a bit odd looking, with blond hair, go inside the space ride with your husband."

I said, "Yes. Mr. Chapman owns the space rocket ride."

"Mrs. Haralson, the space rocket is no longer there."

"Yes, I understood the ride was going to be disassembled."

"Right, but we have an eyewitness report from a workman dismantling another ride nearby, that at about 8:30 a.m., the space rocket took off. He said it literally *took off* into space."

I babbled, "It … took … off?"

The officer nodded, "Yes, the space rocket launched from Shain Park. We have found no trace of Mr. Chapman or your husband. We checked with the city and they said the permit pulled for the space rocket to use at the fair was for a nonexistent company named Malus Industries. No one knows who actually owns the ride or any other person connected with it."

I held my forehead. Officer Dougherty hurried over to me, ready to administer any needed medical assistance. I fainted. The next thing I knew, I awoke on my bed with Officer Dougherty holding an ice bag to my forehead.

Merton groaned, "*Mamma Nu.*" He shouted to Edith to bring him a glass of water with some aspirin.

Alex and I moved to Merton's side and asked if he wanted us to call a doctor. Edith entered, rushing to Merton with a bottle of aspirin and a glass of water. She bellowed that she would see to Rabbi Freyburg's medical needs. She asked gruffly what had been going on during these past meetings. "Each time he meets you, he mentally collapses afterward."

I yelled, "She's the painkiller!"

Alex pointed at Edith and shouted, "M, let's get the hell out of here! She's the Russian assassin Rosa Klebb, ready to make knives jump out from her tits and stab us."

I hurriedly went to Merton and planted a kiss on his forehead. I said, "You are a dear man. I love you."

Alex and I walked backward out of the study. Edith stared after us menacingly. "See you next week," I said.

m meets caroline

I flew to New York to see Caroline, my daughter the social worker who helped the city's downtrodden. The trip was prompted by an overwhelming desire to hug her and kiss her for dumping that opportunist boyfriend. Years ago I should have sent Caroline to *Roma*, where plenty of eligible *cavaliere* live to fulfill the heart's desire of disappointed women. If she had fallen for one of them, a grandchild would have already been born, no messing around. Afterwards, a new direction of interference in her life, such as how to raise a child who listens to elders, like me, would have been launched.

There would be no need to concern myself with the future robot clan. But no, my children decided to be do-gooders for the world, ignoring my need for grandchildren. Helping humanity was more important than Mama. My Alex was right, we raised idiots. My responsibilities were, as a grandparent, to play with the *kinderlach*, and *kvell*. Changing diapers or putting up with tantrums was the parent's job. Caroline and Roman left us with the job of dealing with that *schmuck* Chapman. If they had followed my directions, I would be sitting on the throne and basking in total glory by now.

The flight lasted two hours, enough time to compile a list, since there was so much to discuss. Merton had already explained to Caroline about the mysterious robot, Jonathan Chapman, who came to her office. My part was to fill in the missing blanks: get married to a rich Jewish doctor and have children ASAP. On the subject of marriage, I brought a list of names with me that I generated with Annabelle's help. I planned to present them to Caroline within an hour of arrival.

As to Alex, I left him with the explicit order to call Dr. Green for an appointment. Alex would learn more about ART inside the bathroom at the doctor's office than at a museum. I pulled no punches. I stuck my nose in everyone's business and manipulated the shit out of every living thing. I wanted to return home hearing that Alex left a specimen with Dr. Green, and I wanted to report to my husband that Caroline had agreed to cooperate. "Expect grandchildren in the near future. She's getting married. To whom? I don't know yet."

How the discussion with Caroline would flow worried me. Our relationship since her visit to Michigan with her objectionable boyfriend had been strained. I wanted our conversation to be informative and calm. Why can't people just be calm? I don't understand all this fuss.

The second item on the agenda was the robots and Chapman. The thought of telling her, "Robots kidnapped your father and took him to a mysterious planet named Airets," made me apprehensive. I didn't want to sound crazy. "And by the way, your father brought back microbes that generate lunacy in whomever comes into contact with him." I was petrified she might never see her father again. If infected, I shuddered to think that the microbes might prove too much for her, provoking her to run back into the arms of that bum anti-Semite she just left.

The plane landed late in the morning at LaGuardia, and as I wheeled my carry-on to the taxi stand, I ran the routine in my head to reinforce I was the mother and she was the daughter, despite her big education. I dressed the part of a responsible parent. I wore a beige wool dress, a little warm for August. Caroline was a professional and could afford quality clothes. Did she own any? I carried a brown purse with a gold clasp. I laid claim to price dominance. Later, patrons at a restaurant would easily distinguish mother from daughter, wrinkles aside.

The taxi took me to the Seaford Hotel on West 50th, where I found Caroline waiting in the lobby. She rushed to me when I entered. We gave each other the European double-cheek kiss. The smooches produced no lipstick smears. Caroline said, "Mama, how are you? You look lovely." I replied I was happy to see her. I touched her shoulders and extended my arms, forcing her to stand back, so I could get a full look at her.

I said her blouse looked too much like polyester and her skirt, moderately priced, was too short. "You are a professional and must make a good appearance. I shall take you shopping later and buy you appropriate apparel."

She said her clients were poor and would not look favorably on an overdressed staff member. I said an improved appearance would attract a suitable husband. Caroline looked at me with disbelief. I said to close her mouth. "You might start to drool." I left her standing stiffly and walked over to the desk and checked in. Afterwards, I walked back to Caroline. She hadn't moved.

On my return she lashed out, saying that my mind was on a single track, focusing on the hope she get married to produce a baby who'll propagate a robot. I said, "Well, in that case I'll have to be the one to get pregnant."

Caroline laughed. "You and Dad aren't still having sex at your age?"

She was asking for trouble, but I didn't care. I smiled and said, "You bet we are, and better than ever, two and three times a day." I patted her cheek. "Papa will be getting a well-deserved rest for the next few days."

Caroline went pale, shook her head, as if trying to wake from a dream. "I could've done without that image in my head," she said. "Let's change the subject. Let's do Italian for lunch and talk about the weather."

I said, "Let's."

We took a cab to Il Palazzo, an eatery on Mulberry Street in Little Italy. It was a bit dark inside but welcoming. The *maître d'* seated us in the rear garden, where we had privacy. Once seated, I mused that it lacked atmosphere. Even so, the setting was more formal than the Boca de Pepo dig-in-and-eat format.

"Christ, Mama, this isn't Rome."

"Don't get me wrong, it's very pleasant."

Caroline said she was glad I liked it. I said I was so proud she'd rid herself of that ill-bred anti-Semite. She countered with what if she brought home a black man with dreadlocks. She continued, "I must let you know, I find that look attractive."

I replied, "Ach, those filthy cascading turds? Change jobs and do janitorial work. It will give you the chance to see attractive turds cleaning toilets."

I handed Caroline the list of names Annabelle had helped with. "Maybe there's a name you know that will flow into your heart." Caroline looked at me with distain and crumpled the paper. A busboy passed by pushing a dirty dish cart. She flung the paper in the wastebasket.

She asked how things were at home. "You and Dad, I trust, spoke with Rabbi Freyburg?"

I said we did. There had been a lot of turmoil for me: Roman, robots, and a Rabbi. There was one positive. When I look into the mirror, I notice no more than the usual amount of gray hairs. Caroline asked if Rabbi Freyburg had a problem. She said when she spoke with him, he sounded flustered.

I said, "His hearing since Papa's return has improved. Greatly improved. Poor baby. Usually Merton takes catnaps during Sabbath services. Now he's fully alert and hears every conversation from a far distance. Merton confessed to your father he'd heard gossiping women whisper that he and Edith, his secretary, have been sleeping together. He does have a very comfortable couch in his study."

Caroline said that kind of talk was slanderous. I replied it was plausible. I knew that Merton and Annabelle were on a sex sabbatical. As to Edith, we came to an appointment and your papa took special note of her curvatures. I saw it as a sign that Edith may have been replaced by a robot.

Caroline said, "Mother, you're rambling. Robots are not sexual beings."

I said, "Not so fast, my dear. I slept with a robot who was Papa's alter ego."

Caroline screamed, "Mama!" Heads turned towards us.

A waiter hurried to our table. "Are you ready to order?"

Caroline said yes emphatically. She looked at me and said, "Are you ordering for two?"

I gazed at her and said, "Touché!"

Caroline ordered the Apulian Insalata, telling the waiter, "With no anchovies." She was so vegetarian.

I ordered Salmone Grigliato and a bottle of Chianti Classico for the table. I asked the waiter to tell the chef to make the patrons' entrees less garlicky. He said he didn't smell any strong odor. I said I was sorry. "It's coming from the restaurant next door." The waiter bowed and walked toward the kitchen.

Caroline asked how it was possible to smell something that far away. I replied that I lived with a microbe from her father. My sense of smell had newfound strength. "Did you shower with Camay, darling?"

She smiled and asked what strange effects my remarkable powers had. I replied, "Sex and more sex. I do not want to beat you or Roman to the punch. Get busy." I wanted on our family tree every member to have a child.

Caroline asked, "What about menopause?"

I said that was a thing of the past. With my sexual activity, eggs were constantly dropping. I said, "I'm twenty again."

Caroline remarked that if I had special powers of smell and Rabbi Freyburg had special powers of hearing, what powers did Roman have? I said smoking pot and eating. The important matter, I said, was her father telling me about the godly powers he learned about on his trip to Airets. He said the third godly power was sight. It seemed he was blessed. He sees every minute detail. I dread to think what mischief might emerge.

Caroline asked what was so important about godly powers. I took a deep breath and said her father went to the Garden of

Eden on a mysterious trip. While there, he learned about the different powers. Your father claimed eating was a non-godly power but the most important of all. He told me it was a bigger deal than the difference between living or dying. It was all about cannibalism. Caroline gave a little shriek.

I put up my hand to continue. "He said he planned to disclose all the details in his upcoming book. Papa is in a bible trance." I was on a family power trip. The robots were our progeny and Neanderthals our ancestors. "Chapman came to us, since he traced the lineage to us." I asked, "Are you getting the connection?"

Caroline said, "If Roman or I don't have any children, there won't be any Chapman."

I said, "*Sì*! Or will I have to have more children hoping they will be smarter than you and your brother?"

The waiter arrived and poured wine for my approval. I said, "*Il sapore è buono.*" He filled our glasses and left. We smiled brightly as we toasted to a renewed relationship.

We were about to continue our conversation when I was startled by a voice that projected "Margarita" across the restaurant. I was sure the whole world now knew who I was.

Caroline said, "Behind you."

John Chapman, wearing his Steinway smile, approached us. I said, "John, what a pleasant surprise. Now you can scare everyone." I stood and gave him a big hug. He wore a green casual suit with a loud sport shirt. I touched his shoulders and extended my arms. I said, "John, you are a clotheshorse. Is that a new leprechaun outfit from Hell's Kitchen? Shall I take you shopping after lunch?"

"Hello, Mr. Chapman," said Caroline.

John replied to Caroline, "Now that you know I'm not a client, call me John."

The waiter brought a chair for Chapman and asked if *signore* would like a menu. I looked up at the waiter and said a can of WD-40 would do. We broke into laughter. John said it was so good to see everyone trying to see that he'd be born. I said yes indeed, staring at Caroline. "Aren't we dear? We want our place in history."

Caroline squinted, shooting daggers. She said to Chapman, without turning her head, that I had mentioned godly and non-godly powers. What was so important about them? Chapman said it had to do with why eating certain foods was sinful. Chapman didn't understand why it was such a big deal. He didn't eat. We laughed. He said that everyone in the whole wide world took responsibility for Adam and Eve's actions. Humans accepted the punishment of leading lives of work and suffering. John began to perform, waving his arms and speaking in a falsetto. "Oh me, I'm a horrible person. Flog me."

I applauded. "Bravo! John, you should go into acting."

John said all the robots were trying to improve intellectually. He didn't understand why the Bible didn't tell you what the significance of the fruit was. Most frustrating. "However, Alex found out," Chapman said. "He's so clever. He bird-dogged the answer. He isolated the godly and non-godly powers. The sense of touch was non-godly and had its own set of rules: no stealing, no murder. But what's so horrible about eating? You're eating a salad. What could be so wrong? After you're done, you're not going to fall apart. You're going back to work."

Chapman said a letdown of gigantic proportions awaited. No one will learn the truth. "Caroline," he said, "Do you understand the importance of my not being born? We'll never exist to tell the world your father knew the answer. Instead," he continued, "The world will carry on as a bunch of birdbrains as they have in the past." John got down on his knees, clasped his hands, and pleaded in a loud voice, "You can't let me down."

I sat back, aghast. Merton Freyburg could have heard him six hundred miles away. Everyone in the restaurant went quiet.

Chapman bawled. It was a sin to eat ham, but not sinful if you smelled your *goyasha* Jew cooking it. Your father read a book by Maimonidies that said God saw the suffering of the Hebrew slaves, heard their crying, and smelled the sweet fragrance of the sacrifice. Those senses were kosher: the godly human powers. I sensed that Caroline was getting a taste of what her father and I had been living with the past several months.

That was up until one second before Chapman raised his fist. Chapman emphasized his point by pounding the table. His strength split the table in half. It was a replay of history: the Red Sea split again, this time in New York City with two glasses of Chianti soaring from either side of the table. There could be no miracle of walking on dry land. The principles of physics were in force suggesting you get out of the way before the wine splashed down on your clothes.

The wine landed on Chapman. His suit was a sponge that absorbed every drop. Chapman ran and broke down the restaurant's front door. Once outside, he scampered away. A few patrons lay on the floor, bowled over during his escape. I expected the police would be searching for him.

Avoided were fistfights with the manager or waiter. They strode over to our table in a huff. I couldn't make out who said what. The gist was to leave immediately. I paid the bill for the food and gave them Alex's business card to send the bill for damages. I said, "Make it legible. He'll be able to submit it to his insurance company." I stared at the mess. Was there a morsel of reason in that morass to help me reinforce the importance of Caroline finding a husband? If I were in her shoes, I'd come out of the closet and declare myself gay.

We rode back to the hotel in silence and sat in the lobby. I said that Chapman was a child. As a parent, you had no control over what your child would do as an adult. I impressed upon Caroline that she made me proud, Roman also, by completing college. As to the current situation, your father said a little fine-tuning would help. I said, "My Papa did not approve of my marrying your father. He called me an idiot. But he did not disown me and I will not disown the robots."

Caroline nodded. She said she would try to accept the robotic future. But, she continued, under no circumstances would she be the ancestor of a major asshole. "Mama, is there any way to eliminate Chapman from the equation? Somebody made him. Robots didn't develop from a single cell." I suggested we call her father. I'm sure he'll know what to do about Chapman. Caroline, in a subdued voice, said she was in a no-win situation. "Robots will develop with or without me. You're waiting to be crowned and sit on your throne." I smiled. She said we should go to my room and call her dad.

I dialed home, and Caroline picked up an extension. Alex answered. He asked how everything was. I told him about Chapman showing up for lunch and about the incident. Alex groaned. He said he would sort out the details with me when I returned home. He asked Caroline and me how we were getting along. I burst out, "Splendid. But, I can't wait to return home and make mushy."

Caroline screamed, "Mother! You're creating trauma!" I apologized and told her to tell her father how we were getting along. Caroline, rather anti-climatically and with her voice filled with anxiety, said that she and I seemed to be getting along okay. Her role in the future was in my mind a central issue. She bolstered my thought, saying she wanted to know how the robots came into existence.

"Dad, tell me how it happened."

Alex voiced surprise that Caroline showed such an interest. He said the changeover from human to computer was a long story. Caroline wanted to hear every detail. Alex said, "Your mother can fill you in on the particulars." I said I couldn't. The story was so romantic my passions might cause me to faint. Alex told me to cut the melodrama and refrain from any telephone foreplay.

Alex told Caroline that a spaceship took him to a distant planet called Airets. The head robot honcho was a man named Danziger Kantaphel. When Alex met him, he was a robot. "But at one time, Danziger had been a human: our distant progeny."

I mused that Merton Freyberg already heard my Alex tell the story about how one day Danziger's a human being, and the next he's a robot. Merton's close friend, Alexander Haralson, an intelligent and trusted friend, told him a *Bubbe Meinsah*? Merton had a tough time believing him. He planned to have his hearing checked. At Merton's age, people usually lost their hearing. But then his improved with dire results. He heard what people really thought of him. He overheard congregants accusing him of being a philanderer or a cheap ass, always wearing the same suit. He thought everyone loved him. No way. He heard firsthand that congregants hoped he would soon be known as Merton Freyburg, Rabbi Emeritus. Having a heart attack might be a good way of saving face before being removed from his job.

I awoke from my musings. Alex was still telling his story to Caroline, although he avoided any reference to the effect of my improved sense of smell. He said that on the trip to Airets, he reclined on a lounge chair, sipping iced tea, and viewing a monitor that showed the transformation of Danziger's family. It was like staying at home on a cold and windy Sunday afternoon, cuddling up and watching family movies. The first few minutes were pleasant. Danziger's wedding pictures beamed a happy and healthy couple. Later, pictures with his wife and family appeared.

Caroline said that what Alex told her was interesting, but Chapman was a pain. Couldn't we have some influence on the future and eliminate him? Like an abortion? Alex was silent. "Chapman," Alex said, "is family."

In a bratty voice, Caroline said, "You have no idea how badly he embarrassed mother and me."

Alex said, "Do you expect me to arrange with a future member of the Mafia to have him whacked?"

I blurted that Caroline was out of bounds. I said, "Let your father finish." I said I couldn't wait to get to the romantic part.

Alex continued, saying Danziger was born and raised in Chicago in the twenty-fifth century. He grew up with an ambition to graduate college as an engineer. He was a good athlete, playing mainly tennis and golf. Alex emphasized that robots could do the same. That remark was aimed at me for lending Robot Alex his golf clubs while he was gone. Dan, Alex said, was an analytical type. He applied physics to better his sports games. He likened his human form to a robot operating a prosthesis. Danziger rose to be a top athlete. He graduated college with an engineering degree, top in his class. No surprise: he was a Haralson prodigy.

Danziger became a successful structural engineer. After college, he joined a firm that developed robots designed to work outdoors in cold climates. His first assignment was in northern Russia. As a project manager, he headed a team of engineers that built a centralized plant to house robots that physically maintained iron posts which were drilled into the ground. When a drill bit was worn out, the robots could replace it with a new drill bit and send it back down. Don't ask me what the posts were for but the robots were a godsend.

Danziger worked towards life's fruitions. He married Delores Northcourt and they had four children. They lived their lives by conservative standards, respecting the traditional family as we know it today. In the twenty-fifth century though, they were more the exception than the rule, since families all over the world lived in varied ways. Gay families with children and heads of households without spouses were in the majority. Laws allowed people without spouses to breed through cloning and artificial insemination. Humans were also allowed to consecrate vows with non-human spouses. Being married to a dog or horse was an accepted practice.

Needless to say, the human race had gone into a decline and Danziger felt disgusted to count himself as one of them. To get away from the lunacy, an idea to turn his family into robots germinated. He remembered his days playing sports. As a human, he trained himself to be as robotic in athletics as possible. He wanted to build a flexible robot in which the human soul could reside. The idea needed action. Then, long story short, his beloved wife became deathly ill and that spurred him to action, resulting in a robotic design to replicate her. By then the human race had gone mad. Nobody was safe from the war and disease enveloping Earth.

He built a prototype. He worked diligently, not knowing if his idea could work. It was a beginning. Hardware was important, so were feelings and thoughts. The robot would need to live forever. If humans became extinct, who would preserve their best ideals and values? Cloning was not an option: limited life. A robot brain with a human mind was needed. Expediency was needed too, since Delores' health deteriorated quickly.

Danziger completed the Delores robot. He made sure that everything functioned properly. Delores continued to waste away. He held a short ceremony in her care home, presenting her with a symbolic key to turn on the robot.

Mindful his life would end too, he built another robot in his own image, a companion to Robot Delores. In a world of crazy spousal relations, what was so wrong about robots being married? It would be a love story that never had to end. Their fantasy would be to lounge for eternity at a seaside getaway.

I began bawling and blared, "Isn't that beautiful?"

Mia bambina, I was impressed with Danziger. He was a hopeless romantic like me. A romance writer would never be able to top that. When we spoke about love for eternity, it was only until death. Danziger meant eternity, literally. I loved Danziger with good reason.

My Alex said, "The best place for Danziger and his wife to live was aboard a spaceship. Earth's environment declined toward a state of *kaput*. He made arrangements with space buddies to put the robots he constructed, his wife and himself, on board a spaceship and send it off into space. His rocket expert friends saw a challenge and were eager to help. To them, it was a different type of experiment. It wasn't a spaceship that operated with humans controlling it from earth inside a control room. It was a spaceship that gave its own orders.

Danziger's co-workers and friends had no understanding of the trip's real purpose. The spaceship was launched. Danziger at the last minute rigged its computers so that it would never return. When contact with the spaceship was lost, everyone thought a mechanical failure was the reason. Danziger made a nonchalant remark, "Oh darn." Inside, Danziger beamed a happy and contented smile. He was home free. All Danziger had to do was die.

I bawled uncontrollably. I screamed at Caroline how could she, after hearing about Danziger, let down her parents. Caroline admitted that Danziger was a dandy. But what about Danziger's children? Were they abandoned? Alex piped in, saying Dan, the robot flying about in space, would replicate them. "Caroline dear, one of the children was named John Chapman."

She groaned, "Why not John Kantaphel?"

"He could never get the spelling right, so changed his name by universal proxy."

Before the conversation ended, Alex attributed a saying to Dan: "Frequently wrong, but never in doubt."

chapter

NINE

the problem with eating

I sat on the edge of the bed *kvelling*. My Alex's story relating Danziger Kantaphel's life history, especially the romantic part, was a smashing success. It produced the desired effect. He convinced Caroline the Haralsons were to be the progenitors of robotic life, which at some point in the future would dominate the sum of all intelligence in the universe. Thank God Alex didn't go off on a tangent about his theory of food taboos. Caroline and I would have fallen asleep.

Exhausted from hearing the elaborate biography and the excitement it generated, Caroline wobbled into the bathroom and splashed water on her face. Danziger became her hero. Caroline, in an enthusiastic voice, said, "What a romantic! He thought and cared enough about his wife to replicate her human persona into a robot." I kept my trap shut—after the first meeting with Danziger, Alex described him as a complete ass. I found for the first time in my life to practice the fortune cookie adage: keeping thoughts private sometimes has great virtue.

Caroline finished rinsing. She came to the bed and sat next to me. In an effusive manner, Caroline said she needed a man like that. I put my arms around her and said I would help her. "You'll waltz into each other's heart." She greeted my remark with a small smile.

I felt good about future prospects. The goal I'd had on the flight to New York—to plan on grandchildren in the near future—was reachable. When I returned home, I would say, "Alex, you were good. So good that the sex I will reward you with will be of Koranic proportions." The thought made me perspire. I stood and walked to the thermostat and turned it to MAX COOL. I told Caroline I needed to rinse off.

The phone rang. It was the hotel operator saying a police detective was in the hotel wishing to interview me. I said there was some mistake. The operator in a firm voice said, "Madame, Mr. Kerr Greening, the hotel manager is escorting the detective to your room. They will be there momentarily."

I hung up the phone and an instant later came a knock at the door. I warned Caroline: trouble. I told her to stand in the bathroom doorway until I ask her to come out. I went to the peephole. Two men waited.

I opened the door. The hotel manager was obvious. Mr. Greening was about five feet eight inches tall, wore a black suit with a pinstripe vest and black patent leather shoes. He stepped forward and arched his back. He stuck out his chest, and blurted in a fake British accent, "Madame, are you hiding a fugitive?" His breath stank of peppermint.

A broad-shouldered detective, about six feet two inches tall and dressed in a wrinkled gray suit, stood behind him. He walked in front of the hotel manager with a glare at him, and extended his arm. "Mr. Greening, please step aside so I can do my job." He switched his focus to me. "I'm Detective Marsh Kenworthy. May I come in?" I demanded to know what his visit was about. He said he came to investigate the whereabouts of a man who injured some patrons earlier at the Il Palazzo restaurant after being seen in our company.

I nodded to Caroline that it was okay to come out. I stood aside and said, "Please come in." Detective Kenworthy came in and I barred Mr. Greening with my arm. I said he was not welcome. "It's private business."

"I shall go where I please," he snapped.

Arroganza! My blood vessels pulsated. I told the nogoodnik that he must leave immediately.

Detective Kenworthy barged in between us. He said, "Mr. Greening, I'm the law enforcement officer in charge. I'll speak with ..." he turned to me, "You are Mrs. Alex Haralson, right?"

I said, "Yes, I'm Margarita Haralson, and this is my soon-to-be-engaged daughter, Caroline."

The detective said, "I'll speak with the Haralsons." He leaned toward the manager and asked if that was all right with him. Mr. Greening huffed, made an about-face, and left.

Detective Kenworthy took a seat, pulled out a notebook from inside his jacket, and placed it on the nearby desk. I asked him how long the questioning would take. I said I had limited time in New York and had important shopping to do.

Detective Kenworthy, about forty, was good-looking, with dark hair, but dressed like a *schlump*. His clothes needed pressing and his shoe leather was dusty and cracked. I thought he was a person who could use my shopping expertise. If he wore a charcoal suit and foulard tie, he would look more authoritative.

He said, "Mrs. Haralson, you were seen with your daughter at a restaurant, the Il Palazzo, in Little Italy about 12:15 p.m. Can you confirm your presence there?"

"Yes, we were there."

He continued, "While you were eating, a man dressed in a green suit walked to your table."

"He was a panhandler who thrust a *pushka* in our faces."

The detective said, "Witnesses told me the man shouted your name when he came inside, and you let him sit at your table. You're telling me you *don't know* him?"

"He was ... what you say ... *meshuge* ... *pazzo*," I said, trying to sound as foreign as possible. "He got lucky with his naming. We're giving people, and tried to help feed a homeless man. His face was the color of his suit." The detective frowned and said that he had learned the perp didn't order any food.

Feeling a little cornered, I said, "Detective, my English not good. I not understand all you say. Ask zome questions to my daughter. But before you do, are you married?"

Caroline screamed, "Mother!"

He said, "Yes, Mrs. Haralson, I am—happily." He continued to question me. He was smart to see me as the linchpin. He asked if I knew the man's name. He needed to catch him before he harmed other citizens. I said he was harmless. The detective looked at me in disbelief and said he bowled people down and broke down the front door. "He wasn't 'harmless.'" The detective continued, saying he needed our help, since he had trouble locating this villain. "He didn't leave any fingerprints."

Quaking inside, I muttered, "Wearing that green suit, his name must be O'Toole."

Detective Kenworthy raised his eyebrows. Skeptical, as well as exasperated, he turned to Caroline. "Young lady, he got down on his knees and pleaded with you. He said he couldn't live without you. Was he proposing?"

Caroline gasped and said, "No!"

I cut in, "I would never allow a bum to marry my daughter. Never! She's a virgin and I would be very picky about choosing a husband for her."

Caroline said, "Mother, let's not get carried away."

I said, surprised, "Oh my. So you've already had wedding rehearsals. I'll bet you slept with that good-for-nothing *goy*." Caroline sighed.

The detective pushed into our interchange. "Mrs. Haralson, can we stick to the subject?" He faced Caroline. He had learned there was some talk overheard about godly sense—smelling ham—what was that about?

I said, "Detective, did that nosy waiter give you all this misinformation? The facts are as follows. The man was homeless. He droned on about how eating *trayph* was cannibalism. Have you ever heard anything so crazy? Its roots, he stated, were from the Garden of Eden story." I turned to Caroline. "Isn't that so, dear?"

Caroline looked at the detective and said her parents were into the Bible and would know. Detective Kenworthy began to write in his notebook. When he finished, he looked up and shifted his eyes between Caroline and myself. He said I made up a good story about the cannibalism business. He gave both of us his business card, in case we wanted to call him with more facts. He learned from Mr. Greening that I lived in Michigan. I yelled that bigmouth disclosed confidential information. "Calm down. I trust you want to return home, *soon*. The paparazzi have been making inquiries at reception."

I gulped and started sniffling. It was a threat I couldn't challenge. I said, "You're not going to tell the newspapers what happened, are you?"

Caroline burst in saying we had been under a lot of stress. She pleaded with him to let me go home. She said, "I can tell you this: I know the man. I'm a New York City social worker and he's a client. He's what is called a *golem*. He won't be found."

Detective Kenworthy looked at us in disbelief. With pen and paper ready, he asked, "How do you spell that word: golden?"

Caroline corrected the detective adding it meant artificial human.

The detective repeated, "Artificial human, eh? That's very interesting." He asked how you could tell the difference between an artificial human and us normal humans.

I blurted, "Because the artificial one hasn't got a real *schlong*."

Caroline screamed, "Mother, that's enough!"

"Caroline," I said, "I must get out of here. The paparazzi scares me. If they catch up with me, I might say something stupid." I turned to the detective and said that I must return home. I feigned heart palpitations. "Detective, is there a back way out? I'll feel so much better."

Caroline said she didn't know I was having so many health problems. I looked at her in exasperation. I was trying everything to con my way out of New York and she tattletales to the detective. I neared Caroline's ear. I said softly with a harsh tone, "Do you plan to spill the beans about everything?"

Detective Kenworthy said, "Not so fast, Mrs. Haralson. I've got to catch this artificial human before he hurts someone else."

Caroline offered to meet him at his station and explain what she knew. "Meanwhile," she said, "Let Mama leave for home. You don't plan to press charges against her, do you?"

That would improve the situation for us. Caroline doesn't know all the details. I did. By the time she met with the detective at the station, I would be home. Caroline said that we weren't crazy people, even though what we said sounded crazy.

The detective looked at us for a couple of seconds. After some thought, he said, "You may go home, Mrs. Haralson." To Caroline, he said he expected her to visit him the next day at the precinct. Caroline nodded.

I prepared to leave town. The paparazzi would blast the news all over the world, if they found out the newsworthy ingredient: Chapman was a robot from the future and, most importantly, a relative. "Caroline, be a dear. Please check me out of the hotel." I threw my clothes and cosmetics slapdash into my suitcase. My clothes would wrinkle. I didn't care. Leaving town was my only thought.

Detective Kenworthy said to me, "Let me carry your suitcase."

I thanked him. What a break. I would march out of the hotel with the detective running interference. We left the room and walked to the elevator.

Detective Kenworthy said, "Mrs. Haralson, will someone be able to explain the part about eating and cannibalism? I found that statement fascinating."

I smiled and said, "Detective, for you, anything."

On the flight home, I lowered my seat and tried to nap before landing in Detroit. Hopeless. My mind churned about Caroline, Roman, Annabelle, and dear Alex. Each had a special attachment. For my Alex, I was his daytime dutiful housewife, while at night the slut. For Roman and Caroline, I was their matchmaker. As for Annabelle, at night poor Merton wished she was the slut, while in the day the *schmahta* for synagogue affairs.

Something about Danziger building robots wasn't making sense. But I was too far into the romance to think practically.

Several years before Chapman arrived to convince Alexander to commit to a Garden of Eden adventure, my sister Roma visited me from Italy.

Roma was about two years older. She was adopted when she was about nine months old. With adoption, the unexpected seems to surface. My mother learned six months later that she was pregnant—with me. Roma was the big sister who watched over me. We worked side by side in Papa's bakery. She toiled doing the heavy lifting, while I performed the delicate job of setting up the display cases. We were also salesladies. Our sales pitch was our looks. Men gravitated to us and sales were brisk.

If the number of wedding proposals determined which of us men found more attractive, Roma would win. All I heard were suitors saying to Roma, "*Mi vuoi sposare?*"

Oh, she was a beauty. She eventually married a wealthy Milan industrialist named Julin Capitola. She told me, "Julin is a sweetheart. I love older men with old money." Roma smothered Julin. She awoke in him a sense of purpose outside his business life. Music and art served as the mainstays in their lives. They had no children. Roma was intelligent—a professor of engineering at Politecnico di Milano.

I sat up with alarm. Talking to myself I said, "No, it couldn't be." I remembered Roma's build always being firm and her facial skin being wrinkle free. We were at an age when body parts sag, badly. I reached up and turned the nozzle to let cold air flow on me. I pictured her smile: pretty, but somewhat toothy. Was she a robot? Maybe that's why she had no children and decided to become an engineer. Chapman recruited her to build spaceships.

I was blind, naïve. Chapman could have approached other families. Childless, might my parents have entertained the idea of a child robot? Who would be any the wiser? Even so, one child didn't seem workable: too slow to populate the world. Chapman must have thought about distributing robots by other means.

I blurted, "Oh, shit!" Heads turned towards me. I thought, "They're already here: Elvis Presley impersonators. There are thousands." I wanted to parachute out a door to get on the ground.

Alex must know without delay.

A stewardess came over to my seat. "Is everything all right?"

I said, "No. Tell the pilot to fly faster."

The plane landed in Detroit and taxied to the terminal. Anxiety reached crisis proportions. I couldn't wait to tell my Alex what I discovered. When I deplaned, I ran past the luggage carousels to the curbside. Dear Alex was parked at the closest spot to the exit, ready to take me home. He knew what awaited him. I jumped inside the car.

Alex asked, "Where's your luggage?"

I said I had to tell him about the robot invasion and couldn't wait to pick up my luggage. I said to call the airline and tell them to deliver it.

"Thanks!" His tone was harsh. He didn't hesitate to lash into me, saying he received phone calls from New York. He wanted to know what happened at the restaurant and hotel. Both managers labeled my actions as criminal. "What's gotten into you? Have you gone off the deep end?"

Bringing up the subject about the Elvis impersonators seemed, well, stupid at the moment. I told Alex to think about the positive. Caroline and I reconciled. "Plan to have grandchildren in the near future."

He said, "Whoopee!" Alex said the manager from the hotshot restaurant called him, saying I agreed to reimburse them for the damages after Chapman ripped the place apart: $25,000 worth. They also plan to sue for loss of business reputation. Alex's face went red. Did I learn about how the world worked at the Neverland Ranch with that poor Michael Jackson? He continued to bluster, saying that Italians didn't have exclusive rights to hot-blooded tempers. He said he was ready to call 1-800-SHIKSAS to find a hot babe and dump me. He growled, "Give me your baggage claim."

I punched it into his hand. He said I shouldn't get any funny ideas about stranding him. I must have looked good and mad because he snatched the keys from the ignition. He opened the door and returned with the luggage in about five minutes. We drove home in silence. When we got home, I handed him Detective Kenworthy's card. I said it was a matter that needed his immediate attention. "Caroline is meeting him tomorrow." His eyes after reading the card were shooting daggers.

The paparazzi and the police were looking for Chapman. The next morning, Alex went out early and brought home a copy of the *New York Times*. He noisily opened the paper to page twenty and dropped it on the breakfast table in front of me. My eyes riveted onto an article titled, "Mystery Man on Loose." I picked up the paper to hide behind. The story had a brief description of events at the restaurant. The last paragraph said the New York Police Department was searching for an unknown assailant.

I lowered the newspaper and exclaimed that we should drive up north for a week. I saw it as a chance to distance ourselves from all robot and synagogue business. I wanted peace. I said if we stayed at a cottage on Beaver Island, Chapman would have a tough time locating us. I suspected Chapman wasn't a championship swimmer. "Think about it—just you and me."

"Aren't you forgetting something?" Alex waved Detective Kenworthy's card. He asked why Caroline was taking the heat alone. I confessed Caroline told the detective Chapman was an artificial human. Alex slapped his forehead. "*Oy.*"

I said I had to get out of New York and felt sorry for Caroline. If the details were disclosed, the media would hound us. "*Scusami, amore.*"

Alex asked, "What specifically does this detective want?"

"Chapman's whereabouts," I sobbed.

Alex sighed and began staring out the window at our personal Garden of Eden. Alex regretted that there were no snakes walking around with whom one could make a deal. He decided we were left with no option except to call our attorney, Freeman Wetmore III. He emphasized he didn't give a damn what promises were made to that detective. Freeman the legal eagle would deal with the police. Alex said that it probably was a good idea to head up north.

I gushed, "*marito mio.*" I ran upstairs and hastily repacked my suitcases. When I finished and came down, Alex was speaking to our attorney.

"Freeman, tell that cop neither Margarita nor Caroline committed any crime. Chapman's the guilty party. Have them chase after him.... Yes, I know the police want to arrest him. What am I supposed to do to help? Invite him for dinner with the police waiting in the shadows? ... Chapman is, shall we say, unpredictable. I don't know where he lives. He could be in outer space or in a homeless refuge under a bridge.... I know, I haven't told you about the robots and the trip. Consider it a blessing. Everyone hearing it has gone nuts.... The guy is a dynamo.... There could be two thousand armed personnel ready to rumble. They wouldn't stand a chance. On my trip to Airets, Chapman was my guardian angel. One time, while I was walking through an alleyway to speak with a caravan leader, about twenty unshaved, mean-looking thugs ambushed me. Within a split second, Chapman flew out of the woodwork and started swinging. He bloodied them bad. Make a note: I want the movie rights if the police ambush him. Freeman, I've got to say good-bye. M just came downstairs and is ready to go. I'll call you later about your conversation with Detective Kenworthy."

the problem with eating continued

We dined at Nina's Restaurant on Beaver Island. It had taken us about four hours to reach the boat landing in Charlevoix. We had time to shop on Bridge Street before taking the 5:30 p.m. ferry to Beaver Island. On the two-hour trip on the *Beaver Islander*, we avoided any discussion about Merton, Chapman, and unmarried children. We hoped it would continue forever.

On the way up on I-75, I had reflected about a favorite pastime: sitting on a sand dune with my Alex, watching the sun set over Lake Michigan. At nightfall, I would fuss at Alex to locate Airets. Can't the robots move time so we could enjoy the romantic setting earlier?

In bed at the cottage, more romance for sure would soothe our minds and hearts. I packed a few worn-out dresses. Who would see us: some deer or opossums? I shifted my hairstyle into a ponytail. I didn't care if gray hairs showed. I gushed, "Isn't life wonderful, Alex? I love the thought of making a baby in a primitive setting." I wanted to scoot closer to him—oh, how I hate bucket seats. Being at Lake Michigan, whitefish was the main staple at every restaurant. At Nina's

Restaurant, many whitefish selections, such as whitefish amandine, were on the menu. My Alex warned me to avoid the last item, which was lined with *trayph*: whitefish with crab stuffing. My husband worried about my soul's holiness. I smiled and held his hand.

Alex ordered the whitefish artichoke and savored every bite. I ordered whitefish with cherries. While dining, I reminded Alex that the McAfee wedding was in two weeks. Many of his old clients would attend the party. "You'll be able to mingle and tell everyone about your adventure." Alex looked up and smiled. He began to chew his food with his mouth open. I said his manners disgusted me. "Is that how cannibals ate?" He said he checked off the Eusthenopteron selection on the return card for the wedding. Eusthenopterons, I learned, were the forerunners of humans. There had to be millions of Eusthenopterons. My husband told me, for anything to survive and evolve, great numbers were needed. I then understood why there were so many Elvis impersonators. They were robot forerunners.

I understood his tactic. He planned to initiate a cannibalism awareness program. Alex obviously convinced the McAfees to have the Eusthenopterons as a selection, being big supporters of just causes. The McAfee guests would think the fish dinner kosher and would be curious about its ancient flavor. But Alex would jump up on a table and scream there was a terrible mistake. "I will not allow you to eat the Eusthenopterons. Tetrapods are our brethren!" It defies reason what he'll do to get attention. Atop the table, he'll announce at the top of his voice, "The act of cannibalism includes eating meat from a meat-eating animal. In the food chain, a human could have been dinner."

Alex had calmed down after our New York skirmish, enough so I could talk to him about the seriousness of robotic Elvis impersonators populating the world. However, it came at a price. I prepared myself to listen to another installment about his Garden of Eden adventure. And I had to hang on every word to make Alex feel important. It was unavoidable. By the way, how many installments were there? I needed to ask.

I bent over to his side of the table and licked his arm. "My, my," said Alex, "I can't seem to escape your kind." I said I wouldn't become a vegetarian. And anyway, I said, spaghetti every day could be tiring. Alex complimented me, saying mine never was.

I said, "Alex, I believe this subject would confuse God." He laughed. I continued by saying does God plan to watch His ancient teachings sliced and diced to a point where they resemble a salami and egg breakfast?

Alex said, "I see the cannibal can't stay away from the henhouse or the slaughterhouse."

One time Alex said cannibalism was a symbol of triumph: eating your conquered enemies, one of which might be your father. In time, a symbol took its place, with *trayph* representing the symbolic form of cannibalism. "The Torah," Alex said, "prohibits eating animals or insects, knowing their origins were carnivorous." One reason Danziger and Delores departed Earth was to avoid the risk of cannibalism reoccurring. Human population grew unchecked. And the happy-go-lucky, sexually voracious multitude of masses exhausted resources at an alarming rate, faster than the rate of recycling. All hell broke loose. In desperate times, societies eat humans. A classic Sci-Fi movie from 1973 titled *Soylent Green* featured an institutionalized portrayal of cannibalism. Danziger was a futurist and saw the film as prophetic. That's why he and his family got out of Dodge early.

One evening at home, after his return from Airets, Alex told me about his experiences. I was dumbfounded. I said to him his description didn't match what I saw on Robot Alex's monitor. We compared notes and figured I saw a staged version of family movies instead of having a front seat to history. The conniving robots tricked me into believing Alex pranced about on Airets in an area similar to Miami Beach. Alex waved and ran about on the beach and then dove into the ocean's waves. He appeared to be having a blast. His mannerisms were real as could be: his gait, his smile, his back flip. Alex's impersonator was a robot on automatic pilot. A bunch of *mumzarum*, that's what those robots were. And I thought I had geniuses for progeny.

The real happenings I learned from Alex. Part of his trip to Airets was *schlepping* through swamps. Had I seen the hardships Alex faced, I would have put a stop to them by calling Italy for a bone-cracking *Luigi*, to help me move Chapman and Danziger to a scrap yard. I checked Alex's body for bite marks. There were some. Silly me, I made them. I couldn't wait to get into bed with him later.

Chapman kidnapped Alex and convinced him the trip to the Garden of Eden was for the betterment of human existence. Alex believed him. He flew him 613 light years away from Earth to Danziger's flagship, *Spitzenberg*: a hideaway in the galaxy *Nova Easy Gro*. Alex met Danziger a second time while Danziger relaxed on a chaise lounge and smoked a cigar. Dan said he wanted Alex to experience firsthand all the dangers of life surrounding cannibalism and robotic life. He set him up to view primitive life on Airets.

Alex took the robots for granted, thinking they were model citizens. Dan kidnapped him and substituted Robot Alex. Robot Alex set the stage, telling me: no grandchildren, no fame. Roman and Caroline turned into excess baggage by not being married. The robots knew I was vain and wanted a grandchild. They were right. I *would* go to any means necessary. But they had a plan. It would entail me bearing a child conceived with a bionic man: a donor named Steve Austin. His portrayal on television consisted of a bionic right arm, bionic legs, and bionic zoom lens eyes. They figured he also had bionic sperm. With the real Alex out of the way, Steve Austin would deliver the goods to Robot Alex. That specimen for the ART treatment could make Robot Alex the father with no one any the wiser. They hoped life would change into robotic life at a faster pace. *Mia bambina*, I'm ninety percent sure your father is Alex.

On the short trip from the *Spitzenberg* to Airets, Alex traveled in a one-seat puddle jumper named *Mamma Beam*. Compared to *Northern Spy*, it was a 1960s Volkswagen bus covered with rust spots with hundreds of anti-war stickers plastered everywhere.

The interior parts of the spaceship appeared to be bought at a junkyard. Inside, there was a ten-inch monitor with cracks in the plastic hull and greasy looking speakers attached to the side panels. A towel covered the seat. Alex lifted it and, *voila*, seat springs. Once he was as comfortably settled in the seat as possible, Danziger came on the monitor waving good-bye and wishing my Alex luck. Alex complained about the spaceship's flimsiness. Dan told Alex all was okay. The tin can he sat in was the one he and Delores rode into space. Dan assured Alex it was a reliable vehicle without any dented fenders. Alex learned Delores and Danziger rode in it for fifteen thousand years; the time it took them to reach the outer limits of the first galaxy. On the monitor, Dan said good-bye. His *ta-ta* hand motion Alex said resembled a farewell forever wave.

The robots' plan was for Alex to expire without any heavy-handed evidence. They decided the preferred way was a heart attack; nothing messy to contend with. Alex fumed, saying his life was filled with liars. The government lied all the time. His clients lied to him to fudge tax returns. Now a bunch of robotic con artists lied, arranging and hoping to pull off a hit disguised as a fatal illness. I imagined them calling me, saying they were sorry to report dire news about my Alex. Chapman would have visited to pay his respects and handed Robot Alex the specimen to take to Dr. Green's office.

A computer on the *Spitzenberg* guided the speed and directional controls of *Mamma Beam*. Dan told Alex he might enjoy the opportunity to view space scenery through a window on the way. It would take a couple of hours to reach Airets. Viewing stars and various space objects along the way would be majestic, like smelling perfume. The speedometer popped up on the monitor after Dan's adieu. Once underway, the travel speed of *Mamma Beam*, according to the speedometer, was around twenty-five thousand miles per second. Space objects by comparison traveled at about twenty-five thousand miles per hour, relatively stationary by comparison to the speed of *Mamma Beam*. The spaceship bobbed and weaved. It approached and passed stars and objects at a breakneck speed. When Alex looked out the window and saw how fast the spaceship gained on a space object, he feared a head-on collision. One time, Alex looked and swore a crash landing was imminent. He curled into a fetal position, afraid to look out the window. Dan planned for Alex to die from a coronary on the lounge chair. Finding Alex in a fetal position scared to death seemed suspicious. Alex said for the entire trip to Airets on the puddle jumper, his heart beat so fast and hard, his chest felt like a drum set.

The spaceship landed on Airets and the door opened. Alex dove out to get on *terra firma*. Once on the ground, he heaved for fifteen minutes. Why the robots didn't nosedive the old jalopy into Airets and chalk it up as a fatal accident, Alex never knew. With his eyes directed toward the distant mountain landscape, he saw everywhere snowcapped, contoured peaks. It could have been any mountain range: the Himalayas or the Rockies. His eyesight changed to sharp binocular vision. Reaching out and picking up snow, he swore, was within his grasp. Even so, Alex felt like driftwood isolated in the middle of nowhere. He cried. Who would find him?

Alex surveyed the landscape of flat, barren ground coated with a fine gray ash reaching all the way to the base of the mountains. He picked some up to feel it. He assumed it was fallout from a volcanic eruption. Before sending Alex on his flight, Danziger reminded him that Airets resembled Earth. Right then Alex wished he could substitute a trip to the Land of Oz with its fairy tale forms of life.

Mamma Beam disappeared during Alex's reverie. He said Danziger relaunched it while he wasn't looking, sending it to a repair shop. The robots abandoned him and when he landed he was in a fog. A horrifying thought jolted me. "You didn't see cannibalism on Airets, did you?"

Alex gave me that you-have-not-been-listening look and said, "Of course I did." How would Alex be able to explain his trip to Airets to friends? They'll say he went on a vacation to visit cannibals! Why didn't he visit Santa Claus at the North Pole? We wouldn't have to wait until Christmas to receive a gift. He'd be perceived as a person who, in a flash, jumped from a state of mental stability to a nutcase.

When I told Alex my thoughts, he said there had been plenty of nutcases. He threw out the names of the usual suspects: Moses, Paul, and Mohammed. A shepherd, an itinerant preacher, and a camel driver. They established credibility and jumped to the stable side of the equation. I told him no one would let him jump over the fence from the nutcase side. Alex was in trouble.

I drifted back to Alex's Airets story. He said it was cold and his breath vaporized like exhaust. Dan forgot to outfit him with any long johns. He conveniently forgot to mention the freezing weather conditions. Alex was kidnapped dressed in his light yellow pants and blue University of Michigan crewneck sweater. He wore cordovan penny loafers with woolen green socks—dressed to hobnob at a country club, not do battle with the fearsome Nyphilim. I sniveled, my brave husband. If I knew how much danger he faced, I would have run to his side so we could have died together.

Alex said, "Easy, Margarita." Danziger set him loose on Airets to look for the birthplace of human development, whereof one God in Genesis Chapter I, Verse I, knew. Somewhere in the vast expanse in front of him lay the Garden of Eden. It would not be easy to find.

A child of an ill mother and workaholic father, Alex, in addition to being a robot ancestor, could boast good work credentials. Teenage responsibilities included meal preparation, washing clothes or dishes, and caring for his mother. Trial-and-error and books taught him well. Someone asked, after seeing Alex help me do some household chores, how he learned to operate a washing machine. Alex recoiled; he said the knowledge came in an instruction manual.

Late in the evening, we trekked to a vantage point atop a sand dune. The sun over Lake Michigan touched the horizon, the lower tip beginning to change from a circular bottom to a straight line. An hour earlier, a cloud hid the sun until it burst into the open and began its final descent. Alex's Garden of Eden story would wait. The glow of the orange ball faded into the background. Children played below, running in and out of the water, laughing and jumping with glee, stopping every so often to pick up and throw a stone. We laughed with them. Alex said, Why not? We got up and ran down to the lake picking up flat stones along the way. The water always stayed calm at that late hour. A six-skipper was Alex's best. My throws mustered a four-skipper, an all-time personal best.

In our cottage the next day, we lounged with cake and tea. I sat on Alex's lap and hugged him. I told him to feed the animal in me. "Tell me about the cannibals on Airets." Alex began by saying Airets was inhospitable. No exuberance welcomed his appearance. No marching band paraded down Fifth Avenue in his honor. No mayor presented him with a key to the city. If he went away on a National Geographic expedition to Mongolia, a tour guide would have greeted him at the airport in Ulaanbaatar.

Alex wasn't naïve about danger. Even so, Dan's assurance on the *Spitzenberg* led him to believe he would be accompanied by a guardian angel. Alex hoped he referred to one possessing large muscles and an AK-47.

He heard a loud thunder in the distance and looked skyward for the storm. The temperature rose and he felt perspiration on his forehead. The ground shook and splintered. Gobs of dirt and rocks bobbled about him like popcorn popping. Alex arrived and Airets collapsed. The sky blackened and the wind swirled. Particles from a billowing cloud blew into his mouth and nose. Alex's clothes changed to an ash gray color and he spat out a gob of pasty saliva. Not knowing where to hide, he ran towards a mountain. Seconds later, he heard the latent sound of a volcanic eruption. Alex shouted, "Dan, where are you?" He saw several cave entrances. Without being choosy, he picked one and ran towards it.

Once inside the entrance, Alex continued to run at full speed. The entrance narrowed into a tunnel, but he kept running. He passed what he thought was a wolf. He just kept going. No time to catch his breath. As he dashed further inside the cave, he heard the sound of rushing water grow louder. He rounded a corner and saw an underground river. Without hesitating, he leaped into the water. The water was temperate from the nearby volcanic activity. There was light in the cave but it was dim. He felt safe for the moment.

The river's current carried him through a cavern with high walls. Drawings of a wolf and other animals covered the twenty-foot-high shale rock. He waded to one side of the river and boosted himself out of the water onto the river's rock plateau. He rested with his back against a chamber wall. He was still breathing hard and rested his head against the wall. Every so often, he surveyed his surroundings. The tunnel opened into a larger chamber that looked promising to spread out in, take off his wet clothes, rest. He rubbed his face, noticing stubbly beard. Alex had quickly started transforming into a native.

He decided against walking into the chamber. Human hands had drawn primitive pictures on the wall, which looked suspiciously like large stick-figure men with shock-headed haircuts, biting the heads off smaller stick-figure men, and Alex had a feeling that he'd better not be seen. A tribal group could run in at any time to escape the volcanic eruption. He undressed and laid his clothes in a pile. The warm air felt good. He leaned down and drew up handfuls of water, drank, then rested against the wall. Looking up at the ceiling, he saw more drawings: animals with white-capped heads. He fell asleep assuming these images must be the gods of the shock-heads.

Alex dreamed of being Marlin Perkins, the original host of the television show *Wild Kingdom*, returning on his horse from the wild, dismounting, and telling his viewers about the animals he encountered. He loved that show. When he next saw Chapman, he would tell him he found a new, more exciting calling: a television adventurer. Forget the book.

A grunting sound woke Alex. He remained still, looking about for the sound's source. He was scared that any minute the teeth of a hungry animal would sink into him. Eat or be eaten was a law of business conduct. Now he faced its primitive roots.

He spotted a group of rocks that could provide shelter and walked naked along the river's edge, carrying his wet clothes. As he neared the hideaway, a hissing sound grew louder. He thought the hiss was water dripping onto the warm volcanic rocks.

The chamber brightened. He slowed his pace, carefully scanning for human activity. Every so often, he stopped and listened. As he crept along, the chamber suddenly smelled foul. He spotted an overhead ledge and climbed atop the high perch. From there he was able to see down the corridor, and spotted what were several naked humans with hairy chests and lupine faces. Alex was ready at an instant to jettison his clothes, jump into the river, and swim for his life.

The skin on the lower part of their bodies had a yellowish red cast. The appendages appeared human, and they walked with human gaits. Nearby, on the heated rocks, an animal roasted. Smoke filled the corridor with a haze from lack of ventilation. The rank odor and smoke made Alex want to gag. He suppressed it.

A man and woman approached along the riverbank. They stopped at the spot where Alex had climbed out of the river. He had left several puddles. The couple looked at the puddles closely. One grunted. Both looked in all directions. Alex knew they sensed him. They raised their heads and sniffed the air.

Meanwhile, the other members dragged the dead animal's body to the spot where the two cave people stood. Alex could see it clearly: a human corpse. The biggest caveman lifted an arm of the corpse, twisted it off like a turkey drumstick, and gnawed off a mouthful of the steaming flesh. Alex clamped his hand over his mouth to keep from screaming. Everyone jumped in for dinner. Napkins were their forearms. Disgusting.

The tribe, after eating the human corpse, walked down the corridor toward the hearth. Alex saw them disappear in the haze. It gave him a chance to get away. He hurried down stealthily to the riverbank. When he was certain no one could see him, he slipped into the water and floated downstream with his clothes in hand. He left his shoes behind.

He traveled for days, floating down the cavern river. He avoided food, being nauseous from the earlier scene. Eventually, he saw openings in the rock with bushes growing outside the walls. He ran outside and devoured the leaves and berries. The sun was bright and gave him a chance to dry his clothes.

ELEVEN

a reconnect with life

01101110

110

We left Beaver Island jubilant in spirit. For one week, we called a rustic cabin our home, away from family, friends, phones, and robots. For one week, nothing interrupted us. Birds winging over Lake Michigan and Beaver Island increased our enjoyment. I yelled to them to tell Chapman and the robot clan we say hello. We patronized local restaurants designed in log cabin style. Local men were muscular *longa lokshes*, dressed in checkered flannel shirts. Women wore dresses made of old tablecloths. When we entered, heads turned away. Our dark complexions and sport clothes labeled us as foreigners. Scandinavians settled Northern Michigan. They were a typical clannish group who wished for foreigners to spend money and leave ASAP.

I warned Alex, "If they're eating crab cakes, please don't make a scene and call them cannibals."

He replied, "Eh?"

I suspected Chapman, with ingenuity, could find out the location of our vacation hideaway. He kept his distance, though. On the other hand, we could have used him as a guardian angel to accompany us to the restaurant. I would be amused seeing a show of how he protected Alex. I sensed the local lumberjack population suffered from lack of pugilistic rivalry and could use some competition.

My sexual obsession continued unabated. Alex was my stud muffin. With all the screaming, hollering, and snarling emerging from our cabin, the local animal population retreated deep into the woods. It was a false sense of security. Alex and I played Adam and Eve, running through the trees and ferns in the buff. We lay down on leaves. We knew animal eyes watched.

We had plenty of time to tell whatever we had on our minds. One part I shared was the story of what happened after Alex and Chapman took off in the spaceship from Shain Park. Alex was unprepared for, in fact flabbergasted by, what I said.

After I awoke from my fainting spell, Officer Dougherty told me that TV stations had picked up the story. He said reporters, for sure, would come to my home for an interview. He suggested I drive to a friend's house.

I said I would, right after watching the Birmingham TV news report. The officer stayed and we watched as a TV camera panned Shain Park on the screen. The empty spot where the space rocket ride stood was roped off from the public. Inside, a policeman interviewed a workman. Outside, a crowd milled about the Fredrick Marshall statue. A well-dressed man carrying a microphone approached the perimeter of the space rocket ride area. If I didn't know better, I would have thought him a robot. He appeared muscular and had glassy eyes. I turned on the VCR to tape the news broadcast. While trying to gain his composure he said, "Are we live?"

A background voice growled, "Yes."

"Hi! I'm Branch Pearmain. Workers are dismantling amusement rides all about me." The reporter made his statement swinging an arm in a dramatic gesture. "The Shain Park Fair closed yesterday and I'm standing near the lot recently occupied by the space rocket ride that launched into space. It disappeared." He hesitated. "Yes, it disappeared."

The camera zoomed out and a carny appeared wearing greasy jeans and a T-shirt that read "I love ass fishing." The *b* was covered in grime. He lifted his T-shirt and wiped his nose. The reporter avoided putting his arm around the worker, who needed public health clearance, and kept a distance between them by waving the microphone as if it were a billy club. Bugs flew around the carny. "I have with me Cathead Carter who was working here this morning. Cathead, tell everyone what you saw."

"Well, this here rocket ride took off into space. If I hadn't turned my head, I would'na seen it. You know. Like there was no boom noise. You know how them rockets on TV take off in a fireball. I watched it go'en up and ran for the police. It scared me so that I—BLEEP—my pants."

"Thank you, Mr. Carter."

The camera zoomed to a close-up of the reporter. He grabbed his throat and the screen went blank. Maybe the bad odor from the carny's soiled pants caused the reporter to gag.

Officer Dougherty told me it was too early for the police to make any official statement. He did tell me that the report would confirm two men entered the ride just before the rocket launched. The police would reveal the names later. For certain Alex was one. Officer Dougherty saw him. I gave the officer the name of the robot. How they would confirm Chapman as the other person was beyond me.

I escorted Officer Dougherty to the front door and thanked him for all his help. He said if I needed any further assistance to call him. I nodded, closed the front door, and walked to my bedroom, weeping all the way. I stood on my takeoff leg ready to leap onto the bed and let the floodgates open, when I saw Alex calmly sitting on the love seat. I leaped on him and kissed him passionately and felt his groin. I moaned, "I love it. You're already hard."

Alex went ballistic. "You did what?"

I said, "Easy, my dear. How was I to know it wasn't you?"

The doorbell caused me to pause. I said to Robot Alex, "It'll be the news media. Let's go to the front door and let them see you're home. It'll stun them and put an end to the report you were in the spaceship when it launched."

Alex kept at me. "When did it dawn on you that Robot Alex wasn't the real me?"

I said, "In bed later that night. Let's not get into specifics." Alex fumed. That dirty old robot! He planned to speak with Chapman and have Robot Alex's privates ripped off.

In front of us lay the City of West Branch, where the flatlands begin, the halfway point on the drive home. Bummer. We just drove into the reality side of life: Roman, Caroline, Merton Freyburg, and Jonathon Chapman. I could feel my mind drift from the thought of watching the sunset over Lake Michigan atop a dune to feeling the car's tire drop into the valley of a pothole.

We wanted to go back to the life we shared prior to the Garden of Eden episodes. Celebrating a family wedding, bar mitzvah, or milestone birthday every so often embodied the high point of the low-key day-to-day life we sought. The new part added to our lives was Alex's work to write a great story about the Garden of Eden. It wouldn't be easy. Jonathan Chapman was more than a discomforting jolt caused while flying in turbulent weather. I dreaded the thought that more mischief awaited.

We arrived home in the late evening to find the kitchen telephone ringing, which we ignored. Instead, Alex flicked on the kitchen lights and went back into the garage and brought our suitcases inside. We both yawned, longing for bed. After the fifteenth ring, it stopped. We are behind the times: no caller ID. Alex walked to the message machine and said, "It's full. It'll probably be Merton, all outraged at something overheard. We can listen to him tomorrow."

I peeked out the window, a bit apprehensive that somebody might be driving the neighborhood to see if we were home. Chapman wouldn't prowl the neighborhood. He'd knock on the door at any hour of the night.

We trudged upstairs to our bedroom. The phone began to ring again. After ten rings, we looked at each other. Alex said to let it ring. I replied, what was worse, listening to the phone ring or listening to Merton? Alex sighed. He picked up the receiver and acknowledged he was Alexander Haralson. I rushed downstairs and picked up the kitchen extension. Alex said that yes he was the missing person. I heard the caller ask Alex if he was inside the rocket ship that took off from Shain Park. Alex acknowledged he was. The caller asked if the rocket ship went into outer space. Alex answered with a quick yes, it did. The caller asked about the purpose, "Were you part of some governmental secret mission?" Alex, in a funny-sounding voice, responded by asking what was a government. The caller said the U.S. Government. Alex answered he never heard of it. The caller growled, "You're a jerk," and hung up.

As soon as I replaced the receiver, the phone rang again. I lifted the kitchen receiver again. It was Merton. I asked how he was. Merton immediately started to ramble. He lamented about the current state of his existence, comparing himself to Job. He didn't plan to wear sackcloth or pour ashes over his head. His plan was to walk around everywhere wearing a sandwich board that said *The End is Near*. I looked at the ceiling, hoping God would somehow help me and send down a message suggesting how to end this phone call. I finally burst in a loud soprano voice, "Merton, I understand your frustration." I told him we just got home. I suggested Alex meet him for lunch at Steve's Deli, around noon. "How does that sound?" Merton, in a meek voice, asked if he could come over now. I said, "No," firmly. "Alex will see you tomorrow. Good-bye, Merton." I hung up the phone and ran upstairs. I told Alex that I needed to call Annabelle in the morning. Merton seemed in a bad way.

Alex said, "Thank you for arranging tomorrow's luncheon appointment, Mrs. Haralson."

I looked at Alex. Who was he, Robot Alex? Everything seemed to be unraveling. And we had had such a good time up north. I said, "Anything else, Mr. Haralson?" He put his arms around my waist. As his newly anointed secretary, he insisted I come into his office. He said he needed companionship. I said I wasn't sure if he was my type.

Alex said, "Didn't I tell you that all accountants are better adapted to work with figures than doctors?" While Alex and I cooed, headlights from a car crawling past the house were visible. He said, "We've got company." As soon as Alex neared the window to look, the car sped away. He said he'd call the police.

His next sentence was interrupted as the phone rang. I mused we were home all right. We tried to remain calm between the prowling car and the ringing telephone. Alex said he would answer it and picked up the phone. "Hello." Alex held the receiver in a way that we could hear together.

The caller identified himself as Tyler Rennet, a managing editor with *The Observer and Eccentric*. He said a reporter from his newspaper just called and Alex had told him that he rode in a spaceship into outer space. He found the story hard to believe. "Can you confirm?"

Alex covered the mouthpiece and said he didn't have to wait for the McAfee wedding; he could try the story out on a stranger. So what if he printed it? Alex could say he was drunk when the reporter called. I shrugged why not. Try it out on the reporter.

Alex said to Tyler, "Yes the story is true." Tyler asked who were the people who took him into outer space. Alex said, "Robots." Tyler asked if Alex went willingly. Alex replied that it was complicated but essentially, yes.

Tyler asked where he met the robots. Alex said walking around Birmingham.

"How did you meet them?"

"One approached me and asked me if I wanted to meet my ancestry from fifty thousand years ago. I said yes."

Tyler said he thought robots were futuristic. What would they know about ancient history? "And why did they approach you, versus me?"

Alex said they weren't robots that went about all day long and shot laser guns. They were a different class. They went to school to become cultured.

Tyler asked how he would know if he met a robot. He never saw anyone walk around Birmingham in a metallic suit. Alex replied they're dressed like ordinary people. Walk about town and make it a point to shake everyone's hand. If on an occasion you hear a crunching as if the bones in your hand are breaking, coupled with excruciating pain, he's a robot.

Tyler asked if Mrs. Haralson knew about these robots. Alex answered yes. Tyler said, "And you met your ancestors." Alex answered he specifically visited his cannibal ancestors.

"That must have been a hell of a family reunion."

"We ate well."

"Some roasted guy?'"

"Oh, you're a comedic managing editor."

"Weren't you afraid they'd eat you?"

Alex answered that if history was any measure, sons sometimes killed over-the-hill fathers and feasted on their remains. So logically, his Neanderthal ancestry should have been more afraid of him, he being the progeny. Alex said he was raised a perfect gentleman with high moral character—a statesman, not as a cannibal. Anyway, Alex said, they were limited to eating one father per lifetime. He said, "I learned who the tribal elder was, and discovered that the gentleman had been designated as dinner shortly before I arrived."

Tyler said it was a miracle Alex came back in one piece. Alex attributed the reason to being careful not to call them Neanderthals. For some reason they did not like that nomenclature.

Tyler wanted to know whether the robots divided into genders. Alex answered they were *its*. Each one was characterized by both male and female traits. "Look Tyler," Alex said, "They didn't take showers or have men's and women's restrooms." Alex looked significantly at me and said, "Going over and touching their chests or groins to determine gender might be misinterpreted and would seem to be a social no-no." I grimaced and planned to give Alex a head *klop* as soon as he got off the phone. The Robot Alex incident was not soon going to be forgotten.

Tyler wanted to ask more questions. Alex said he was tired and ended the call. When he finished, I said curtly, "Keep the receiver off the hook. I don't want an interruption." I folded my arms. "Did your remark about touching their chests or groins have anything to do with Robot Alex?"

Alex said, "No, dear."

I said, "Good. Women were not born with oversexed traits."

Alex retorted, "Oh, really!" He said what did I call my sexual fierceness: an environmental means to an end? Frolicking? I scoffed and told Alex to watch his mouth. Otherwise, it would be a lonely evening. It wasn't much of a threat. I was worn out and wanted to go to bed. Having sex would have been punishment for me. He looked relieved.

Around 3 a.m., I woke Alex. I said I wanted to hear more about how he escaped the cannibals. Exasperated, his reply was, "Can it wait?" I imagined the hairy bodies and the odor that emanated from them. I nuzzled his cheek and whispered in his ear. "No, it can't."

He hesitated and then propped up the pillows, with a sigh, "All right."

Alex made his way to an open area along a river basin. A waterfall was in full view in the background. He quickly and aptly named it Margarita and Alexander Haralson Falls. Alex said he felt uneasy surveying the wide, open spaces at the waterfall. He saw himself as an easy meal. Besides the cannibals, surely hungry animals with keen eyesight, hearing, or sense of smell, prowled. Could your father have been more obvious in the open with his blue sweater?

Danziger told Alex they would keep close tabs on him. If lost or in danger, they would rescue him. After the encounter with the cannibals and being transported in the spaceship *Mamma Beam*, my Alex felt like the brunt of their jokes. Alex was alone with no flare to shoot. In every direction, everything looked the same: mountains and more mountains. I whispered in his ear, "Danny boy tried to lose you again." Alex smiled and nodded.

He trekked up an ascending ridge, searching for a hiding place among the rocks, even though he was exhausted from physical exertion and lack of sleep. The ridge was an obstacle course of large granite boulders. Once atop the ridge, the view of the waterfall was dazzling. Plus, it was a good lookout spot; he could see if any spaceship landed to whisk him away. As nighttime neared, he found a nearby crevice with an overhanging ledge on which to rest. It seemed safe, better than entering a nearby cave that was dark.

In the morning, he awoke to a grunting sound and froze. Footfalls grew louder every few moments. He said he felt hunted all right. Bushes rustled. The stalker wasn't walking in stealth. It didn't matter. Alex had no chance against the cannibals. They were strong and carried knives; he was no match—an apple to be cored. After an hour, the footfall sounds tailed off. Alex peeked around the crevice's bend. He saw a child with a satchel on her shoulder, picking berries. The tension eased and he was able to slump back and breathe a sigh of relief. After waiting another fifteen minutes and hearing no footfalls, he stuck his head around the corner. He shouted, "Oh shit!"

A chrome-plated, five foot two inch T-Rex Cyclops with hands on hips, bent over and said, "Alex, where the hell have you been?"

Alex replied, "Whoa. Do I know you?"

She said she was Roma. Her appearance paralleled a no-nonsense dominatrix with handcuffs and whips in her utility belt and a menacing stance, looming over him. The last time he'd seen Roma, she stood against the wall in *Northern Spy* as a computer. Alex sensed she wanted to rough him up, but he felt a degree of safety. Any animal or cannibal who ventured near to harm or kill him needed to challenge this bitch to a fight.

Alex said, "Roma, my dear, am I glad to see you."

She said, "I'll bet you are." She lifted him up off the ground, grabbing the neck of his University of Michigan sweater. With Alex firmly in tow, she clopped over to the ridge where they could see the waterfall and *Mamma Beam* at the base. Her metallic finger pointed towards the falls. She asked why he didn't wait by the falls for her to pick him up. Alex asked was she referring to the newly named Margarita and Alexander Haralson Falls. Roma said, "Don't be a smart-ass." Alex asked what the big deal was. She found him. Didn't that make her happy?

She let go of Alex's sweater. He dropped and hit the ground with a thud. Pain ensued. Alex looked up and said, "Roma, you are a major league bitch. Is that any way to treat your elders?" She growled at him.

While kissing his cheek, I said to Alex, "You bring out the best in people." Alex said Roma was a typical woman: no concern or common sense. I gave Alex a *klop*. "Enough of you." I plopped my head on the pillow and folded my arms. I said to continue. He then shared with me what it was like living with Neanderthals.

Roma picked Alex up off the ground and took him to the place where *Mamma Beam* awaited. Roma opened the door and flung him inside. "When the spaceship crashes, and if you survive, stay on the trail into the mountains. Do you think you can do that?" Alex replied it was okay not to say good-bye or wish him well.

The spaceship soared off into mountainous terrain. *Mamma Beam* darted close to crevices and cliffs. Alex reached for the radio's voice transmitter to broadcast "mayday." He screamed and begged for his life. Nobody heard him because the transmitter's attachment was cut off.

Alex landed safely and dove out the door, kissing the ground. He found the trail and walked to the Neanderthal encampment. They seemed friendly from the start. All his relatives came out to see the distant relative from Michigan. Some walked around him and others leaned in to get a good sniff. Alex, feeling welcomed and seeing family members who were a bunch of hairy, club-swinging brutes, broke the ice by crouching in a pugnacious stance, bobbing and weaving. They screamed to each other, "*Oy vey*, what a crazy cousin!" Their Yiddish was protolingual, made up of grunts mostly, not unlike that spoken in Detroit.

Once the ice was broken, everybody rushed Alex, wanting to greet him. Some pounded him on the head or shoulders like pile drivers. With the ground being soft and mushy, he sank about a foot, bruised, but lucky not to be a fence post. Some broke out into a dance routine, looping arms and skipping about.

The strongest and most articulate was Party Adam, apparently the chief. He and the rest of the family hugged Alex to show welcome and affection. They were pals from the first minute. During their initial greeting, they faced each other and the Neanderthal placed his hands on Alex's shoulders, smiling at him and looking him over from head to foot. He grunted *ugh* several times; he seemed to be saying, "By God, you've grown." Alex wondered how Neanderthals could evolve into *kibitzers*.

Everyone beat up everyone else. Alex learned the Neanderthals' language. It was easy. All it took to be conversant was to say *ugh*. The number of times in a row *ugh* was said or the tone of voice indicated what was meant. Orders were given with kicks, punches, or slaps. Hungry was the only word pantomimed: pointing to one's stomach or a hand eating food. Alex learned *Ar* meant Airets. Apparently the Neanderthals gave their planet a name.

The Neanderthals made Alex feel right at home, home being a cave. A corner in the rear was reserved for guests. Even the wooly skin Alex snuggled under couldn't overcome the strange noises and strange odors. Rotting garbage smelled better. Alex assumed the latrine area was nearby or dead animals rotted around the bend. Did Neanderthals have any cleanliness traits? Alex said my sensitive sense of smell would enjoy a smorgasbord because ventilation was nonexistent. During the night, the Neanderthals snored and grunted up a storm. Noisy kids were quickly quieted with a bop on the head. Most of the clan slept near the hearth, which was by the entrance. That area also served as the dining room and ceremonial grounds. At night, three strong men covered the entrance with a stone slab. No animals or enemies could mount a surprise attack.

In appreciation of the hospitality shown, Alex gave Party Adam his University of Michigan sweater, literally the shirt off his back, as a present. The people took turns bobbing and weaving in circles around the hearth, swinging the sweater like a flag over their heads. A carbon copy of a strip club, the sweater substituted for a bra. In return, Party Adam gave Alex a bearskin coat to get *farputst*, the coat being the equivalent of a tuxedo.

Seeing the Neanderthal physiques up close, Alex thought them more brutish than they appeared in pictures. When the men stood together ready to go hunting, a street gang best described them. A tall people, Alex estimated each member measured about six feet five inches, and they were muscular from hard physical labor under harsh conditions, not by weight lifting.

Airets was fifty thousand years behind Earth's development but one million years into the future. Being in the future, Alex said, we know more about the past. The further time advances, the more we know. Alex traveled to the real Garden of Eden. The timing was perfect. No digging up the ground was necessary to find artifacts. Being taken to the Garden of Eden rewarded and motivated Alex to keep the generational lines rolling with grandchildren.

The next morning I called Annabelle. Merton had told her some facts about Alex's trip into outer space. She said, "I can't believe it. It's impossible for anyone to travel to another planet. The technology hasn't been invented. Anyway wasn't the purpose of Alex's trip to visit the Garden of Eden? What's that got to do with another planet?"

"Annabelle," I said, "I know it's hard to believe." I told her when Alex first recounted his adventure I thought he had gone mad. When events started to unfold in the beginning, he led me to believe he was going to an ancient archeological site in Turkey and northern Iraq. I saw pictures of him swimming on a plush beach. When he returned home, he told me this convoluted story about his going on a spaceship to a planet where ancient history took place and the Garden of Eden existed.

Annabelle said, "And you believed him?"

I told her yes. But I kept an insane asylum's telephone number on speed dial. As I heard more parts of the story, everything began to make sense. I knew that by themselves, a raconteur's narratives, without some evidence, didn't make a story true. How would I find out if I wanted to?

Annabelle asked if Alex had changed. I said, "Oh, yes. Believe it or not, he has been acting kinder. We were in a restaurant and Alex, after finishing half his meal, asked the waiter to pack the remainder in a styrofoam box along with a plastic fork. When we left, he walked over to a homeless person sitting on a walkway and handed him the package saying, 'Enjoy your dinner. This should help you gain some strength. Maybe someday you can help another troubled person.' Alex said it so kindly that the homeless man looked up in amazement. The homeless man said, 'Thank you.' It didn't mean Alex had to like him."

Annabelle said it didn't sound like Alex. Knowing his past attitude, he might have walked over to that person and kicked him, with an abrupt comment like, "Quit this begging crap. Get off your lazy ass and get a job." I sighed. That sounded more like my Alex.

I said I was sure she knew we returned home the previous night. I knew Merton was eager to meet Alex so I had arranged a luncheon meeting. Annabelle said, "You're a dear."

I learned from Annabelle that Merton at first thought Alex's story a concoction fabricated by a very mentally challenged person. It wasn't a matter of it being hard to believe. It was utterly impossible. In time, Alex's story grew plausible, especially when Merton's hearing became hypersensitive. Merton concluded to Annabelle it had to be the only explanation.

Merton heard Alex's tales about a futuristic world filled with robots that evolved into sentient electrons. He worried that nothing filled their lives with joy. They had every inspirational idea or object gleaned since the beginning of civilization at their disposal. Art, music, architecture, poetry, whatever, evolved into a yawn. If he had to say what bothered him most, it was a fear that religion would come to an end, replaced by a philosophy that everyone in the world will act without faith-based inspiration in any form. He said since recorded civilization began, religion, whether from a gene or other type of indoctrination, has been the driving force in society to bring order to the world. In a Sabbath sermon many years ago he said, "We may drive religion out of existence by letting the world be ruled by non-believers." And now, disclosing that non-God-believing leaders will be robots living in the future would be lunacy. Wholesale panic or the sack?

I told Annabelle that I sympathized with Merton's dilemma, him being a respected leader. Now everyone's finding out Merton believed Alex's adventure to the Garden of Eden. I said I suspected anyone who has heard him must want to throw a net over him. When Alex returned and told me where he had been, I wanted to do the same. Annabelle laughed.

I said the gentlemen, as we spoke, were having lunch. I couldn't wait to hear the details of their conversation. I said, "Call me if you need me."

Roman, clean-shaven, his black hair combed and shiny, came downstairs dressed in sporty clothes. His stomach appeared thinner. I suspected smoking pot was becoming a thing of the past. I said, "Are you going anyplace special?" He told me he had a date for lunch. I said, "Don't go to Steve's Deli. It's reserved for your father and Merton." Roman said he wasn't going there. If it was someone special, I offered to pay for a hotel room after lunch.

Roman said, "Mother, will you relax. You'll get grandchildren."

I felt better.

TWELVE

the holy language

I peeked out the living room window to see if Alex had come home from Steve's Deli. The news of our contact with robots had leaked about town. Each time I checked, I kept seeing neighbors mowing their front lawns, some every two hours. I didn't know grass grew that fast. They pretended to be busy, but I saw them glance at our house at every opportunity. Finally, Alex drove into the driveway in his Cadillac, ever so gently so as not to scrape the car's bottom. He couldn't bear the thought of any repair below his insurance deductible. I'd heard him say, "If you get into an accident, make sure it's a *doozy*." Alex got out of the car and waved to a couple of neighbors with accompanying shouts, "How are you?" and "How's the family?" They returned halfhearted waves. I would explain to Alex that they were mainly interested in catching a glimpse of a robot.

My Alex walked cheerfully from his car into the house. Relieved to see him, I walked up to him and gave him a hug. I said, "Let's forget *I love you* and start right in with *lunch with Merton*. From your grin, I sense it was a success."

I could see in Alex's smile his mind was a storehouse flooded with news. Instead he teased me. "*Lunch with Merton*. Is that a sequel to the movie *Weekend at Bernie's*?"

I stepped on his foot. "Say something before I strangle you!"

Alex talked Merton out of lamenting his sorrows by wearing

a sandwich board around town. Alex begged, "My foot, please."

I removed my foot and helped him settle into a chair in the breakfast room, while I rubbed his neck, I said, "Now talk."

Alex explained that Merton felt his soul was punctured and deflated. Hearing us describe a future universe controlled by soulless robots was incomprehensible. How could he continue to live in such a world? Stripped away was a lifetime of Judaic beliefs, layer by layer. Precious possessions, held so dear and used to comfort and inspire his congregants. The robots had no idea or concern about the Garden of Eden. They said, "What is it: a Chinese restaurant?"

Merton pictured himself a male Lady Godiva riding nude on a donkey through town, mocked as he passed the viewing throng of laughing robots with chattering teeth. Merton said, "These idiots will someday own the power to rule the universe." Merton started to blubber. Alex handed him a napkin and asked Merton if he had any Xanax.

Merton spoke as if he was carrying a burden in his head weighing two trillion tons. "The donkey will have it easy," said Merton. "It only has to carry my trim, muscular frame." Alex suggested Merton's doctor prescribe stronger medication, like Prozac.

As Merton continued to talk, his voice escalated and reached a sermonic climax that reverberated throughout the deli. "Dear God, make room for another troubled soul." Alex asked Merton to hush. When he did, Alex asked where Merton learned to speak using an evangelistic tone. Merton told him, "I've been watching Christian TV stations."

Alex groaned. Other patrons stared, open-mouthed, like frozen fish. The owner of the deli, Steve, was slicing corned beef. He stopped for a second and peered over with squinted eyes and raised eyebrows. Alex returned a thumbs-up sign to indicate that he had the problem under control. Alex worried that Merton's next outburst could set off a nasty scene. Steve was known to act out his hot temper. He'd approach bad-mannered customers with a knife in his hand and say, "Get up from the table, leave your sandwich, pay your bill, and get out!"

I asked Alex who was eating at the deli. He said it didn't matter who was there. The world tapped into the goings-on from outgoing cell phones. Alex swore he heard in his mind computer keyboards clacking at the synagogue office, drafting Rabbi Merton Freyburg's resignation. The board of trustees, he envisioned, would have it prepared, demanding his signature as he walked through the door, returning from lunch. Alex hoped they would allow a face-saving reason, "Rabbi Freyburg resigned to pursue other interests."

Alex mentioned that Ralls Jenet, the manager who ran Willfongs Jeweler, was eating there with a cabal of salesmen. After waving hello to Alex and Merton, he leaned inward to his luncheon partners, told them something, and they broke out in laughter. Alex was incensed. He stood and walked as if going to the bathroom. He approached Ralls' table and said, "Enjoying your BLT, you cannibal?" Ralls looked over at Steve. Alex looked around at Steve and said to Ralls, "If he comes running over with a knife, I'll make sure it goes in your *kishkehs*." He went back to his table.

I said, "Alex, that was gutsy."

Alex said to watch the newspapers. He felt the sordid details of the luncheon engagement would make headlines. "No doubt reporters ate lunch at nearby tables." It seemed everyone knew he and Merton scheduled a date to eat lunch at Steve's and had waited for them to arrive.

Alex told Merton he needed to straighten up his act. "How are you going to officiate at the McAfee wedding on Sunday?" In Merton's present state of mind, the McAfees were Irish Catholics, and he would officiate a *goyasha* wedding, giving the bride and groom the sign of the cross.

I said, "I'm having lunch with the girls tomorrow. I'll bet they'll have a gossipy account."

Alex replied, "No doubt Annabelle will be hearing Merton's version. You'd better call her when we're done."

Alex continued that he sat quietly with Merton, feeling disconnected and at a loss as to how to help. In the past, the two were never at a loss for words. Alex wondered what he could say to break the ice. Could Merton come to his senses alone? Impossible! Alex decided to use a scattergun approach. Fire off five things and see which one got a reaction. First, Merton had to calm down. Alex told him he wasn't in the pulpit and the patrons around them weren't his congregation. Merton lowered his head. Alex forged ahead saying he'd hate to see Merton embarrass himself. "The world isn't falling off a cliff." Merton promised he'd stop saying stupid things.

He said, "Alex, tell Margarita I won't walk around town wearing a sandwich board."

"Merton," Alex said, "I'm glad to hear that."

Merton sat quietly reading the menu. Alex hoped relating another part of the journey might shock him into regaining his senses. Alex said, "Merton, I have more to tell you about my adventure."

Merton became indignant and barked, "There's more?"

Alex hadn't told him everything and Merton looked at his friend with a suspicious eye. Lunch with Merton turned into a debacle, with Merton already unhinged from hearing about the robots. Alex decided to ambush him with more of the Garden of Eden story. "Merton, let me finish. I'm not trying to slight you. My only purpose is to help." Alex suggested his story was so completely off-the-wall that Merton would forget all about his own silliness. "My craziness will surpass anything you've heard before. If you'd like," Alex said, "Feel free to testify at my insanity proceedings."

Then Alex dropped the bomb. He told Merton he had experienced a theophany. "I spoke with God on Airets."

Merton's mouth flopped open. Alex said Merton immediately morphed into Mr. Rational Person, the old Merton we knew and loved so well. "Alex, I can help you." He offered a crash counseling session, right over a corned beef sandwich, and attended by an eavesdropping deli congregation.

I, along with Merton, was shocked to hear about the theophany. I became light-headed. We moved from the breakfast room into the living room, and I flopped onto the sofa. I was confused and started to sweat. I thought Alex's adventure centered on the five senses. Now a story about a theophany emerged. I said to Alex, "Tell all, great warrior. I want to hear why God decided to speak to you, when he had ten billion other choices."

Apparently Roma shuttled Alex over to a city named Scratchy, and dropped him off with some of the local currency. Alex equated its location to be Karachi on the Indus River. He joined a caravan scheduled to travel westward over desert and mountains toward Mount Ararat. The trip would take about a month. "Somewhere in that expanse," Roma had told Alex earlier, "is the Garden of Eden." The caravan departed and all Alex had to do was ride the camel to a paradise he dreamed about and loved. My Alex could feel it: every second, the Garden of Eden was getting closer.

Along the route the caravan came to a rest stop. The setup reminded Alex of a truck stop on an interstate highway. They took an off-ramp along the main east–west travel route and the caravan halted in a designated parking area. Everyone dismounted and the camel drivers made arrangements with the local tribe to rent some space in a large community tent for the travelers to use for eating, meeting, and praying. Private tents for sleeping were available for a fee. Otherwise travelers slept in the stable area with the animals. Alex chose the former.

Alex wore a burnoose, which did a good job of protecting his face and head in the desert valley. In addition to hot weather, strong winds made the sand swirl. When he removed the hooded part of his burnoose at the rest stop, his face and hair were coated with sand and it felt like sandpaper. It was sticky sand. Sweat was the bonding material.

Alex said I'd have been right at home with my powerful sense of smell. Everything stank to high heaven: people, camels, Alex, his clothes, and his feet. A contest to judge who gave off the worst horrific stench could spawn a yearly TV special: *The Smelliest Human*. I would be a judge.

Sleeping tents and eating areas were owned and manned by a local tribe. The camp operated a retail center where supplies were available for purchase to restock caravans. In addition, it sat at a crossroads where caravans coming from various directions converged: a bus terminal. Patrons from one caravan could transfer to another.

Alex narrated his travels crossing over several mountain passes before descending into an orange colored desert valley. Dry, scattered bushes and thick clumps of scrub grass served as the most practical form of bottom-wipes. Alex thought it a perfect spot to construct a golf course. He loved the idea of convincing the robots that cold weather and high winds would make it a challenging venue. He hoped, while they were playing golf, a sandstorm would erupt and the sands would shift and bury Chapman, Danziger, and Roma permanently.

Alex met up with Camel Adam, the caravan leader, soon after dismounting. He asked how long they would be staying. He learned the stopover would be about five days. The animals needed a rest, as did the hired help. Camel Adam suggested Alex could use some too. He also told Alex he had to wait for the arrival of another caravan with transfers before they could restart.

While they spoke, Alex caught sight of large military tents in the distance. He learned from Camel Adam that the tribe that ran the rest stop lived there. Their leader was a man named Elder Adam. Alex learned the tribal leader was a good businessman with honest values, which earned him the respect of travelers. However, everyone felt safer at the truck stop. He learned it was dangerous over there: they ate people. Alex wondered when humanity began to view fellow humans as something other than the next meal. Alex acknowledged Camel Adam's report with a nod and left. He paid his fees and walked to the private tent area with his gear. He found a suitable tent and labeled it as his personalized "EconoLodge." He made a pillow with his gear. With the wind constantly blowing, it made for great air-conditioning. The flaps had to be left open. Lack of privacy was the tradeoff. Alex was tired and collapsed.

I said, "Alex, you're so transparent it's disgusting. You traveled a million years into the future to live among smelly animals and the first thing you worried about were fluffy pillows." I pulled Alex on top of me and kissed him feverishly. I said I didn't mean to interrupt.

Alex continued, saying in late afternoon, the bright sun beamed into his face and jolted him awake. Everyone was walking toward the campfire, attracted by a horrible smell. Alex thought a garbage dump was on fire. He realized it was dinnertime. The smell was foul; the menu was garbage stew, *drek*.

While he stretched, he noticed in the distance the local tribal family sitting together. It was strange, since they didn't move from their sitting positions with their hands resting on their knees. Alex wondered whether it was a religious ceremony. Were they praying? It reminded Alex more of a yoga session. A sound reverberated from the campsite, *YAHWEH*, a word Alex knew well. His interest piqued. Where did they learn that name for God? What religion did they practice?

Alex tried to force some dinner down. The food was awful, seasoned with cockroaches. His stomach grumbled with starvation. He remembered Camel Adam saying the tribe ate humans. Maybe Alex should have dined with them. Leave it to Alex to find out the trivial fact that humans tasted like pork. At the time, he said the thought didn't seem so bad.

He threw his food to the camels. Alex was a gas machine, burping and blowing wind. He walked a distance of about a mile from the camp to find a place to retch in private. It was a struggle. It felt as if he carried lead weights in his stomach. After heaving, he found a comfortable rock for sitting. He closed his eyes to relax.

A sound broke his calm: "YO-HO!"

Alex was startled. He thought it sounded like a human voice. He looked around. No one was there. What he saw was little wind cyclones hovering close to the ground blowing past him. Another cyclone passed. "YAWWEH!"

The words were familiar. It was God's name, the same one used by the tribe. How could those words made by the swirling sands sound so human? At the least, he wished a trusted friend sat next to him to corroborate what he'd heard. The story of Moses speaking with God at the burning bush embraced trust. His theophany was believed: no witness, no tape recorder. How did he get away with it? Alex walked briskly back to camp in a disbelieving state of mind. Once there, he saw a group of seasoned travelers sitting together. He walked to them. He introduced himself and asked if anyone ever heard or understood the words that emanated from the sand swirls?

They shook their heads and shrugged their shoulders. He knew what he'd heard and was very determined to pursue the voices. Since the sun had already set, he decided to wake early in the morning and return to the area where God's name was spoken. Starting there made the most sense. Alex walked to his tent, eager for a good night's rest. Before lying down, he brushed off the sand coating his clothes, since he planned to wear them to bed. Camel Adam warned him that clothes left about were as good as gone.

When light broke, his eyes were already open, having slept more with anticipation than soundness. He jumped up from his bedroll and stretched, raring to go. Everyone seemed fast asleep so he tiptoed away from the camp.

As Alex walked towards the previous evening's resting place, the temperature warmed quickly. The conditions were ideal for whirling sands and hopefully for again hearing a voice in the wind. Once away from the camp, Hebrew words reverberated in a loud bass voice. "I AM GOD, YOUR GOD." Alex looked up and noted the source of the sonorous voice: a canyon. He believed the words were meant for him. Awestruck, Alex understood its intensity as a demand, a beckoning to travel to the distant mountain range. What he should do there was unclear. He watched huge sand swirls weave intricate patterns above the mountain peaks, a seductive dance. Alex imagined himself fearless in the middle of that tempest. He was kidding himself. He would be scared out of his mind. The small sand swirls about him scared him enough, teasers by comparison. It appeared a face-to-face encounter with God awaited. Alex accepted the invitation, hoping every answer to every biblical puzzle would be answered.

I told Alex I was excited listening to his account. "So you told Merton this story?" Alex nodded. I begged, "Tell me more. So you went to the mountain?"

Everything he saw and heard felt like the source of things he had been taught as a child. There weren't any stand-ins, like Charlton Heston ascending a papier-mâché mountainside. The whole scene played out for Alex's benefit. He was the center of attention.

The wind picked up and tiny cyclones passed near Alex. Again he heard, "YAHWEH." A small cyclone approached the vicinity and Alex ran and lunged to touch it. He was spun around several times and thrown to the ground in a daze. He couldn't believe such a small whirl had such power.

A larger cyclone spun near and said, "MY HOME IS HEAVEN ABOVE. THE GARDEN OF EDEN IS MY EARTHLY PARADISE." Alex screamed.

A loud angelic voice reverberated in the canyon, "ALEXANDER HARALSON, *KOOM AHERST*." Alex couldn't believe the cyclone decided to speak in Yiddish. Who was going to believe what happened? Alex thought, no one, which included himself.

Alex had to find a way to journey to the canyon. He ran back toward camp using every ounce of energy. Soon he tired, slowed down to a walk, and flopping to the ground. Another large cyclone appeared. "DO NOT BE AFRAID. I PROTECT ALL."

Alex replied, "You're kidding, right? Why would I not be afraid of a disembodied voice?"

While Alex caught his breath, a glance to the side revealed a young boy hiding behind a nearby bush. He stared and then smiled. "Hello, young man." No reply came. "Are you feeling okay?" Again, no reply came. Animals were in view. A shepherd, Alex thought. He might be a child that belonged to the main family tribe. Alex jerked his head towards the herd. "Are those your animals?" The young man turned and looked without acknowledgment. Alex remembered what Camel Adam said about staying away from tribal members. He kept to himself until he caught his breath. Then he rose and walked toward camp, smiling and waving good-bye to the young man. Alex looked back and saw the young boy running to a horse tied to a bush. He mounted it and galloped away.

As Alex walked, the rising sand swirls in the distance brought on by the howling winds set the stage. A voice spoke from the mountain. "COME CLOSER. YOU ARE THE CHOSEN ONE." The highest authority had invited Alex to hear something profound. God would address Alex in his holy language. In the distance was the meeting place.

"This is quite a *Bubbe Meinsah*," I said. I trust it will be incorporated into your book for our robotic grandchildren to read.

Alex replied, "Oh yes."

"Good," I said, "Now get me to the mountain."

Alex went to Caravan Adam and asked how he could secure an animal and a guide to take him to the mountains. Alex was directed to find Stable Adam at the community well. Alex met him and hired an animal. Stable Adam said, "About the guide … hmm, let me think. Well, yes. Camel Coat Adam could guide you. When do you want to leave?"

Alex answered, "Now," impatient as always. You can't keep God waiting.

Within an hour, Stable Adam returned with Camel Coat Adam leading two mounts with short reins. The horses had thick muscular legs and walked sturdily. By eyeball comparison with Earth horses, Alex estimated these as larger with a more upright neck and head. Camel Coat Adam held the reins tight as the powerful horses pranced, ready for action. Alex had practiced riding horses in his teens and loved the activity. He asked what their names were, but they didn't have names. To Alex, a horse without a name was sacrilege. Alex called his horse Akaro and jumped on his back. The other he named Descio. Camel Coat Adam mounted him. They rode bareback. Alex pointed in the direction where he wanted to go: the mountains. Descio broke into a gallop, Akaro followed. As they headed in the direction of the mountains, the wind swirled hard and the sand pelted Alex's face. Alex rode toward heaven. With each horse's stride, cyclones appeared with faint words. Alex glanced at Camel Coat Adam.

His eyes were focused on the task. When their eyes met, Camel Coat Adam pointed in the direction of the mountains. Alex acknowledged his gesture with a raised fist.

They reached the mountains after an hour's ride. Camel Coat Adam pointed to a cave entrance and they dismounted. Once off, Camel Coat Adam grabbed Alex. Camel Coat Adam indicated that there could be hungry animals inside. Alex thought, kick out the humans, lions he could handle.

Leading the horses, they entered the cave, which protected them from the brunt of the hollering wind. There was enough light inside to see by. Suddenly, a voice erupted. "I AM YOUR GOD."

Alex stiffened. He snapped to Camel Coat Adam, "Did you hear that?" The guide said he only heard a whirling sound.

Again the voice blared: "OF EVERY TREE OF THE GARDEN, YOU ARE FREE TO EAT. BUT AS FOR THE TREE OF THE KNOWLEDGE OF GOOD AND EVIL, YOU MUST NOT EAT OF IT."

Alex, unnerved, backed against the cave wall. His body and hands shook. He pleaded, "God, please help me," knowing he was in God's divine presence. The guide saw Alex's fright, with concern. He suggested they return to the main camp. "No," Alex blurted. "I'll be okay." Alex knew returning to camp was the smart thing to do. But he put it out of his mind. This journey was the big show.

Camel Coat Adam said he knew where there was an underground river. "You can wash and cool yourself." Alex smiled and nodded. Leading their horses, they walked deeper into the cave's interior. Alex felt the air turn damp and cool. They came to a flow of water and Alex bent down to drink and rinse the sand from his face.

Alex heard Camel Coat Adam say, "Young Adam." Alex looked up and saw the young boy he spied earlier in the brush.

Camel Coat Adam ran to the boy and asked if he was okay. The boy said he was. Young Adam said he saw them approach. He came to lead them to a place of safety. A fierce storm was approaching. Alex thought, isn't what was going on outside already a fierce storm? Young Adam said Blanket Adam camped with a fire burning and food cooking. They began to walk. Young Adam said, "Stay together."

Young Adam glanced at Alex who returned a knowing nod. Young Adam looked significantly at Camel Coat Adam. The look said to Alex that he remembered who he was and silently asked what an outsider was doing here. Even so, Young Adam looked at Alex and beckoned, "Come quickly."

Alex rubbed Akaro's nose to reassure him as the passage became pitch black deeper inside the cave. Instead, Akaro tried to bite off his arm. "Okay, have it your way."

Young Adam said, "Keep your hand on the wall." He said they would be nearing a bend where light would come from another passage. The young man's confident demeanor impressed Alex. In time, Alex reached Young Adam's hearth with his protector, Blanket Adam. Camel Coat Adam and Blanket Adam greeted each other with hugs and smiles.

Camel Coat Adam said, "*Shalom Aleichem*. It is great to see you." Blanket Adam replied, "*Aleichem Shalom* to you."

Camel Coat Adam said the sand storm erupted unexpectedly. "Your hearth," he said, "speaks that we're safeguarded."

Blanket Adam asked what brought him to the canyons. Without hesitation Camel Coat Adam introduced Alex, saying, "Meet Peaceful Heart." Blanket Adam asked if Alex was hungry. Alex nodded. Blanket Adam began to cook vegetables in a pan. It wasn't appetizing, but looked edible. Young Adam and Camel Coat Adam stood aside and conversed.

Alex had told Camel Coat Adam his name was Peaceful Heart at the community well when they first met. All his life, it was referred to as his Hebrew name. Alex would change the custom when he returned home. His soul always lived in God's holy space and his Hebrew name would be reclassified to be his spiritual name. The trip was beginning to make a significant impact. His idea flew in the face of tradition.

Alex walked near a small opening to the outside wind. He sat and listened to the buzzing noise that whistled. No voices spoke, yet the sound of the wind continued to frighten him. As a child, Alex remembered hearing a similar sound while sleeping. It awoke him and he lay shivering. Someone was at the front door. Alex blurted, "*Go away!*" Everyone's eyes were riveted on him. Red faced, he said he didn't mean to startle anyone.

Within a raging wind, a gentle and firm voice spoke, "I AM YOUR GOD." There was no hiding place. Alex lay on the ground and listened.

"IT IS NOT GOOD FOR MAN TO BE ALONE. I WILL MAKE A FITTING HELPER FOR HIM."

Alex covered his ears with his hands. For about fifteen minutes, he heard faint sounds and faded into a trance. A tap on his shoulder startled him. Blanket Adam said that the food was ready. A bit groggy, Alex stood and walked to the hearth to eat.

After a few bites, Alex felt alert. He inquired whether everyone was related. Camel Coat Adam said of Young Adam, "He is my cousin." Alex glanced at Young Adam, who lowered his eyes when he saw that Alex was looking at him. From confidence to shyness; he was reticent, seemingly, not wanting to admit openly that they had met.

Alex asked if they were related to Elder Adam. Camel Coat Adam spoke, "We all are."

Alex commented, "I trust I'm a friend."

Camel Adam inquired, "Why would you think otherwise?" Alex said he'd heard the tribe practiced cannibalism. Blanket Adam said they ate their enemies. You'd have to do something terrible, like steal. Stealing an animal from any tribal member was not permitted. The punishment was death and to be eaten.

Alex told them he observed a ceremony and heard the word YAHWEH used. Blanket Adam told him it was the name of their God. Blanket Adam pointed to a nearby wall. On it was a carved statue, an idol. Alex thought they would someday learn YAHWEH was a portable God, and hear his words listening to the wind. Alex felt pleased. He was way ahead of the tribal members as he understood every word the wind spoke. He was the chosen one to visit the Garden of Eden. How great was that?

Camel Coat Adam spoke. "Help us understand something, Peaceful Heart. Who spoke to you earlier?"

Alex answered, "God."

Young Adam, with brightened eyes said, "You heard God?"

"Yes." Alex told him God had a holy language, which he knew and was able to speak. "Today was the first time he spoke directly to me."

All asked with anticipation, "What did he say?"

Alex felt tempted to preempt history at this point and declare a commandment, the missing one in his opinion: *Thou shalt not nosh thy brethren*, but he decided to keep it simple and truthful, and merely said that he was told to go to the Garden of Eden.

Everybody smiled. Camel Coat Adam, pointing at Young Adam, said, "He has told certain tribal members about talking birds. We are skeptical. Is it possible?"

Alex said, "The young man raises an interesting possibility." A mynah bird could be taught to speak. As to other birds, he told them he'd heard birdcalls many times. "I never thought they meant anything other than one bird communicating to another." Alex said he didn't know if they were messengers of God. "A few moments ago, the wind's noise was a language I understood." Alex said that for him it was God who spoke.

Young Adam said, "I believe birds speak a language."

Alex encouraged him. "Keep working. You'll find an answer."

Alex turned to me and said, "How about that?"

I didn't know what to say. Alex had heard God speak to him. "Wow," I said. "And Merton sat quietly and listened?"

Alex said Merton went off on a short philosophical binge saying never had he heard such a story about the origins of language. He was taught it was a collection of organized babble. Merton said Alex was in the right place at the right time.

I said, "Now there's the old Merton I know, listening, thinking, analyzing, and imparting important ideas. He regained his composure."

Alex arched his back and extended his arm. He mimicked Merton saying, "Alex, it was the beginning of the monotheistic eternal God's divine presence. Everywhere I go, I will carry the knowledge of God being always present. I'll be alert, as he may want to speak to me. No longer will the passing wind fail to gain my attention. I know the language. I'll continue to pray. Maybe he'll deliver a *Divar Torah*. I'm a believer. The power of God resided in the wind, the most powerful force on earth. Who would have believed it? Water moved where the wind blew. Absent wind, water stood still. I used to think water was the most powerful natural force on Earth. Now I've learned wind holds that honor. Being a force everywhere in every corner of the universe demonstrates his majesty."

All eyes were directed at them. Alex leaned in and said, "Merton, you're preaching to the choir." Alex suggested they go for a walk. There had been enough trouble for one day.

Merton agreed and said, "Maybe we'll meet up with a robot."

Their stroll through a mall started quietly. Merton broke the silence. He said he sensed Alex had more to say, which Alex acknowledged. Alex began, saying he was by the hearth when a buzzing noise caught him off guard. Alex walked toward the cave entrance.

"I AM YOUR GOD."

"Peaceful Heart!" It was Camel Coat Adam. He yelled, trying to overcome the wind's noise. "Do you hear God?"

Alex nodded.

"WHERE ARE YOU?"

"I am here."

"WHO TOLD YOU THAT YOU WERE NAKED? DID YOU EAT OF THE TREE FROM WHICH I HAD FORBIDDEN YOU TO EAT?" Alex was scared, but God spoke again. "FEAR NOT. I WILL PROTECT YOU. GO FORTH TO THE GARDEN OF EDEN. THERE, YOUR ANSWERS AWAIT." Alex fell down and reached forward. Then the bomb dropped. "I COMMAND YOU: DO NOT EAT THE FLESH OF YOUR OWN SPECIES."

Alex thought, See, I was right all along—that's not written in the Garden of Eden story. In fact, it wasn't written in Exodus. It was a missing commandment, perhaps a stolen one. Right, I'm always right. Alex was overcome with his own awesomeness, and fainted.

Merton said, "Oh my, you heard a missing commandment from God." Merton fell to his knees and said, "*Oy.*" He asked Alex who forgot to write it in the Bible. Alex shrugged his shoulders and said he thought Merton was the Bible *maven.* While still on his knees, Merton grabbed Alex's shirt and said, "You were surrounded by cannibals and they didn't make you eat part of a human carcass?" Alex answered he only saw it. Merton said, "Phew." Merton was relieved. If Alex had, he might be the Michigan version of Hannibal the Cannibal.

Alex helped Merton stand. Merton asked how Alex put all the logic together. In a pompous voice, Alex said, "My cranium, my dear Merton, my cranium." Alex said he had a special insight for him. The key part of dietary laws started with what was found in nature *not* attached to the ground. We answer the question, "If it's a vegetarian species, like the locust described in the eighth plague, they're permitted. Simple logic, Merton."

Merton was worried about Alex. How can he be so smart about cannibalism and so dumb about Elder Adam's family? "They were a bunch of cannibals and you're *schmoozing* with them, as if they're clients. Give me the logic to that."

Alex said to consider him a lucky guy. Anyway, Alex said the story concluded with his regaining consciousness. The wind still blew hard. Blanket Adam saw that Alex was awake and came over to him at the entrance and offered him water. Alex sat up, still a bit dizzy, and drank. Alex saw the family members staring at him intently. One member asked if he was a holy man. Alex answered that after being face-to-face with God, he was.

Young Adam wished Alex could stay longer, but prayed for his safe journey. Alex told them he dreamed many times of seeing the walking snakes inside the garden and shake hands with them. They all laughed and bantered, "The shrewd ones." Blanket Adam said the crawling snakes were the only ones they saw. Alex said he made some new friends for life, even if they were cannibals.

Two days later, the storm ended. Camel Coat Adam and Alex mounted their horses. They said, "Good-bye and thanks." The ride back to the camp was made leisurely and in silence. Alex was still in awe. At the main camp, the storm had ripped some tents apart. The community tent was partially collapsed. The EconoLodge tent was nowhere to be found. Some animals from the caravan were coated with dust, lying on the ground near death. Injured people lay on the ground. Alex looked about to see where he could help. He spotted Caravan Adam covered in sand and ran to him. "Are you okay?"

Caravan Adam grunted something about the connecting caravan. He said, "Don't worry. Caravan leaders know the routes well and know what to do when emergencies happen." Alex had cultivated another friend.

Within a week, the caravan from the south came plodding into view. The two caravan leaders met and decided to wait two days before again departing. That would allow the recent arrivals to rest. Then the drama would go into its next act, hopefully the final.

I said, "Touching and eating are the human senses, the others the Godly ones." I told Alex I was starting to understand. Listening to my most learned husband, ancient people figured out the reasoning of linking God and spirituality to the five senses. He took the compliment most pompously.

He wanted to play golf. With his improved sense of sight, he was sure his golf score would improve. I wondered, "Did the real Alex come home?"

THIRTEEN

alexander treks to the garden

On Saturday night, we had Frank and Georgia Stansill over for dinner and bridge. The relationship sustained itself with Frank and Alex being the best of friends. The compatibility of our social activities consisted of a harmonious male–male and loathsome female–female relationship. The men cheered each other for every well-done action such as a golf shot. Georgia and I sniped at each other at every opportunity. We avoided each other at every chance encounter. If I sighted her while grocery shopping, I went to the opposite side of the store. If we passed each other walking in downtown Birmingham, we looked away, never stopping to chat.

Frank and Georgia lived about four blocks away. For Alex, the distance was three blocks too far and for me about a thousand miles too close. Nothing ever satisfied Georgia in the twenty-five years I'd known her, a real *draykop*. I felt sorry for Frank: he lived with her. I doubted the temperature during marital relations ever warmed the bedsheets out of an ice age deep freeze. I saw in Frank enthusiasm and passion expressed in our social contact. I imagined he needed to be pounced on by an overheated wife, but it could never happen with Georgia. Since my heightened sexual sensations, I thought everyone should get properly laid. That included Frank and Georgia and Merton and Annabelle. My Alex and I were in a world unto ourselves.

Saturday's visit started as a typical get-together. We first ate supper. Georgia complained that my cooking tasted awful. She said the linguine was hard. "It's undercooked and the sauce tastes harsh with too many ingredients." You could set your watch to the time when she started complaining. Why was I surprised? It didn't matter how careful or how much effort I spent preparing dinner. Appreciation was a dirty word. When we dined out, she always sent her entree back to the kitchen, never prepared to her liking. Anyway, when did she become an expert in Italian cooking?

In the past, I always tried to be civil and not say anything, but this time I couldn't hold back. Fed up with Georgia's antics, I said, "I prefer everything hard: my linguine and my play toys." Alex looked up from his plate glaring at me. Frank chuckled.

Georgia gave me a curious look and said, "What was that about?"

After dinner we settled in the family room to play bridge. Alex and I stood no chance against the Stansills. We were the Washington Generals of bridge. The Stansills ranked high as bridge players, having won many major tournaments. The game concluded with Frank trumping and making his bid. Alex burst out, "Well-played, Frank and Georgia."

I looked at Georgia. She smiled triumphantly. She turned her ugly puss to me. I said, "It appears you've skewered us again. You can cook me to suit your taste." Her face changed to an expression of disdain. Alex looked at me, shook his head in disbelief. I said to him, "We lost again, but we had fun, though not as much fun as we'll have in bed."

Alex tried to deflect the conversation by saying to Frank, "I don't know if we'll ever beat you. We could use some bridge lessons."

Frank said, "Alex, you thrash me every time we play golf. I admit you're a better golfer, even with my side trips to the driving range."

I looked at them while they spoke. They resembled each other in their attitudes, mannerisms, and political viewpoints. It was frightening. The left side parts in their hair matched. I was happy for Alex and Frank. A better friendship wasn't to be found. They laughed at each other's jokes no matter how corny.

My personal feelings about Georgia were reinforced when we went to the Stansill's for dinner and bridge. She cooked beef stew, it being her specialty. I would characterize it as pig slop. We melded as women taking care of the home front while our husbands built careers. When asked by people what I thought of Georgia, I was kind when I stated our relationship was pedestrian. Verbal combatants on many subjects, Georgia ranked our home's décor of contemporary furnishings as rubbish-in-progress. I classified the Stansills' antique home décor as a here and now garbage dump.

When Alex returned from his adventure to the Garden of Eden, Georgia's comment was one that I will never forget: "It's beyond my understanding. How could you let him go to a strange place with strange men without getting references?" I told her the touring company, Malus Industries, and the tour guide, Jonathan Chapman, came highly recommended. However, I admitted she had a point. I could never imagine anyone else giving Chapman a favorable recommendation. Georgia continued, "Alex is back in town and going around talking like a lunatic. I don't understand anything he says about the Garden of Eden, and when he talks about it, I get a headache." Luckily, Frank and Alex's friendship wasn't impaired by their feuding wives. In fact, Frank understood everything Alex said about the Garden of Eden.

I thought about Annabelle. Now there was a friend. She never criticized Merton for the lunacy he displayed surrounding his sensitive hearing. I knew why I hated Georgia so much. The rest of Betsy Deaton's group of country club friends had the capability of saying something nice every so often. This bitch couldn't.

Frank started his professional career having graduated as an attorney from Harvard Law School. A career opportunity opened with a transportation company. He began work as their legal counsel, and in time was promoted to president. After forty years of service, Frank planned to retire. His retirement date would be the completion of some unfinished business projects. Alex and Frank had great business minds. I once asked Alex why they had never gone into business together. He replied, "We'd never be friends."

After playing cards, we sat in our living room eating cake and drinking tea. Even though Frank and Alex were carbon copies of each other, the thought of extramarital activities with Frank, which was creeping up on me for all sorts of reasons, seemed absurd, yet persisted. Frank and Alex had noticeable differences. Frank's scent was a mint aftershave, artificial and cheap. Alex's scent was a swampy musk, he-man and outdoorsy.

Frank asked, "How's your book coming along?" Alex replied he worked at it every day. Alex admitted that he had some difficulty clarifying the events when he left the caravan and rode to the Garden of Eden.

Georgia interjected in her most polite manner, "Do we have to hear about it? I'm getting a headache."

Frank chuckled and turned to her. He said, "I find Alex's trip fascinating."

Georgia snapped, "You would. You don't know any better."

I quickly interjected, "Well then, Alex will be quiet and won't say anything about the trip. Instead, I've got a bit of personal news that relates to Alex's trip." Georgia groaned. I said, "Alex got a call late today from Wolf Winslow's office. He wants *Alex* to appear on his talk show."

Frank shouted, "Wow!" Georgia went limp in her chair.

"I was preparing supper, when Alex ran into the kitchen and gushed, 'Guess who just called?' I replied, 'Deep Throat?'"

Alex and Frank laughed, while Georgia sat *ungabluzen*. I swooned. Who could believe it? Wolf Winslow actually wanted my husband to appear on his show.

Underneath, I was happy yet apprehensive. I'd seen some of Wolf's shows and heard about him from friends. I felt his interviews were somewhat superficial. Alex was a deep-thinking individual. I wanted him to conquer the viewing audience by transmitting some of Airets' erotic essences through cable TV lines. Sexual upheaval would break out *en masse*. What a glorious thought.

Wolf would need to ask thoughtful questions. In those moments, Alex was at his best, relaxed and lucid. Wolf had better not reach the low depths of a Geraldo Rivera by asking Alex to speculate. Or if Wolf asked silly questions, Alex would attack and be perceived as the bad guy. He couldn't care less. In the end, my man would be on top. How I would control myself was another matter. After the show ended, I imagined dripping with perspiration waiting to pounce on Alex. I wouldn't care if we made love while the TV cameras broadcast to a live audience.

Wolf Winslow's shows were interviews of people with high current media interest. The format was similar to Larry King with Wolf's unique focus on topics with a Michigan connection. So here's Alexander Haralson, a person who was born in the twentieth century, lived in Michigan, and happened to travel to another planet. This story must have caught the attention of Wolf's media staff and was irresistible.

Frank piped up that he was seated next to a soon-to-be celebrity. He sounded excited. Being president of Air Etic Transportation, Frank had to give plenty of TV and radio news interviews. In his college days, training courses on how to handle an interview didn't exist.

Alex said he delivered plenty of speeches on accounting, followed by question and answer sessions. Frank said if he went ahead with the interview, his advice was to loosen up and take a couple of shots of liquor beforehand. Frank continued, saying the media today was much different. "You'll have to answer all questions, even if they're petty or have an agenda." Frank said he hired a voice coach. He felt his training helped his interviews go smoothly.

Frank said he wanted to hear more about Alex's adventure; specifically the part Alex had encountered trouble writing. Georgia's face turned red as she looked and growled at Frank. I had had enough of Georgia's multitude of complaints for one evening.

At that point, I wanted to drive her home. But Mr. Charisma was ready to speak, and when he spoke, everyone listened, including her.

One problem was to explain how he went one million years into the future on a planet that lived fifty thousand years earlier in Earth time. Alex said his real problem was delicately describing some horrific happenings. He said no politically correct police patrolled. The natives' lifestyle was limited to killing and eating animals, screwing, sleeping near a fire, and running from predators.

Georgia slithered in, "What happened if someone got sick?" Alex's expression to Georgia was stoic. He shrugged his shoulders and said, "They died. Medical care was a shaman dancing around the patient, chanting."

Frank interjected, "I see that all the time on TV documentaries."

Alex said, "Frank, stop talking about Shabbat Services. Give Merton a break." Frank and Alex roared. I remarked I'd like to take them to the synagogue, drop them off, so they could repent. Georgia added that while they were there, Frank and Alex should apologize to Merton. I thought, oh God, for once, we agreed on something.

Alex said that he would apologize to Merton. But Frank had heard the board had been unhappy with Merton recently. Congregants reported he seemed to know everyone's business. Alex gave me a significant look and said, "I'll bet Merton can hear every word of our conversation." We laughed.

Alex continued, describing a place named the Bath Water Oasis, where the caravan and Alex separated. Camel Adam told him the trek to the Garden of Eden was about thirty-six miles over rough terrain. Alex had a sore butt from riding the camel in the caravan; he speculated that another camel ride would cut off circulation to his legs. Even so, he would endure the torture from any animal. He wanted to get to the Garden of Eden.

My Alex checked his provisions. When he looked in his knapsack, he saw some overripe fruit and stale bread—a bleak situation. My Alex was dust-covered, sunburned, wearing torn clothes, feeling aches and pains, and out of the local currency Roma had given him. The thirty-six-mile trek was impossible without transportation. He realized that his entire adventure's success or failure was at a critical stage. He desperately needed more food and an animal. Alex's second choice for his next meal was grazing the surrounding scrub grass.

I interjected, "Next time, my darling, you won't be so critical when you sit down to dinner and find a tuna sandwich."

"My love, I'll never again take you for granted."

Georgia squealed, "Will you get this story over with. I want to go home." I told her I would drive her home. Georgia said she wanted to go home with Frank.

Frank said, "Relax Georgia. All we'll do at home is watch TV and doze off." I smiled. Frank confirmed my suspicions. They weren't going to spring into action.

Alex continued that he was in the middle of nowhere with no money to buy food or an animal. Where were his guardian angels? They had deserted him. Alex sighted in the distance some shepherds at a well with donkeys grazing nearby. If he had some money, he thought, surely they would sell him what he needed: food and a donkey. He dropped his knapsack on the ground, ready to sit, rest, and think. He noted a strange "thud" that came from the knapsack; certainly one not made by stale bread. He looked inside. He found a heavy bag of gems. How had it gotten there? Alex looked skyward, "Thank you, Lord."

Everything looked bright. The shepherds would sell him what he needed, plus he could hire a guide to lead him to the Garden of Eden. Looking into the distance and seeing the mountain range, getting lost seemed easy. Alex walked to the shepherds watering their sheep: a father and his two daughters. Alex asked if the man owned the grazing animals. The man said he did. Alex asked if it was possible to buy one and obtain a guide.

The father walked around Alex while his daughters stood watching. Finally the father asked Alex his name and where he was going.

Alex told him his name was Peaceful Heart and his destination was the Garden of Eden. Alex wondered why the father didn't just ask for all his money. He would have given it to him.

He circled Alex several more times, scrutinizing every detail. It seemed he was estimating the value of every thread of clothes no matter how decrepit. When satisfied, he introduced himself as Pony Tail Adam. He turned to his daughters with a gleam in his eye. "Meet my daughters, *Shmendrik* and *Schlump*." He used gestures as if selling used automobiles. They dared to smile at my husband. Alex mugged a sour expression and muttered, "Man, are they ugly." In a beauty contest, the donkeys would win.

Alex thought, "He's not going to make a *shiddach* with the two ugly daughters and a donkey, is he?"

I chimed in, "I have two unmarried children. I'd like to arrange marriages for them." Then all my efforts would be channeled to make my future *machatunim* pay for the weddings.

Frank was dumbfounded. "What about the donkeys?"

Alex said Pony Tail Adam's daughters were top priority. The donkeys were a bonus. Georgia said, "Didn't you tell him you were married?"

Alex replied that we were talking about fifty thousand years ago. Unmarried daughters were considered grazing animals available for sale. Alex said the thought entered his mind to let them carry the provisions while he rode a donkey.

Georgia interjected, "Alex, you should take Frank back with you. I'm sure the Adam sisters would be an improvement over Margarita and me."

Alex said to Georgia, "Never. I will never part with my *baalebusteh*."

I said, "*Marito mio*, you are so kind. But get on with the story."

The father informed Alex it was a package deal: the donkeys and the girls.

Alex was stuck negotiating with a con artist. He dreaded taking the daughters as part of the package. But what other choice was there? There were no cabstands or rent-a-car counters. Pony Tail

Adam's daughters and the donkeys appeared to be the only option. Alex tried again. He told the father he was only interested in the donkeys. "Please keep the daughters." The father shook his head. Alex said if he was forced to buy them, he would pawn them off on a passing caravan as slaves. The father said, "Okay, if you want."

Georgia pointed menacingly, "Wait till I report you to NOW."

Alex said, "It was the father's idea to showcase his daughters. Report him."

Frank said, "Must you politicize everything, Georgia? The times were primitive. Pony Tail Adam had options."

Georgia shrieked, "That's horrific!"

So Frank sided with Alex. The ride home would be a screaming match.

Frank asked, "What was the outcome?"

Alex put his arm around Pony Tail Adam and showed him some of the gems he had in his pocket. "Two donkeys and five days' food, and they're yours." Pony Tail Adam smiled and looked at his daughters. Alex shook his finger, "No, no, no."

Pony Tail Adam nodded his head, "Yes, yes, yes."

Alex prayed for Roma to come and save him. He didn't have forever to negotiate. Selling the daughters to a passing caravan loomed larger every second. But what if there wasn't a passing caravan? Alex's mind was working deviously like a biblical hero. He knew if he took them, there would be opportunities along the way to get rid of the sisters. Somewhere along the route Alex would make a sharp left turn and the sisters would be forced to take a hard right-hand turn into a den of wolves.

Frank shouted, "That's murder!"

Alex replied, "Let's call it recycling."

Frank said, "Where are your moral values? If you'd explained your predicament to Pony Tail Adam he would have understood."

Alex bellowed, "Do you think cannibals worry about other people's predicaments?"

Alex said Pony Tail Adam knew a rich or stupid American when he saw one. Alex lamented that conquerors stole women.

"The winners didn't pay." Alex said he hadn't fought or won any war. And he didn't want the sisters for free.

Alex was the man I married because I loved him and felt he would care for me. My father, prior to our engagement, wasn't interested in what I thought. He said that all women cost money and wanted to know Alex's finances. If I got divorced, he wanted to be sure I returned home with a sizable bank account. He also thought all men play around. I told him Alex was a religious man and would be *fedele*. I realized that my father resembled the Pony Tail Adam. The only difference was I was prettier than his daughters. I started to get the feeling that there might be a message in Alex's story; then I thought, Naaaaaa.

Pony Tail Adam laughed. "You are a tough customer." He told Alex his brother-in-law, Palm Tree Adam, would return in another day. "He will take you to the Garden of Eden by the main road. You don't need to buy my daughters. Just make sure you give him all the gems in your possession."

Alex replied, "Gladly."

Frank noted that matters became anticlimactic. Alex said he felt conned but relieved. When it came to money, every cheating or lazy brother-in-law sided with family. Those Adam brothers had a racket.

I was not worried that Alex would be unfaithful. Georgia irked me, saying, "Since Alex was away so long, those women must have become better looking by the minute. When you have only pigs to screw, in time they grow wings." I chided Georgia for such a heartless thought. I *so* wanted her to go home.

Alex said, "Frank, did you want me to finish the story? Or did you want to go home with your lovely wife?"

Georgia said, "Well, I never!" Frank said he did not appreciate the sarcastic remark.

Alex replied by asking did Frank think everyone was born with a pure heart. "You could act any way you wanted in that world. Wake up, Frank. Here's the rest of the story whether you like it or not."

Frank and Georgia sat quietly.

Palm Tree Adam arrived from the Garden with returning pilgrims. They seemed unhappy; not a good sign.

Alex, in country club mode, joked with Pony Tail Adam that he was lucky to have not sold his daughters. He would have taken them to the Garden of Eden and made them run around nude, hopefully catching pneumonia. Or he'd have put a snakeskin jacket on them and fed them forbidden fruit ... laced with poison.

Apparently, one returning pilgrim witnessed the exchange. He came forward and said to Pony Tail Adam, "You sold me one of your daughters. She tried to kill me along the way. Now you're trying to sell her again?" Before leaving, Alex elbowed Pony Tail Adam and called him an old rascal, extracting a laugh. Best to keep on the good side of the local mafia.

Mardi Adam came over to him and said, "Good-bye, my friend. I wish you luck." Alex thanked him for his assistance, although he couldn't quite recall who he was. They hugged, and while he was close, Mardi Adam whispered, "Be careful! There is great danger. The Adam brothers hope you die from the harsh elements or fierce predatory animals." The Adam brothers weren't above doing to Alex what he considered doing to the Adam sisters. In reality, being supper for the wild beasts wasn't a danger. Alex said he counted on his guardian angels. During his adventure, they had pulled his ass out of the frying pan more than once. Alex just wished they'd hung around so he'd be more reassured. Was he to expect a rope to appear from nowhere and wrap around a leaping beast's neck and yank it away just as its flaring jaws were ready to sink into his genitals?

Frank cringed and placed his hands to cover his privates and said, "Ouch."

Georgia said, "I want to know if you ate any human body parts."

Alex replied, "I'm partial to elbows."

She said, "I'm serious."

Alex asked if she was worried if he got enough to eat. "As to your question about eating humans, the answer is no." Alex ate mainly fruit and berries. The main source of protein for Neanderthals was relatives, people like Uncle Irving and Grandpa Mortimer.

Georgia said to Frank, "I'd like to go home. Hearing about cannibalism and eating Margarita's dinner has made me sick."

I wanted to strangle her. That was the only way to cool me off. What a dud. Georgia broke up the evening. I wanted to hear Alex continue. Cannibalism was a gruesome subject, yet he was adept at keeping the adventure's subject matter lively. We said our good-byes to the Stansills.

Alex and I hurried to our bedroom. While undressing, my mind returned to Alex's discussion with Frank. I walked to Alex and put my arms around him. "You didn't mess with those Adam girls, did you?"

"No. But you can't conceive how tough the situation was. All the gems I had in the knapsack were turned over to the Adam brothers. They even frisked me. Otherwise my passage to the Garden of Eden would have been in doubt. The only downside is I arrived at the garden with no money in my pocket."

Alex was high on his pedestal. I noticed that his eyes spellbound anyone who heard him. Like his narration spellbound Frank Stansill. What was I, chopped liver? At the grocery store or hair salon, I met some friends and acquaintances, and told short versions of Alex's adventures. It drew either boredom in the form of yawns, or pyrotechnical laughter. I experienced what a stand-up comedian faced. Did anybody believe anything I said? "Alex, I'm a failure. Is it my accent?"

"You're too hard on yourself. Maybe you'd like to take my place on the *Wolf Winslow Show*."

"Do you have to make things more difficult?"

"When I become famous, all you'll have to do is smile and answer reporters' corny questions: 'What's it like being the wife of a universe traveler?' With your bright smile, anything you say will be golden."

"Thanks." I continued thanking Alex for visiting Dr. Green's office to leave a specimen. "I'm scheduled to visit him tomorrow. Soon, my dear. Soon."

FOURTEEN

the garden of eden comes into view

Stanley Whitescarver, the voice coach recommended by Frank Stansill worked with Alex in the living room, helping him to prepare for his upcoming interview with Wolf Winslow. Prior to hiring Stanley, Alex grumbled to himself at the idea. He felt he could easily learn by himself the skills needed to do a successful interview. Determination was an inbred trait, he said. Alex reviewed his old speeches from handwritten notes, and watched the tape of his college graduation address. Alex realized after reviewing them, his old speeches and old manner of delivery were dated. Wolf Winslow would clobber him. Alex ran to the phone to call Stanley.

Stanley, a bit snobby, made it clear to Alex that he considered himself a *communication* coach. "I am not a speech or voice coach," he said. "Those expressions are misnomers from an Orwellian world."

I watched Alex as Stanley told him this. Alex raised his eyes toward the ceiling. Other people might interpret his expression as indifferent. I knew it to be his patented façade before he unleashed a biting remark.

"Really," said Alex. "I'll be learning how to converse and you're saying there's a difference between communication and speech. Is that anything similar to the difference between a specialist and a general practitioner? I thought all doctors were trained to relieve pain."

Stanley replied, "Alex, do you mean all medical degrees are not created equal?"

Stanley's specialty was training business professionals on their speech and demeanor in advance of media appearances. He trained clients to sound as articulate and intelligent as possible. In private business meetings, business professionals are usually feisty or domineering; annoying traits that subordinates endure, definitely not recommended in public appearances. Most businesses hire a public relations person to field questions from the media. They spared the entity from being labeled a bunch of *dumkopfs*. Confronted with product recalls or other problems, corporate reputations can be destroyed. Only an executive's appearance can serve to calm the troubled waters. The audience, if not detecting a sensible and sensitive executive, can paint the corporation in a negative light. Since Alex worked alone, he was the designated spokesman. Chapman and Danziger were the *dumkopfs*.

Being the first training session, Alex recommended that they begin by viewing his taped college graduation speech. He decided not to let Stanley see his written speeches. Alex realized they were dry. Why add gasoline to the fire? After watching the tape, Stanley lifted his nose and said Alex appeared to be a bit rough around the edges, his gestures and his voice stilted. "I would rate it, though, a C+. You're going to have to do better on the *Wolf Winslow Show*. Oh, and feel free to call me Stan."

In Alex's situation, because of the esoteric nature of the subject matter, Stan felt Alex needed to establish to the viewing audience that he knew more about the Garden of Eden than anyone. Stan said, "Believability will follow." Wolf's reputation was well-known by Stan and he suggested that Alex be prepared for off-the-wall questions. A low opinion of a guest would fuel questions to disorient you. Stan continued, saying Wolf was a womanizer. "Since you're a guest without tits and ass, watch out." Stan said Wolf would see Alex as red meat and do all in his power to have him perceived as a castrated wimp. I thought if that happened, Alex's book publishers, the robots, would be kicking themselves. I imagined Danziger hanging Chapman from a very long rope: good-bye toothy smile.

I told Stan that he didn't need to worry about Alex shaping up. My Alex wasn't afraid to put his reputation on the line. "Didn't Alex agree to be interviewed?" I said money wasn't always the issue. Alex had a following as a person of sensibility and a deep sense of self-respect. So far nobody knocked him off his position when it came to believing that he went to the Garden of Eden.

Stan said, "Wolf will try."

Secretly I wanted Wolf to expend a great deal of effort. Let him have callers who were shills. I had great faith in Alex.

While Stan and Alex worked in the living room, I planted myself in the dining room. There is a wide archway between the rooms. I could see and hear everything. The living room was rearranged with some of the sofas and chairs pushed aside against the walls. Stan brought studio props that simulated how the studio set would look, which included upright stools with back rests. He placed them in the middle of the living room. Stan informed Alex upright stools were a Wolf Winslow trademark. Stools with backs lulled the guests into feeling comfortable and not prepared for his attacks. If you fell off during the interview, Winslow won.

Stan brought a TV camera and I asked if it was real. He acknowledged it was and showed me how it worked. Stan said, "I'll be taping practice sessions." Afterward, I went up to Alex and whispered we could star in our own porno flick. Alex replied that showing off my tits and ass to Wolf might distract his attention so he'll ask easy questions.

Stan wanted to start by rehearsing an interview, learning how Alex verbalized things. He could then cut in and make suggestions. They sat on the stools. Stan, acting as a stand-in for Wolf Winslow, started out by saying, "Good evening. My guest is Alexander Haralson, a traveler to a distant planet named Airets to explore the Garden of Eden. Welcome, Mr. Haralson."

Alex nodded and said, "It's a very long and unusual story. I think your audience would be most interested in hearing about the last leg of my journey into the Garden."

Stan said it was as good a starting point as any. He warned Alex, saying Wolf may have other ideas about where to begin. "Don't arrive with an agenda." Stan said, "Go ahead. Please tell us some of what happened."

Alex spoke about the caravan ride.

While he rode with the caravan nearing the Garden of Eden, he looked out into the distance and thought, somewhere in that vista, it was there. The desert in front of him was a rocky, semi-arid plateau, with foothills to the yellow and green rolling mountains in the background. Scrub bushes, brown from lack of water, quaked in the wind. The Garden of Eden's reputation for beauty was well-known. However, Alex thought its curb appeal needed a makeover.

Stan said, "Your cynicism is appealing. Go on."

Alex frowned at Stan before continuing. Ideas loomed such as maybe God would speak to him again saying, "Alex, welcome to my heavenly home. Make yourself comfortable." Alex speculated God might add that Alex brought plenty of baggage. A lifetime of beliefs being important, but for now, put them aside. God would say with brevity "Alex, you're at bat in the bottom of the ninth inning with the bases loaded." Everybody watched in anticipation. The game was his to win. "Alex, you have the credentials to complete the job, the culmination of everything you've worked and prayed for."

Stan groaned. He said it sounded a bit like *Pilgrim's Progress*.

Alex muttered, "We're not doing a book review."

Stan got off his stool and said, "Alex, please put some faith in me." He placed his hands on Alex's shoulders and adjusted his posture. "You're not sitting correctly. Lean toward the center.

Sit straight and look like you're reclining and relaxed at a Passover Seder. Let's continue." Stan sat on the stool, asking what the exhilaration was like.

Alex said, "You're asking was I happy? Unbelievably happy! The Garden of Eden was within reach! *Moi*, Alexander Haralson, would soon be breaking bread with Adam and Eve."

Stan suggested Alex spit out the *b* in each word: breaking bread. Stan continued with, "What thoughts do you have about the biblical story?"

Alex commended Stan, saying he was a great straight man. Alex said the words of Genesis were on a huge digital screen scrolling across the distant mountain. It reminded him of watching the latest news flash across the ticker atop the Times Building in New York City. Occasionally, he looked about while riding his camel. But every time he raised his head to the mountain, he saw another biblical passage.

I saw Stan jump down from the stool and place his hands on his hips. Stan pointed to Alex. "Let me stop you here. You're too tense. Your mind and body aren't coordinated. You want a relaxed appearance, with a voice that resonates with authority." Stan said it was difficult, but Alex needed to speak with passion while keeping a low-key demeanor.

Stan said the preliminaries were over. They would do an actual show simulation, as if being broadcast. "Focus on your posture and demeanor." He told Alex to rearrange the chairs face-to-face about five feet apart. Stan said when he imitated Wolf he'd raise his right hand, and he'd raise his left hand when he imitated a caller.

Stan said, "Let's start." Seated in his chair playing Wolf, Stan said, "We have many callers on the line with questions. Bethlehem, Pennsylvania, you have a question for our guest?"

Stan raised his left hand. "I do. I heard you go both ways on creation."

Alex looked at me and said, "Sir, if we're talking creation, not sex, it's two ways."

Stan glared at Alex and shook his head in disbelief. Playing the caller, he said Alex couldn't have it both ways. Alex said calmly yes he could. Inside a synagogue, it was six days, outside fifteen billion years.

Stan shouted, "Much better." Stan said he would now challenge Alex. "I need to see, close up, how you will handle yourself when Wolf tries to back you into a corner." Stan warned Alex the worst possible situation would be for him to appear nervous to the camera. Even if you're calm inside, you're toast.

Stan raised his right arm. "Alex, you appear to be a man of reason. Don't you think your position is off-key? The world is digital: on or off."

Alex replied, "Ha! Well-said by a spokesman for secular enlightenment." Alex pontificated, "You believe that understanding creation and moral underpinnings were perfected by your analytical *mavens*, and then canonized. Was that it, Wolf?" Alex continued, saying Joseph Campbell believed many scientific theories were formulated thousands of years ago. And to paraphrase Albert Einstein, science kept revising those theories with the passage of time. "Let me sermonize. You're no better than those fanatical religionists who froze their beliefs in the Dark Ages."

Stan burst out, "Great! You were aggressive right on cue, in the heart of the situation. Your underlying message to the caller and audience was direct and concise. 'I'm no asshole and won't tolerate listening to ignorant questions.' Trust me," Stan continued, "if you keep up this level of intensity, Wolf would be wise not to allow through any Tweety Bird questions. He wants a successful show as much as you do."

Stan raised his right hand and said, "That's quite a statement, Alex. Let's go back a moment to what you said earlier. Genesis' digital screen is rolling across the mountainside. Tell us what it said and what were you thinking."

Alex said, "Some important moral values were formalized in the Garden story. For example, the prohibition of adultery was described as '... a man leaves his father and mother and clings to his wife ...' Another value implied was the prohibition against sodomy. The Bible says, '... for Adam no fitting helper was found,' i.e., no funny stuff with the sheep."

Stan's mouth dropped open with a puzzled look. "Isn't that stretching it a bit?" Stan said Alex needed to bone up on his subject matter. "It's sensitive stuff." If Alex didn't sound well-versed, they would burn him in effigy around the planet.

Alex said to tell that to the priest in the Garden of Eden who told him about the prohibitions. Alex said, "Was that close enough to the horse's mouth?" There was no book written for Alex to carry home. The Garden of Eden story was carried forward as an oral tradition.

Stan asked, "How?"

Alex said Adam, the high priest, wore a belt with gems attached to it representing the rainbow. Each gem told a story. Alex heard one of those stories in a ceremony. A Sabbath sermon, if you would like to call it that. The high priest pointed to the green stone and told the story of vegetation's creation. Alex asked the priest how he acquired the gems. He replied that they came from contributors. "Hey, Wolf, doesn't that sound just like how we do it now?"

"Okay, Alex," said Stan, "you maintained good eye contact with the camera. Your answer sounded factual and sincere."

I remained nervous, even with Alex's apparent rejuvenation. The anxiety of the *Wolf Winslow Show* proved too much to comprehend and endure. I tiptoed from the dining room to the den. I spotted *How to Win Friends and Influence People* and started to flip through some pages. I realized it wasn't going to help. A book on verbal warfare seemed more suitable. Something with an up-to-date sadistic vocabulary seemed even more appropriate and necessary for Alex to study.

I fidgeted for something to do. I promised myself I would go to Borders bookstore after supper to get Alex a how-to book on meanness. I spotted the telephone and dialed Annabelle. She answered.

I screamed in a low voice, "Help!"

Annabelle laughed. "So Alex is driving you crazy?" She continued, saying Alex drove Merton nuts, and now you. "Relax, Margarita. Considering you were the one who helped me cope with Merton's difficulties, it's my turn to help you. Sit on a chair and take a couple of deep breaths. Forget about the show until it's over. You'll get a video copy of the telecast. You can then watch it in bits and pieces, sort of sneak up on it."

I told Annabelle she was right. But I couldn't. I wanted to jump out of my skin and cuddle under Alex's. Annabelle said since I was still inside my skin, go for a bottle of Chianti. "Drink a few glasses. It'll calm you down."

I said, "Annabelle, sometimes you're impossible." I hung up the phone, picked up a book, and threw it across the room. I went into the kitchen to find a calendar. How many more days before Alex appeared on the show? I found myself sweating. I went back into the dining room.

Stan, as Wolf, said, "Christmas, Mississippi, you're on with our special guest, Alexander Haralson."

Stan stood and walked in front of Alex, saying to keep talking. He wanted a front view. He raised his left arm. "The scriptures say God created the world in six days. I heard you say earlier that the world was created over a span of time. Why should I believe you?"

Alex broke out laughing with the remark. He said the concept of creation in the Bible was written so seamlessly you could swear that everything happened within a week. Alex addressed the biblical fundamentalists watching the show, saying he was sorry to inform them, but he heard from reliable sources that the age of the planet Airets was calculated to be fifteen billion years, and the Garden of Eden he visited was fifty thousand years old. These same persons were unable to confirm the long-held theological view of Airets' age being about six thousand years. When I asked how they could be so sure, they said, "Our thinking came from the future. From that vantage point, we know more about the past."

"Short and to the point. Good. Did the Garden of Eden settlers know about creation?" Alex said they thought God was omnipotent, and as such, completed the *gansa megillah*, the job of creation, including humans, in short order. Ancient settlers needed a beginning. We do too. "Anyway, it was good folklore. What a tale!"

Stan, as Wolf, said, "Blessing, Iowa."

Stan, imitating a caller, said, "What part did morality play?"

Alex said it was a dog-eat-dog world in a literal sense. Cannibalistic taboos were nonexistent. If you hadn't eaten in a couple of days, Aunt Fanny started to look appetizing. Stan slapped his forehead, suggesting Alex tone it down. Children will be watching.

Stan, mimicking Wolf's affected style, said, "How did morality start?"

"You had to be in authority to make changes. From the start, leadership is political. Hey, Leibowitz, don't be *shtupping* your sister, we got enough idiots in the clan already! Morality initially gets decreed by politicians, who have the foresight to set up standards for local needs. Good idea not to eat shellfish caught in an estuary next to an urban center. Prohibitions kept societies intact. Priests came later and ratified the standards to cover all bases."

Stan said, "Let's go back to the journey. Did anything unusual happen along the way?"

Alex said he saw returning pilgrims, and was struck by their reticent and indifferent expressions. "I asked the caravan leader, Palm Tree Adam, what was wrong with those caravan passengers. I thought visitors to the Garden of Eden would return ecstatic." Palm Tree Adam said they had been exiled. Alex asked, "What did they do?" Palm Tree Adam said they ate the forbidden fruit. Their eyes were opened.

Alex asked if the same thing would happen to him. Palm Tree Adam said, "Probably. When you meet the Serpent and he tests your will, you'll understand the difference between human and Godly powers. Let the Garden priests explain them."

"Wow," said Stan. "I'm impressed with your adventure." As Wolf, Stan said, "Jerusalem, North Carolina! Go ahead."

Stan, as a professorial caller, said, "You hired a guide to take you to the gates of the Garden of Eden. That sounds too convenient."

Alex answered, "You're right." He continued, saying a commercial enterprise was in play. What else could he say? Riding with Palm Tree Adam to the Garden was the same as riding with a busload of tourists to Disneyland.

"Has your wife heard about this whole adventure?"

"Indeed she has." Alex replied, saying that I thought the most intriguing story was about how the biblical passage, "… from dust you came and to dust you shall return," developed. Alex learned from the Garden of Eden powers that every living thing exists in God's space. Our physical presence displaces a part of God's world. When our mortality ends, we are buried and the borrowed space is returned to God.

Tears flowed from my eyes. I said, "Alex that was so beautiful." He blew me a kiss.

"Christian County, Missouri, you're on the air."

Stan, aping an Ozark accent, said, "Did you carry any weapons? I mean, did you kill anyone?"

Alex replied, "The only thing I have ever speared in my life was an anchovy in a salad bowl."

Stan remarked that he noticed Alex's hands were quiet. He saw no sweeping wrist motions to emphasize a phrase. "That's good." Alex asked Stan how he could add something he felt was important if a caller didn't bring it up.

Stan said, "Just ask Wolf before the show to include it." Stan warned that if it were a subject inappropriate for family viewing, Alex might not want to *shtik*. "Let's rehearse more. How did your wife react when you returned?"

My Alex said how wonderful and understanding I was during his trip, looking out for the family. Alex said when he returned, I was eager to hear about the trip. "What she heard made her a more spiritual person." It brought tears to my eyes. I wanted to run and give Alex the biggest kiss, which I did.

After things calmed down, Stan asked, "Who took you to Airets?"

Alex replied, "Robots." It sounded crazy even to me. I watched as Alex explained about the robots. With every passing minute, his poise kept wilting. He might have been getting tired.

Stan's chiding might have caused his adrenaline to flow harder and now he was out of energy. It also might have been about Alex being uncomfortable talking about the robots. Suddenly, Mr. Charisma, on his present subject, wouldn't be able to convince anyone that grass was green.

I recalled earlier doubts I expressed to Alex. "You're under stress. Appearing on the *Wolf Winslow Show* might be a big mistake. Cancel your appearance."

He refused. "I'm not a quitter," was his reply.

Stan looked at me and said, "Let's take a break."

I asked Stan, "All seems to be going along, improving?" Alex breathed a long sigh and flopped back onto a sofa.

Stan commented, "We need more time together." He said by the time the show taped, Alex would be well-prepared. Stan turned to Alex. "I see a problem." He said when there's a break in the action, it does not mean Alex could relax. "The microphone and camera will still be running. You need to have an alert appearance at all times." The show began the minute he walked in the studio's door and won't end until he left. "We're talking hard work." Alex acknowledged Stan's comment with a nod. I went back into the dining room.

"Alex, continue on from where you left off. I want to finish our session with your reaching the Garden. I'm fascinated."

Alex said, "Palm Tree Adam's caravan was on a plateau. Ahead was the climb to the top of the mountain and the Garden of Eden. From our vantage point, the Garden was not visible." The rise was the highest and steepest he had ever seen. Alex estimated five hundred feet. Climbing the Sleeping Bear Dune in Western Michigan was tame by comparison. Once the caravan started the climb, it seemed endless.

As the caravan went up the incline, a full arc rainbow came into view. Alex said it was breathtaking. He kept his head up, hoping to spot the Garden's wall. He was so close he could taste it. Alex wanted to dismount his camel and run to the garden's gates. Once inside the gates, Alex planned to stretch out his arms and hug and kiss everything. His happiness needed expression. No one anywhere on Earth had ever achieved such a goal.

"Squinting into a bright sun, I hoped to see something. Maybe someone might spot us and wave." Alex swore he saw gates about forty feet high with large carvings of animals. His exhilaration was sky high. Alex shouted to alert the welcome committee. "We were the next arriving busload."

"In reality, I was in a daze." The caravan reached the top of the incline. They stood at the edge of a farming village, a pastoral setting edging up a mountainside. A road bisected a ridge filled with golden wheat on one side. On the other side, a brownish yellow plant was growing in long rows. Toward the end of the planted area was a forest. Rooftops were visible through the surrounding trees. Alex guessed they had to be the trees that made up the Garden of Eden. It was scenic and inviting.

In a mellowed tone, Stan said, "I wish I had traveled with you."

Stan sounded strange. I stared at him. He lay stretched out on the couch with his head on the armrest, looking up at the ceiling with his mouth open. My Italian blood boiled. So Alex has landed another fish. Stan, our superstar communication coach, was reduced to just another dreamer. Alex's magical powers had done it again.

Alex was looking away from Stan, unaware of what happened. Alex continued, "After we reached the center of the village, I saw another planting area going up the mountain. Beyond it was a forest that stretched right up to the mountain peak. Atop the mountain was a thick mist projecting a rainbow. The agricultural area and the forest formed concentric circles. The urban area of ten buildings was the center. It was spectacular, a total contrast to my dream. Where did I get the idea of a gate and walls?"

Alex turned around and saw Stan. "Margarita, he's in a daze." Alex opened his palms. "What did I say?"

FIFTEEN

blue sky,
blue water

We lay on the living room carpet, facing each other with our heads resting on sofa pillows. The heat from the fireplace warmed our feet while we held hands. I said I felt like we were inside a Neanderthal cave. Alex replied the cave where he stayed wasn't a luxurious hotel with rooms to indulge oneself. Neither was the EconoLodge at the rest stop.

The events of your father's lunch with Merton stayed fresh in my mind. The revelation that *caro mio* had spoken with almighty God knocked me over. Imagine, *bambina*, your daddy having talked to his maker. What a spoiled kid you'll grow up to be. I took deep breaths, as my mind evoked the story's images. The air was full of his scents. Alex brought back the tang of the horse he rode with fury into the canyon. I smelled the mist of the river he drank from inside the cave. The effect was a compulsion to demand kinkier sex.

Our sex in the past had been great: romantic and passionate. With my insides *su fuoco*, it was all going to change. I said to Alex that I insisted on overstepping our normalcy by using chains and whips on him.

Alex shrieked, "Bondage! Are you nuts?"

I told him his stories transformed my mental state to that of a cavewoman. I've turned into an insatiable sexual savage. I wanted to beat him into submission. I said, "Our bedroom will be a dungeon and I will shackle you to the bedposts. Then I will ravage you!"

Alex sat up. "What the hell is the matter with you, M?"

I pushed Alex onto his back and I quickly nuzzled up to him. My action switched between nibbling an earlobe and sniffing and kissing him feverishly. "I smell the scent of a prehistoric animal. I have a need in me that won't subside. Too bad you couldn't bring home about fifty of your hideous-smelling Neanderthal brothers. I'd screw every one of them to death."

Alex jerked up. "I'm going to drive you down to Cass Avenue and leave you on a street corner. A *nafka*, that's what you are."

I said, "Lie back. We'll have more fun here."

Alex cried, "Help!"

I licked his neck, stopping occasionally to inhale under his arms. Alex said, "I just took a shower. How can you smell anything besides soap residue?"

I played down his remark by saying, "Your primitive stench is dreamy."

I broke out into a frothy sweat and couldn't wait. I climbed on top of Alex, zipped down his pants, and sat on his erection. I said, "No more sweet talk, my dear. From now on," I said, "we'll perform with raw animal mentality."

Alex moaned and I screamed. My orgasm caused a shout loud enough to awaken the entire neighborhood. I yelled, "Let them call the police. I'm only beginning." My Kegel exercises paid off. Heaven descended and became an addition to our house.

After hours of torrid sex, we rested. Alex asked if I had decided to tell some of his stories to my friends. "And what'll you do when your libido skyrockets?"

"Yes, I want to tell a story. And if it's at a restaurant and I get hot," I said, "I'll screw every waiter in the place."

My turn to tell a tale came in the form of an invitation. Betsy 'Boa' Deaton arranged a luncheon at her lavish country club for a few of her nearest and dearest friends. If Alex could drive people crazy, why shouldn't I join in on the fun? I saw her invitation as an opportunity and accepted. I would try to dominate the conversation by talking about Alex's experiences traipsing around Airets. That would not be easy. Betsy's luncheon chatter encompassed a mishmash of petty and self-serving topics. The time would be filled hearing about who cheated on whom, who got divorced, the latest vacation taken, the newest restaurant patronized, and how much money out of indulgent husbands' pockets was spent on clothes. They also talked about their efforts on behalf of needy organizations. Their thank-you notes acknowledging the donations to their causes were petty. They wanted their generosity recognized with pictures in the newspaper taken at the charity galas. The same group of boring women posed with toothy smiles. Pictures taken alongside their husbands were nonexistent. Adulterous, haughty, charitable, and gossipy described these women. I failed to understand how it was humanly possible to be simultaneously kind, sinful, and obnoxious.

Betsy knew Annabelle Freyburg was my friend, being members of Congregation *Beth NeeSaw Emet*. But she would never be invited to such a gathering. Thank God! With Annabelle's delicate nature, I envisioned her in tears in five minutes from Betsy's taunts. Annabelle would excuse herself, bawling her eyes out as she left. For me, Annabelle had always been a mainstay; my bomb shelter. With these women, I would need to be hers.

Once these women heard my story about the Garden of Eden, I envisioned mockery exploding. The noise might collapse a chandelier. I needed to experience the storytelling challenge firsthand. The luncheon was timely and most opportune. I would be compelled to defend Alex's wacky stories. Not all wives agreed with their husbands on all private or intellectual matters. I did. There was no way to prepare for the awaiting challenges and ridicules. I fit the category of being behind the times on many subjects. For one, trying to understand how scientists deduced that the Earth was spherical and not flat eluded me. I needed to show personal toughness to overshadow my lack of knowledge. I imagined wearing, under my outer clothes, a dominatrix outfit to the luncheon.

The perfect garments to be dressed in for the battle were a tight leather tank top, short shorts, and riveted boots.

Beverly 'Cleopatra' Coffman and Flora 'Bull Run' Carbal were other attending executioners. I thought hot-blooded Italian women were the tops when it came to emasculating husbands or trampling humans fitting the miscellaneous category, which, according to them, amounted to about 99.99 percent of the world. Beverly and Flora conveyed their despicable derision in expert fashion. Everything was fair game. They earned the big mouth monikers given them.

Billie 'Geronimo' Garvis was also an invitee, being another member of the ignoble quartet. If Beverly, Betsy, or Flora said anything negative about someone, Billie, with impeccable timing, would howl with laughter. Avoid them like a plague was the safe play. I, however, knew my audience and would be up to the challenge.

I planned to tantalize them with a description of my glorious sex life. They didn't need to know the catalyst was Alex's stories. Sex lives with their husbands, I suspected, consisted of a couple of faked caveman grunts at best. I would embellish on our all-night, non-stop action. I'd say, "It didn't require me taking him to the hospital to patch up the wear and tear, and no, Alex didn't take any medication to enhance his sexual accomplishments."

We gathered prior to lunch in the foyer of the country club, with everyone arriving according to a pecking order. With Betsy Deaton being the hostess, protocol dictated she arrive first to oversee any final preparations and to await her guests. She adorned the table with a lilac arrangement and placed a sample vial of BVLGARI, *Rose Essentielle* perfume next to each place setting. Being an accountant's wife, arriving on time at the appointed hour, in this case noon, was standard for me. Beverly and Flora arrived about ten minutes later. Billie arrived twenty minutes late complaining about the road construction as if that lame excuse caused her tardiness. We were led to a table by the *maître d'*. As we walked to the table, all eyes were riveted on us wearing our expensive ensembles. It's as if a street gang entered.

Since Betsy would pay the tab, she had privileged rights to

speak first. "Margarita dear, tell us about your children and of course ..." she looked at Billie when she commented, "... we'd love to hear about Alex's adventure."

"My children are wonderful. And my Alex, I couldn't ask for better."

Beverly said, "Alex, the accountant, a stud. Get real."

Betsy followed, "I've heard Roman is stoned in perpetuity."

I said, "I love your insurance phraseology. Your husband must come home every night with a cute expression. Roman is a new man. He had a bout with smoking marijuana. No longer. He's straightened around and is practicing at Beaumont Hospital in the Internal Medicine Department. And the girl he's dating is so lovely and sweet."

Flora said, "Is she popping over to the hospital every day to get popped in a linen closet?"

I said, "If you mean to share an empty patient room for awhile, I dare say it's possible. They're adults. Anyway, I don't approve of linen closets. They're tacky."

Flora smiled. "Who is the young lady?"

"Shirley Newton, Tracy and Arthur's daughter. She's beautiful, intelligent, and earns a good salary."

In unison, a mantra chanted, "Oh, Margarita, I'm so happy for you." When the chatter subsided, all noses lifted.

Beverly inquired about Caroline.

I said, "She, too, is beautiful, intelligent, and earns a good salary. As to who she's dating, we're hoping."

"Maybe Caroline would go out with my son, Mason," said Billie.

She referred to Mason Garvis, D.D.S. Even with his degree, his occupation was unclear. I couldn't remember the printing on his personalized license plate: 2TH DOC or TENNIS BUM. I said, "Have him call Caroline," thinking I had to do my part to make the atmosphere appear polite. So far, the opening salvo was successful. My children's good news plunged a dagger into their *stomaci*.

A waiter approached our table to take our drink orders.

Billie said, "Your other children, I've heard are metallic."

I smirked, ready to answer the taunt, when I noticed the waiter. I became unsettled seeing the waiter's sideburns and hairdo: an Elvis look-alike. He made no pretense. His eyes stayed welded to me, ready to hear my answer.

I said, "I don't know what parts of Alex's trip you've heard about. He did meet a robot named Danziger."

Billie said, "What Jewish mother names her newborn Danziger? Was he named after a new emotional complex?"

Laughter erupted.

Unruffled, I took a sip of water and said, "He wasn't born. He was a self-made man."

The laughter stopped with a change to hard stares. "What?" they chorused.

I said, "He constructed replicas of himself and his wife in robotic form."

Everyone echoed, "Where are they now?"

I said, "Probably flying around in outer space."

Billie choked with laughter and blurted, "Is that where you're flying now?"

More laughter. They groped for revenge and struck a lucky blow. Even so, I was ecstatic. They paid attention to me. I said, "Would you like to hear about when Alex saw the creation of the world?"

Flora said, "Oh my, another doozy?"

Beverly rushed in saying, "The creation of the world! I daresay Alex isn't old enough to have been around."

Billie held her hands across her mouth tightly, so as to control herself and not burst with laughter.

Beverly said, "It's too bad I didn't invite Annabelle. She could be your cushion, delivering applicable rabbinic parables."

I breathed a sigh and said, "So could Alex. May I start?"

Flora said, "Of course."

Flora wasn't paying the bill, so her go-ahead was ignored. I looked at Betsy who gave an approving nod. I said, "I know you will think this story sounds crazy. The incident happened as Alex headed to the Garden of Eden. He traveled by camel with a caravan led by a man named Caravan Adam."

"My dear, I thought we were to talk about robots," said Beverly.

I wanted to strangle Beverly, but maintained an air of calm. "Let me clarify. The robots took Alex to a distant planet and left him. The planet was inhabited by prehistoric people whom he befriended."

They all looked at me with disbelief.

Betsy's mouth spouted. "What's this have to do with creation?"

"My dears, listen to me." I waited for a moment's silence. "He wasn't an accountant sitting and working behind a desk. His temporary occupation was adventurer. Unlike you, lounging on your back in Florida, he was on a trail ride."

Betsy remarked, "We do the same thing: get mounted, keep in rhythm, and get dismounted when finished." Laughter ensued.

I cringed and continued, "Here's what happened."

The caravan went up a mountain slope, rounded a bend, and neared a ledge about five hundred feet wide. A deep blue ocean came into view. Alex recalled it being spectacular. The caravan leader came to a stop at an open space. In our terminology, we call it a scenic view turn-off. Some travelers were pilgrims, who dismounted and ran to the edge of the cliff. Once at the precipice, they prostrated and ululated, "Whoopee." Alex dismounted and stood his distance, being afraid of heights. Even so, Alex's curiosity piqued. What happened that prompted the pilgrims to act strangely? He spotted Camel Adam, a caravan worker, and asked him what they were doing. He told Alex that they were praying to the god that created Airets.

He watched the wailing and body fanning for about thirty minutes. Mardi Adam, another worker, returned to the camels and grabbed Alex's arm. He walked him towards the ledge, while pointing to the ocean. It made Alex nervous. He tried to wiggle himself free, chirping about beautiful scenery and that his father loved photographing impressive scenery.

Mardi Adam waved frantically with his hand. He motioned to Alex to follow his arm and kept pointing toward the ocean. "Look there," he said, "We are in the center of the light."

Alex pointed in a different direction, towards the sun, and said, "Mardi Adam, the sun is over there."

Mardi Adam again pointed to the horizon. "The light is there when God opens the heavens."

Alex filtered through his biblical mind. *Let there be light.* Was the *light* the horizon? The great lights were created on the fourth day. He asked Mardi Adam what he meant.

Mardi Adam said, "Do you see that we sit upon land? Do you see the water beneath us? Do you see the sky above?"

Alex nodded.

"That circle in the distance joins them," said Mardi Adam.

Alex jumped with excitement. "Do you mean the horizon is a distant seam holding the sky and water together?"

Mardi Adam smiled, nodding approval.

Alex's thoughts raced to comprehend everything he heard and saw. The color was blue from top to bottom. It meant that at some juncture in time, the sky and water were joined together. Dare Alex even suggest that God opened the joined parts like a clam, to reveal the world? *Let there be light.* Alex recalled the biblical passage, "… *made the sky, and it separated the water below the sky from the water above the sky.*"

Betsy said, "Who did Alex fool around with? Was it with a cavewoman?"

I replied, "Sorry, I don't have any information for you to take to your sex therapist, but I do have information for your jeweler."

In a chorus, they said, "Well, tell us already."

Alex asked Mardi Adam, "*Where* is God?"

Mardi Adam said that God opened the air and we entered his domain when we were born. Our skin is coated with his presence. "*He's* portable wherever we go …"

Billie let out, "Can we get past the skin cream part?"

I retorted, "Okay. Let's go to the death part: from dust to dust. It's exciting. Alex learned why Jewish funerals are held quickly. The soul departs the body at burial. At that moment, the sacred air space where the person lived was returned to God. The soul needs to be freed."

One of the cabal said, "Now it's Alex, the death *maven*."

I said, "I, too, am an *esperta*. Do you know the first thing you should find out immediately after your husband's death, besides the location of the key to his safety-deposit box? Make sure you find out who else he was *shtupping* before he croaked. Even babies can hire an attorney and get in on the action."

I told them, as I said, a clam shell opened long ago and Alex saw the hinge that banded the blue sky and the blue ocean. God's heavenly home and the firmament lay somewhere between the two expanses. This was probably the reason why blue became the dominant color for Jews.

They got more interested when they learned Mardi Adam opened a small pouch and removed a lapis lazuli stone, holding the gem between his thumb and index finger and raising it up to the sunlight. He said, "I hold in my hand a fragment of the sky and ocean, from when the great division occurred." Alex mentioned it sparkled with a pulsating brightness.

Betsy said, "Any man walking about with expensive jewelry in his pocket needs attention. Could Alex introduce him to me?"

Flora asked, "My dear, what social diseases did they carry? I trust you had Alex examined."

Beverly chimed in, "Margarita, are you okay? You're perspiring." I was drenched. The odor came from the grime I pictured caked on Alex's sun-baked face. The cavewoman needed to be excused from the table and return home for a matinee. Alex predicted telling the creation story to Betsy Deaton and her pit bull friends would fuel my libido. I imagined Alex's nude body covered with spaghetti, topped with marinara sauce. I would be a predatory animal eating her prey. No knives or forks. My head would lower towards his stomach and I would pretend the spaghetti was his viscera. Enough of Betsy and her friends!

I couldn't restrain myself from saying, "I'm sorry, I must leave. I feel weak." It was an opportune time to leave. Dessert and coffee were ready to be served. I stood, eager to depart from this brackish cabal. I said, "It's been a delight seeing all of you and, Betsy, thank you for being a gracious hostess."

Betsy said, "We must do lunch again soon. Next time I'll invite Annabelle and someone from Kaufman's Funeral Home. We must be better prepared on money matters."

Billie broke into hilarity. I shook my head and muttered, "Crazy bitches. They believed me."

I walked to the club's entrance and gave my ticket to the valet. While waiting for my car, I felt I had let myself down, as my power of persuasion failed to induce any movement towards some form of madness. These bitches listened in condescending fashion. What a bummer. I sniffled. I wanted them to drool with envy about my successful children and my glorious sex life and take a knife and commit *hari-kari*. I should have said to them, "Alex and I are in our senior years and we can't get enough of each other. Top that. I dare you." How do you make inroads with a group of self-serving women? The valet brought my car. Like the waiter, he was an Elvis look-alike. He wasn't here when I arrived. Oh my, get me out of here. Chapman must be spying on me.

On the way home, a wild thought hit me. Was Alex lucky? He saw everything from the three dimensions of time. I was jealous of his ability to juggle past, present, and future events to his advantage without any consequences. He stuck his jaw out to the world, daring anyone to hit him. He walked in the middle of a busy avenue, with drivers hitting him head-on, knocking him twenty feet into the air, and taking personal blame for the accident.

A driver might say, "Are you okay Mr. Haralson? Let me call an ambulance for you."

Alex stands up straight, as if no harm was done, dusts off his clothes and says, "Don't call an ambulance. I'm fine."

The driver would then ask, "Don't you think you should walk on the sidewalk?"

Alex, at his best, would say, "Why?"

Walking in the door, I started to strip off my clothes. I yelled, "Alex, your happy harlot is home. Get ready to be devoured."

Alex yelled back, "You skinned me alive yesterday, go away."

I went to the refrigerator and found the leftover spaghetti gone. I yelled, "Alex, did you finish the spaghetti?" I went upstairs in a huff and saw Alex standing at the top. He stood in a panic seeing me wearing only my bra and panties. I said, "Why aren't you undressed? Robot Alex, all is forgiven!"

Alex said, "You know ... you need help."

I said, "I know. I've made an appointment with Merton to see him tomorrow. Now off with those *schmahtas* and get back in bed. I mean business."

Mia bambina, I am sorry your ears hear too much you don't understand. I will try to soften my words.

the ghost sitting and watching from the corner

I sat in Merton's waiting area before my appointment with Merton. I dreaded admitting to him the extent of my sexual appetite and its impact. I would justify my actions by telling him how badly I wanted a grandchild. And he would hear I planned to use every means possible to achieve it, which included having another child myself. Annabelle knew my state of mind. I pictured her as a sad ghost sitting in a corner of my bedroom and watching Alex and me roll around in bed.

My children were dating, but slow to announce any engagements. I had *shpilkes*. I pestered them mercilessly, "So? When?"

They replied, "We'll announce an engagement when *we're* ready."

I fumed, slammed down phones, and pounded counters. I yelled to whoever would listen, "I disown my offspring! Losers!" Migraine? You have no idea! I lay down and put a cold compress on my forehead.

Sitting in the waiting area, Edith seemed indifferent. This cow rolled around more than a pinball. One time she's overly cordial, another time a grouch. Something else changed: the door to Merton's study. When Alex and I first visited after the robots arrived, it was a steel barrier to a sanctuary. Now it seemed to be a revolving door to an asylum.

Merton invited me in and I sat down in front of his desk. However, two new palm trees sat behind Merton's desk. The top leaves reached the ceiling. It was an even greener study now, even though plant pots had been removed from the floor, revealing the putting-green carpet. I made sure Merton looked at me when I surveyed the trees. I shifted my eyes towards Merton and asked how he felt. I said, "Is synagogue business back to normal?"

He looked fatigued, but he said, "I'm okay. It's okay. What brings you to my office alone?"

I looked up at the trees and heard Annabelle say, "Go ahead, Margarita. Get it out in the open. Tell my husband you've become a tramp."

I thought, "Goodness, this was Annabelle's new hiding place to hear all the news." To Merton I said, "Rabbi, I've turned into a slut." I told him my behavior had spun out of control. Alex and his robot *banditi* fried me well-done on both sides. I told Merton I suffered humiliation while having lunch with Betsy Deaton and her muggers. "I bragged about my unmarried children and whom they were dating and about my wonderful sex life. For them, hearing about the greatest adventure in my Alex's life ranked as boring as a bedtime story. I could have generated more excitement talking about liposuction.

Merton said we were in the same boat, having both gone off the deep end. At Steve's Deli, he heard Ralls Jenet whisper to his friends what a jerk he was. Merton said, "Do others in my congregation think of me the same way?" Merton started to cry. I looked at the trees. I could smell gefilte fish with ozone mixed with cigar smoke. It seemed Danziger joined Annabelle to listen. I suddenly wondered, were the palms representing the sacred trees of Eden, with Dan being the father and Annabelle the mother? Symbology lay heavy on me—I wanted to go back to being a numbskull.

Merton calmed down and said Alex took Ralls Jenet's *shusking* as a personal affront and took action. Then, when Alex told him about the theophany, Ralls recovered part of his senses. "For now, M, we're trying to grab onto a side of the swimming pool."

I said, "Right now I despise myself." Merton, obviously not impressed with my becoming the queen of slutdom, said he was sorry, but there was nothing he could do to help. "In time, you'll sort matters out." I was speechless, so Merton changed the topic. He'd thought a lot about Alex's theophany. "I'm sure you've heard the story."

I rolled my eyes.

Merton said Alex was on the right track, interpreting cannibalism's meaning. He didn't bring back all the answers, but, nevertheless, Alex's thinking was provocative.

I said, "What you're saying is that the missing commandment wasn't narrated."

To which Merton responded, "Ah, clever old M. Thou shalt not *nosh* on thyself or thy brethren." The general practice terminated before the Garden of Eden, but was implied in the story. Merton said the concept of bodily holiness drove the eating prohibitions.

Merton went on to say he planned to utilize some of Alex's material for his sermons. Merton gave me an example. He said, "Hopefully, it won't overheat you."

I smiled approvingly.

Merton said, "Evil behavior wasn't prohibited because it was distasteful. Dostoyevsky wrote in *Crime and Punishment* that compassion functioned outside science. Moses customized Godly principals into laws so everyone could live within a sphere of safety, without having to look over their shoulders every minute." I nodded. Merton continued, "And you *didn't dare* admit to hearing voices such as angels telling you right from wrong. Inmates in insane asylums vocalized those ideas." He turned to look at the trees. He said, "I swear I just heard someone say, 'Merton, what about you hearing voices?'"

I thought to myself, "Annabelle keep quiet."

I said, "Alex said the ancients had scientists."

"That's true," said Merton. "Modern science has been a disappointment." He said, "Tomes about creation filled bookshelves.

What they didn't write about was how cannibalism ended. It's an important subject to discuss. But, the *mavens* decided the agendas. The scientific community should have formulated a god. Instead of seeking money from foundations and governments, a Sabbath collection box would be filled to the brim beyond their wildest dreams."

I told Merton I had another confession. I planned to have another child. My gynecologist, Dr. Green, would administer ART treatments. Alex already left a specimen. Merton, shocked a little out of his fog, said he didn't realize the depth of how determined I was. He said, "It appears that Roman and Caroline will not fulfill their parts." I said I couldn't wait to see their faces when I announced I was pregnant. When that happens, my next step: fire Roman and Caroline as my children. I looked at the trees. They were odorless. Merton sat quietly.

After the meeting with Merton ended, I drove home. My mind was focused on Alex's story instead of the road. Something was strange. How had Alex avoided being someone's supper? Did he have guardian angels? He lived among cannibals, a despised foreigner, an intruder asking questions that were none of his business, and he returned home safe and sound with no bite marks.

Alex was working in his office. I ran in, tore off my clothes, and jumped him. Kissing him feverishly, I said, "Alex, I'm hot and wet, just the way you like it. I need to hear more about Airets. It's stimulating. I need to satiate myself."

"Did you see Merton?"

"Yes. Don't slow things down. Indulge me."

"Okay, okay," he said. I snuggled into his arms.

Alex began his story while I lowered his trousers. He said when he landed on Airets, the robots eavesdropped on him from a distance, hearing and seeing everything. That was how Roma found him in the mountains. Alex said he never observed them.

In a sexy voice I said, "Those sneaky bastards." I nibbled Alex's ears. "Keep going."

Alex said everyone meant business: the robots, the Adam brothers, and Danziger. Everyone wanted to kill him.

I said, "You're safe with me."

Chapman told Alex what happened at the campsite the evening after hearing the creation phenomenon explanation. Camel Adam and Mardi Adam, the caravan workers, met. Camel Adam said, "Many people expressed interest in knowing about the passenger, Peaceful Heart. And Peaceful Heart is aware of everyone's interest."

Mardi Adam replied, "Before I took Alex to the ledge, he asked me what everyone was doing. I told him the worshippers were celebrating Airets' creation."

"Yes, people noticed you conversing with Alex."

"I told Peaceful Heart how Airets' creation happened. I meant no harm."

Camel Adam said he understood. He also said a caravan traveler named Ibn Shah Adam, known as the traveling priest, told him that Peaceful Heart tried to strike up a conversation. Alex said to him, "I am traveling to the Garden of Eden." He asked Ibn Shah Adam if he ever visited the Garden of Eden. Ibn Shah Adam said no, which was a lie.

Camel Adam continued, saying the trip took great endurance and Alex appeared physically able. Mardi Adam said Alex appeared intelligent: smart people understand quickly and ask good questions, such as, "Where is his home?"

Camel Adam heard Alex say he was from Michigan. "Meecheeghan? Where dat?"

Mardi Adam said our caravan boss, Caravan Adam, thought Alex possessed great wealth, so plotted to rob and kill him. Mardi Adam learned Caravan Adam spoke with Guru Adam to set Alex up. Guru Adam invited Peaceful Heart to his tent in Scratchy. Mardi Adam learned Guru Adam and Alex spoke privately about morality. Peaceful Heart said some laws Guru Adam advocated were manipulative and dictatorial. Guru Adam was incensed. "Who was this big mouth?" Camel Adam said Guru Adam's punishment for insolence was death. He sent a gang to finish off Peaceful Heart.

I jumped. "Wait a moment. Just who was Guru Adam?"

Alex said, "The high priest of a large population in eastern Asia. His home turf was Scratchy, where the caravan started." Alex traveled there after being informed by the robots it was the gateway to the Garden of Eden. Guru Adam's power was based on an army backed by a trading empire. His decrees consolidated the empire's economic power. Alex said, "A prehistoric barbarian—just what the world needs." Alex said Guru Adam sent a goon squad to kill him. His squads were many and fearless.

Mardi Adam mentioned to Camel Adam that Peaceful Heart was alive. Camel Adam said Peaceful Heart had protectors. They counted less in numbers than Guru Adam's death squad, nevertheless they were proficient in combat and equally fearless.

Alex went on to say that Danziger's protection squad looked like hungry wolves with grayish teeth and fierce eyes. They all looked alike and stood tall with hands that resembled iron. Danziger's protection squad passed three of Guru Adam's goons on the way to find Alex. One protector grabbed a killer around the waist and pulled him close. The killer later said he never had encountered such power. He couldn't budge free. The protector applied pressure, and said in a raspy voice, "Leave Peaceful Heart alone." He applied more pressure, grabbing and clutching the killer's throat, choking him with his other hand. The protector asked if he understood.

I asked, "How did they get inside Scratchy's walls undetected?"

Alex said he didn't know. The other protectors then went face-to-face with the other killers. Guru Adam's killers were told Peaceful Heart was to be protected on the voyage. The killers then ran to Caravan Adam, who then contacted Camel Adam to make sure that all went well.

Alex said Camel Adam ordered Mardi Adam not to say a word to anyone, but Alex could be the leader of his God's invading force. Camel Adam said he tried to be friendly at the ocean, hoping it would stave off an attack. Camel Adam said Guru Adam will get even. Guru Adam said Alex's trek up the mountain to the Garden of Eden would be his last. He devised a plan to outsmart

Alex's protectors and finished by saying, "The scavengers will eat well."

Camel Adam liked the plan. Upon their return journey to Scratchy, they would tell Guru Adam Alex's fate. Afterwards they would even the score with his guardian angels.

Annabelle called and was I glad. I needed a break. She asked how the luncheon had gone with the country club girls. I told her they acted the same: complete carnivores. "Telling them the story of creation only heated up my libido. I excused myself."

Annabelle rejoined, "Oh, me."

I told Annabelle I mentioned to Merton I wanted another child. I paused for Annabelle to say something. She said nothing. When I realized Annabelle wasn't going to say anything, I said Merton could fill her in later on the details. Annabelle asked if I had seen a doctor about fertility tests. I told her I had an appointment to donate eggs. Annabelle wished me luck.

I told Annabelle that the robots plotted to kill Alex. I sniveled. Annabelle said, "Oh, my." I said my jerky husband thought the robots put their arm around him as a sign of friendship. When in fact, they plotted to kill him. They were executioners getting to know their victim. I bawled. Annabelle said she would come right over. I said no. I would be all right. "Thank God Alex went to the Garden of Eden. If he went to find Moses, we might not hear from him for forty years." I said good-bye.

I climbed back on Alex and said I wanted to hear more. He said he tried to be friendly. Mardi Adam asked Alex to tell him more about himself. Alex said he came to find his dream, the Garden of Eden.

Alex went further, saying he knew the caravan workers didn't trust foreigners. He told Mardi Adam the seeds of beliefs were nurtured from parents and teachers. "Someday, tolerance and respect of other ideas will evolve." Alex continued, saying so far on this trip, everyone's survived quite well. We are fellow human beings, part of collective nature like trees and snakes and birds.

My husband, the anarchist, said this.

Alex told them where he lived. He had breakfast with men of means and others who were common laborers. "We eat and talk at the same table. When everyone leaves, each returns to his way of life with the same old hatreds and bigotries." I spoke with a patronizing voice, "*Thy kingdom come. Thy will be done, In Airets as it is done in Heaven.*"

Later in the day was my appointment with Dr. Green to harvest my eggs. I was preparing to go to the hospital when the phone rang. It was Dr. Green's office calling. The nurse on the phone explained that they had two specimens labeled Alexander Haralson. I called Alex to come downstairs. I explained to him what the phone call was about. He said he made one trip to Dr. Green's office. I said to the nurse to give Dr. Green a message. "My husband will drive with me to the hospital to deliver another specimen."

After hanging up the phone, I said that was strange. "I can't imagine how another specimen got mislabeled with your name." I patted his cheek. "Plan on getting it up in about thirty minutes." I cuffed Alex's chin. "Don't worry. I will see to it there will be no mistakes."

the robots return to michigan

With a month remaining before Alex's TV interview with Wolf Winslow, excitement filled our home. The telephone rang continuously. Everyone conferred best wishes and luck. Frank Stansill called, saying in a fired up voice, "TV ads have started." We learned PBS ran commercials that listed Wolf's upcoming guests. Brooks Patterson, Oakland County Chief Executive, and noted author Elmore Leonard were scheduled to appear earlier. My Alex's name sat on the bottom. It would rise closer to the top with every passing week. Local newspapers called to schedule interviews with Alex. It didn't take a genius to figure that *Alexander Haralson* appearing in print would make him the newest entry in a *Toast of the Town* roster.

All Birmingham was abuzz. When I drove about, some downtown stores displayed signs that read, "Don't miss the spaceship ride at next year's Shain Park Fair." In our neighborhood a steady parade of cars drove by honking their horns. I stepped outside to see the excitement. I thought, at first, it was a wedding procession. Instead, shouts of "Good luck" and "Alex is our hero" trumpeted. I waved back with a big toothy smile. Some well-wishers whistled and shouted, "We love you, hot mama!" To my admirers I blew kisses. The gaiety lasted for hours. Thank God they had enough common sense to disperse at night to let us sleep. I recalled Alex relating his exuberance when he trudged the last leg of the journey to the Garden of Eden's entrance. I had the same feeling. I would count down the days until the show. At zero, I imagined a rocket ship igniting and being propelled in a blaze of glory to outer space.

I felt happy for Alex being the center of attention. He earned it. His adventure initiated the tumult. Wherever he went, everybody knew him and wanted to shake hands with the returning adventurer. When asked how he felt, he told people how great everything turned out. His facial expression beamed a smile of satisfaction that resembled Chapman's. That scared me. In front of people congregating, I felt like whispering to him, "Why don't you tell everyone that robots are your progeny?"

All this happened to a boring accountant living a boring retirement. Inside this boring existence, a Jewish accountant thought about why there was no specific prohibition of cannibalism in the Torah. To Alex's credit, I never heard any clergy or intellectual say or write anything about the subject. When Alex told me what rolled around in his head, *I* deemed it important. He guessed from the lack of scholarly works on the subject that the human race thought it boring or meaningless; its most useful purpose being to induce sleep. To my Alex, it was a caffeine fix. Who else would jump out of bed in the early morning to meet a robotic guru who said he would take him to the Garden of Eden to answer the question?

For me, however, I endured second place. At malls or restaurants, the conversation converged on Alex. I assumed the role of the stupid Italian housewife supplying human interest. Many times I was asked, "What spaghetti sauces do you cook that are Alex's favorites? Could I get a copy of the recipe?" And another, "We can't thank you Italians enough for introducing pizza to America." That remark fried me.

All preparations proceeded smoothly. Stan and Alex reinstated their communication coach–pupil relationship in preparation for the show. Stanley Whitescarver's dreamy mind returned to Earth. Stan mentioned sleeping it off, whatever that meant. Alex forgave him, saying, "I can't wait to get going again." Alex's lessons proved productive, and Stan stayed focused, leading me to believe the interview would be a triumph. I observed a few sessions, impressed by Alex's improved demeanor. He exhibited a powerful presence with relaxed motions, strong posture, and fluid speech.

Stanley Whitescarver was the communication coach, while at the same time I was the sex coach. My job was to deliver the greatest satisfaction and pleasure to Alex. I'd heard that great musicians played their best after sex. The musicians caressed their instruments with tenderness to produce the sweetest tones. No doubt they projected the biggest and most enthusiastic smiles to the appreciative audience.

My part also included being seen as the wife of a celebrated and renowned universal traveler. I envisioned hobnobbing in circles of biblical experts. With me at his side, we would attend parties in his honor, or speaking engagements that featured my Alex. Accepting cheers with overhead waves would be our trademark. I would not be seen wearing any cheap off-the-rack clothes at these events. The solution was a new wardrobe. No one perceived me as Alex's *shleppy* wife. I would dispel any impression that my only function in life consisted of lounging around all day, cooking spaghetti, and servicing Alex. I planned to be shown off as Alex's trophy wife. True, my age worked against me. But I planned to be a fighter. I imagined with Alex's charisma, women would try to steal him away. Being *farputst* would give off a warning to any young hussy that tough competition awaited. I realized I had an advantage, being his wife. I planned to continuously paw his shoulders or arms in public. The Linda Dresner shop in Birmingham would have the elegant designs that would shape a statement to the world of my importance: I'm dripping with money. It would be my first stop.

I noted at times my adrenaline level dropping. With all the happenings, it came as no surprise, going to bed exhausted. I fought it though, knowing *mio caro* needed a daily dose of sexual rejuvenation. Sometimes I was so tired I felt like giving passersby the finger instead of kisses or waves. I thought, why be bogged down with silliness? Do something constructive: go shopping.

I parked my car in the garage nearest downtown Birmingham. As I exited, Shain Park came into view. It was the site of the now-famous Shain Park Fair where Alex met our progeny, that idiotic robot, Jonathan Chapman, at the rocket ship ride. The more that memory faded, even if he was family, the better for everyone. I focused on shopping for some new outfits to face the adoring world I imagined. I felt a toughness and focus that reminded me of the dominatrix robot, Roma.

In the Linda Dresner shop, I spent about two hours looking for outfits that would make a splash, and purchased a perfect one for about $5,000. I planned to wear it to Alex's interview. I bought a suit with a six-button jacket trimmed in velvet and pearls. It had a pleated, wool, street-length skirt. Betsy Deaton and her friends would gag with jealousy if the TV camera happened to pan my way during the interview. The country club girls only cared about what I wore. I planned to tell Betsy after the interview that I tore it into strips for dusting cloths. "It's a *schmahta*."

The big expense so far was the new diamond bracelet I bought the day before at the Douglas Shubot Jewelry store, and I wasn't finished. A pair of black suede pumps at L'uomo Vogue to complement my suit would be my next visit. I couldn't wait to see Alex's face when he received the bills totaling about $20,000. My prepared remark, if he complained, would be, "You do have a book deal, don't you, Alex?" And I'd caress his cheek and murmur, "You're having the best sex ever, aren't you?" Could there be any answer other than yes? Case closed.

I decided a small bite of lunch was in order, to reward myself for working so hard at spending money. Expensive dinners loomed on the horizon so I needed to stay thin to be able to fit into my new outfit. A Cosí restaurant, located a couple of blocks from the Linda Dresner shop would curb my hunger. Its menu offered smaller meal portions: perfect. While I walked there, I felt as if I was being followed. I glanced about and saw a crowded street but no one I knew. Inside the restaurant, I sat by the sidewalk window and every so often I peered out and saw happy faces.

I concentrated on eating my sandwich and a glass of iced tea. Smaller meals had other advantages. Finishing quickly meant I'd have more time to shop. "Where should I go to put another dent in Alex's bank account?" Oh yes, I remembered, the shoe store. In an instant, my earlier uneasiness returned. I looked around the restaurant trying to catch someone staring at me. Customers filled the tables conversing or reading while eating. I didn't recognize anyone. I thought I might be a bit paranoid about being followed. If so, whoever followed me had the wrong person. They should follow Alex, the VIP.

I finished lunch and headed back to the parking garage. Eyeing Shain Park, I saw mothers with their children at the swing sets. In the distance, I saw a man sitting quietly on a park bench. He turned his head toward me and smiled. I stopped in my tracks. I recognized him immediately: Jonathan Chapman. I couldn't believe it. We looked at each other eye to eye, longer than momentarily. He gave me a short wave. I stared at him while debating whether to go over to him. John, I knew, was a determined sort. If I snubbed him, he might come over to our house and knock on our front door.

I called Alex on my cell phone. I whispered, "Guess who's sitting in Shain Park?"

Alex replied, "Jesus Christ."

I said, "You've got the initials right."

Alex screamed, "Oh my God! Don't talk to him. Come home immediately. I'll call the police."

I verbally spanked Alex, saying, "A lot of good that will do. Are you expecting the police to walk up to him and say, 'The city has an ordinance against well-groomed businessmen sitting on park benches. We prefer the benches be used by our model citizens: heavily tattooed teenagers with blue-dyed hair'?"

Alex admitted I was right. I said I would talk with Chapman to find out why he returned. Alex said he would be my shield and hurry over to protect me.

I said, "Relax. I'll be fine."

Alex said to make sure there were no cars or spaceships nearby. "He might kidnap you."

"I'll be careful, darling."

Alex continued, "And don't let him fill your head with any of his cyborgian *chazzerei*."

I cried, "Enough, Alex!"

We hung up. I walked over to where Chapman sat. It was the site of the spaceship ride. A marker acknowledged its location, "From this spot Alexander Haralson flew into outer space."

Chapman stood and extended his hand. "I'm Jonathan Chapman."

"Do I look like a dingbat with memory loss? And put your hand down. You won't be crushing my fingers, so you may as well find someone else to bug."

Chapman laughed offensively like a mad monkey.

I told him I knew his problem. He was too stupid to know when he was being insulted. "Get lost, *please*."

Chapman said he needed to speak with Alexander. I broke into laughter. I said, "He doesn't want to talk to you robots. And that includes that sneaky progeny potentate Danziger. You guys are ancient history."

"We started him on a new career. Doesn't that count for something?"

I told Chapman to tear up the silly contract between Alex and Danziger. "If you guys play rough, Alex will hire attorneys to have it voided."

Chapman said, "Do you mean he's on his own?" And then he asked, "Doesn't he need our help any longer?" I said yes to the first question and no to the second. "We're cutting out the middleman: *YOU*."

Chapman sniffled and said, "You're a meanie."

I reminded Chapman about a few past matters. I said he made Alex a celebrity. Word about his trip to Airets eventually got out. Competing publishers and promoters of speaking engagements offered deals to load his pockets with big money, as compared to Danziger's puny offer. I said while he sat on the bench waiting to be a nuisance, I enjoyed myself, shrinking those expected proceeds. I said, "Do you understand? He doesn't need you now, nor do I. And another thing, do you remember the incident in that New York restaurant when you did $25,000 worth of damage? Consider it your crowning jewel of stupidity. Could we say good-bye civilly?"

Chapman whined, "Well, Margarita, the bargain we had with Alex was the exclusive rights to the Garden of Eden secrets."

I said to Chapman, "Buy ten copies of Alex's book when it's released. It'll open up all the classified information." I finished by saying, "John, come by our house after the book gets published. I'll make sure Alex autographs a copy for you."

Chapman chuckled. He seemed more in control and said, "We know he made it to the Garden of Eden on Airets."

I said, "You're twisting my arm. Of course he made it to the Garden. You knew that. Weren't you or a family member his guardian angel?" Chapman said he was talking about what happened *inside* the Garden.

I said I missed something. "You were never inside the Garden watching over him?"

Chapman replied, "No."

I said, "Okay. So Alex was on his own. He's a big boy. Why was that troublesome?"

Chapman wanted to know what happened when Alex met the Serpent. "Did he break down and eat the forbidden fruit?"

I said Alex told me everyone who encountered the Serpent ate the forbidden fruit. "The failure rate was 100 percent. How else could you go through life knowing good and evil?" I continued, "The most religious person in the world would cave in and eat the forbidden fruit. It didn't matter whether or not Alex met the Serpent. He was toast either way."

Chapman harped, "What if Alex failed?"

I said, "Call in to the *Wolf Winslow Show* and ask. He'll answer the question." Chapman said if he called, Alex would know it was him and may not say to him what he told me. I said, "Chapman, I'm lost. What do you want? If he ate some forbidden fruit, so what?" I told Chapman what I heard. "Alex told me the Garden of Eden was like any other small town where you check into the local hotel, you have the bellman take your luggage up to a room, and you go the local bar for a few drinks and to eye women. Think of the garden as a close-knit neighborhood town. Everyone in town knows everybody else in some way, a bit incestuous, definitely. What else did you want to know?"

Chapman demanded more. I said that was it. What else was there? I said the more *I* wanted was more of that animal odor Alex brought back. My sex drive had skyrocketed 1000 percent. I thought about bottling and selling it as a commercial enterprise.

Chapman shook his head. "You're not being serious, Margarita. You must listen to me. Alex might have eaten human flesh."

I said, "John, that's not possible." I told him Alex would never do such a disgusting thing. Alex was only after why cannibalism was the missing commandment. Anyway, the Tree of Knowledge and knowing good and evil was symbolic. So what?

Chapman asked, "Did he ever explain the tree's significance to you?"

"Yes, in part. He mentioned Godly and human senses. The Godly senses are sight, hearing and smell. I'm all *fardrayt* what they all mean."

Chapman said, "And did he tell you the human senses are touching and tasting?" I asked Chapman where the discussion was taking us. He said, "Well, for robots, senses don't matter."

I said, "Congratulations Chapman, you're not a cannibal. My interests lie in spending money and getting laid."

John said, "Eating is the part that needs clarification."

I said, "I sense you're not coming up for air."

"Please don't interrupt me, Margarita. Robot Alex was to take your Alex's place. He was going to fool them. If the Serpent gave him human parts, ingesting them would be like dropping them into a trash can. But if Alex ate them, the transgression would be the equivalent to dropping an atomic bomb. You'd agree, that's significantly more sinful than eating a slice of bacon."

I told him my prehistoric ancestors were cannibals. I couldn't change that fact. "And as for me," I said, "I wasn't."

Chapman insisted, "It's got to be cleared up. We need to take Alex back to the Garden of Eden on Airets." I growled, "Over my dead body."

"We have to." Chapman said, "Humankind was given a sec- ond chance. The first *farshtunkener*, Earth Adam, made a mess. Alex could reprieve everybody, being chosen the designated Adam of Airets."

I said, "Send Robot Alex. Make sure *he* meets the Serpent."

Chapman's voice elevated, saying the Serpent had extraordinary powers of sight. He could see mites in clothing and could discrimi- nate who's who by their hair follicles. He would know Robot Alex was a shill. And we have to know what happened the first time.

I said, "You just said the Serpent has extraordinary powers, so he would have tumbled onto Robot Alex immediately. You're nothing but a con man, Chapman, and I may be just a housewife, but I'm not a complete idiot."

"Actually, you are," Chapman said. "I must insist, I'm afraid. It's back to Airets with your Alex." I could have punched him.

"Can't it wait?" I said Alex was scheduled to appear on TV at the end of the month. "Check with me after the show."

"Margarita, we're your progeny. Do you want us to carry for eternity the burden about our ancestor Alexander, the cannibal? I must speak with him on the matter of the Serpent."

I called Alex on my cell phone. There was no answer. I looked at Chapman. "He's not home."

Chapman said, "I know." His answer shook me. I never heard Chapman speak so glibly. I was ready to pee in my pants.

I said, "You know? How?"

Behind me I heard, "Margarita, is everything all right?"

Startled, I must have jumped five feet into the air. I turned and said to Alex, "Don't ever do that again."

Alex smiled. But his smile looked different. On a closer look, his face definitely changed: robotic. I expected the Alex I knew to put his arm around me and hurry me away from Chapman. Instead, he stood still and gazed at me with a smile.

I said, "Alex?" I faced Chapman and said, "This is not my husband. Where is he?"

"On his way back to Airets. This time," Chapman said, "We'll be with him when he visits the Serpent. No mistakes."

I said, "Right now, I'm furious. Take me to him immediately!"

Chapman said it was not possible. "Perhaps we'll have him home before the *Wolf Winslow Show*. He must visit the Serpent with us." He said he hated to sound harsh, but if Alex didn't supply him with the information he wanted, the Alex standing next to me would be the one making the TV appearance.

I shrieked, "A goon squad, that's what you are."

Chapman said he would think about allowing me to communicate with Alex. "Go home with Robot Alex and wait. When we have our answer, your Alex will return."

I said, "And afterward you will never visit us again?"

Chapman said, "Don't you like us? Deep inside, we're party animals."

"Chapman, get lost. The highlight of your robotic lives happens when the electrons of your essence dance the Hora." A strange odor struck me. I moved my nose near Robot Alex and sniffed. I said, "You smell of semen, you horny bastard."

I looked about for help and saw no one. The swing sets stood limp. Where were the police when you needed them? Being in a tough situation, I cried, "Annabelle … Merton … Papa. Where are you? I need help!" I turned to Robot Alex, saying he'd better not try any funny stuff with me at home. "Plan to sleep in the garage and hump the drain."

I said, "Chapman, please, can I speak to my Alex?" He smiled and said, "Maybe."

I took home my new husband, Robot Alex. I thought about calling Annabelle. If I explained the situation, she probably would advise I go along with Chapman. "Alex will come back." What choice did I have? Where was Roman; out with his new honey, Shirley? I felt like meddling to break them up. The robots didn't deserve us as ancestors. I worked to get Caroline and Roman on the path to marriage. Now I had to work on my progeny. They were off course. *Vay's meer.*

I asked Robot Alex why Chapman had worked himself up about Alex committing cannibalism. He explained they wanted a pure ancestor, one who followed the rules, who didn't symboli-cally eat his father.

I asked, "What rules?"

Robot Alex said, "What grows with roots attached to the ground, directly or indirectly, is always permitted: vegetables and fruit. It's the unattached where the prohibitions emerge: fish, birds, animals, and insects. I remember reading that the eighth plague was locusts that ate all the grasses and fruit; they were vegetarians. If any species wasn't, it was assumed they ate human flesh."

I listened, but could feel my eyelids closing from boredom.

The phone rang. It was Dr. Green's office. The nurse said someone at the hospital mysteriously dropped and broke the recent specimen bottle. They apologized and asked if Mr. Haralson could come to the hospital to donate another. I looked at Robot Alex and growled, "It was you. That second bottle found in Dr. Green's laboratory. Was it yours?"

He replied, "No, it was Steve Austin's." He must have seen my nostrils flare because he said, "I can see you're upset. Let's not overreact, Margarita."

I screamed, "You're dead meat." I went to the garage to find a sledgehammer.

a very long distance call

I awoke from a deep sleep on my living room sofa. I rubbed my eyes, yawned, stretched, and looked at my watch as I sat up. I realized the time was the next morning. What happened? I remembered Robot Alex lulled me to sleep by droning on about the Garden of Eden's meaning of cannibalism over and over. I looked around the room. There he was, sitting and waiting for me to wake up. He said "Good morning, Margarita," and immediately started to recite his boring monologue:

"The entire body outside and inside must avoid any sinful activity. It's easy to understand that hitting is sinful touching. It's the inside that's more difficult to understand. If you believe in God's omnipresence, you understand that we inhale and exhale a Godly essence."

I shouted at Robot Alex, "Will you shut up!" As soon as I finished, Robot Alex went back into his mantra.

"Eating is the part that needs clarification. What grows with roots attached to the ground, directly or indirectly, is always permitted: grains, vegetables, and fruit. It's the unattached where the prohibitions emerge: animals, insects, birds, fish, and humans. Humans were eaten as part of a staple diet or a delicacy by many of the aforementioned creatures. Let's start with insects. I doubt they are a favorite meal of yours. Certain species of locusts may be eaten. They are vegetarians. The eighth plague was locusts that ate all the grasses and fruit."

I shouted, "Poor Merton, I know what he's going through. I will buy him earplugs."

Robot Alex droned on, "Fish follow the same pattern. No scavengers, such as lobsters or shrimp. They have eaten human flesh. So have the birds that are flesh hunters. Land animals are permitted if they have split hooves and chew their cuds. Priests in the Garden decreed that eating any form of life that ate humans for nourishment was forbidden. And any human eating such forbidden creatures is committing an act of cannibalism."

If Robot Alex wanted to keep me engaged in a conversation, he should have spoken about the clothes I bought at Linda Dresner, offered some ideas to marry off my children, or suggested how I might outsmart the snobby women at the country club. Imagine him. He thought his job consisted of protecting me, making believe he was the real Alex, and preventing me from running and screaming through the neighborhood that robots had kidnapped my husband.

He sat in front of me on our expensive living room chair. I told him the furniture was for invited guests, not for an uninvited guest to park his oversized fat ass. I guessed his weight at around three hundred to four hundred pounds. I said to him he could have stood all night. I growled, "Get up!" He didn't budge. I walked over to him. I looked down and saw a small tear in the upholstery. I screamed, "Get your fat ass up." After a few moments of no movement, I grabbed a heavy vase and swung it at his head. The vase shattered. His head remained intact. "You *maiale!*" I went back to the sofa, sat down, and sulked.

I said, "Robot Alex, the next time you repeat that Garden of Eden poop to me, I plan to do something to put a dent in your armor. Don't ask me how, but you can count on it."

Robot Alex surprised me and started confiding the reason Alex was kidnapped and taken back to Airets. His story sounded very similar, starting with Genesis, Chapter I, Verse I.

He told me the robots felt they belonged to a new generation of humans. The robots desired a starting point just like us normal folks, by asking, when did the robotic human race begin? They acclaimed Danziger and Delores' sentimental takeoff from Earth as the robotic version of Adam being molded out of clay. He took it another step further, to the story of the Serpent. Humanoids lacked physical senses. What sins could they commit? Who could tempt them? And what fruit would open the eyes to test temptation? The answer was simple: none.

Robot Alex said, "We robots have no *saychel* and are no better than self-running vacuum cleaners." He lamented, "What are we? We are clusters of electrons without an identity." Robot Alex never stopped, and said all robots perceived the void with dread. Danziger ordered them to do the next best thing: let a proxy engage the Serpent. Alex was perfect. "Let him take all the heat. If he fails, it's no skin off our backs."

"You ungrateful bunch of self-serving tin cans; after what my husband has done for you," I huffed. "My Alex landed in a cold climate without proper clothing. He avoided cannibals looking for a tasty meal. He met his Neanderthal relatives and lived in their pigsty of a home. He traveled over mountains on a camel. He was left in the middle of nowhere to fend for himself." I thought, was there a person in the entire universe who would return from such a trip ecstatic? Yes, I knew one. Who would allow anyone to treat him so shabbily, to be a guinea pig and love it? Only one person would: Alexander the Great Haralson. Your father came home delighted, happy. *Oy.*

I rose from the sofa and placed my hands on my hips. I imitated Roma and spoke with her tone of voice. "Listen to me, you robotic runt. I want to talk to my husband right now." When I again received the silent treatment, I ran toward the front door. When I reached it, he stood there, barring my way out.

He started to touch some buttons on his chest, so I kneed him in the groin. Pain shot through me and I collapsed on the floor. I yelled, "You molester! You brute!"

He said, "Let me call the spaceship."

First he picked me up and carried me to the sofa. He was a *shtarkeh*. He rubbed the sore spot. My knee felt better. It began to tingle and I launched into a reverie. Two different visions of Alex ran toward me: one my husband and the other Robot Alex. They were spiritually the same person: interchangeable. Physically, they looked identical on the outside but were night and day on the inside. Evolution divided them by light years. If I ever ran away to Airets, Robot Alex was my man.

I said softly, "Are you in touch with the spaceship yet?"

A metal lid rose on Robot Alex's chest and revealed a monitor. On it, a man sat strapped in his chair. It was the real Alex.

I said, "Hello, darling. I can see you on the monitor."

Alex said, "Margarita, I'm so happy to see you. Are you okay?"

"I'm fine." I rubbed the top of the robot's head. He was still messaging my knee. I said, "I miss you. Are you all right?"

"Yes, I'm fine. I miss you. You won't believe it, but we're six hundred light-years apart and yet you sound as if you're sitting next to me. I've got to admit, our progeny are communication whizzes. I see a new business in the future."

I took away my hand, looked directly at Robot Alex, and said, "My progeny, the whizzes." *Mia bambina.* Everything will be remembered for you: communication transmissions and video camera tapings. How else could I remember the small details of my story?

Alex said, "'M, You look tired." I said I was.

He said, "Get some rest." Alex turned around and said, "Danziger, say hello to your mega-grandma minus several thousand generations."

In a digitized, unemotional bass voice Dan said, "Hello."

Alex turned back and said, "He's not much of a conversationalist."

I said, "Alex, all I see are computers. Where are the robots?"

Alex said, "That's what I told you. Our progeny, Danziger, and all the other grandchildren, are computers stuck to a wall."

I sighed and pleaded, "I need you. They've made my life hell by building a robotic duplicate of you."

Alex said, "Ask him if he's going to make the mortgage payments. If he says no, ask him to leave and call the police."

Still looking at Robot Alex, I said, "He watches every move I make and goes everywhere with me." I said to Alex I didn't mean to whine, but I was in a no-win position. I wanted to break away from Robot Alex. "I'm afraid he might get some ideas of romance. I don't know what's worse: his droning on about cannibalism or trying to sweet talk me." I didn't mention that every hour Robot Alex threatened me, saying to stay put and not call the police, he actually thought he was saving his damsel in distress.

Alex said to tell him to shut up, and to feel good about not having to feed the son-of-a-bitch.

Alex said the spaceship would be landing on Airets in about an hour. The plan was to drop him off at the Serpent's house without any side trips. Alex said, "I'll try to get home ASAP."

I sniffled, "Alex, be careful."

Alex replied, "I will. Anyway I'm with my guardian angels."

I said, "*Oy*, Alex, wake up, will you!" I told him Robot Alex told me the purpose of his trip. I said, "How do you plan to answer Wolf Winslow if he asks what transpired between you and the Serpent?"

Alex said he didn't have a choice. Whatever he said would be heard by Danziger, who planned to transform into a bird and circle the meeting place trying to be inconspicuous. Alex said if he made up a story on Wolf's Show, Dan would deviously and immediately give the press a videotape of my meeting with the Serpent.

I said to Alex, "Wait a minute, someone's calling." I ran to the den to answer the phone.

"Hi, Annabelle."

She said, "Is everything okay? I received a call that Alex wasn't feeling well."

I said, "Annabelle, hold on for a minute." I walked back to the front door carrying the house phone. I said, "Alex, can you call me when you land? Annabelle's on the phone. We have women matters to clear up."

Alex said, "Sure. Hold on a minute. Danziger, could I call home after we land? My wife wants to know that I landed safely." On the screen, I heard no response. Alex was waiting for Danziger to answer him. Alex returned. "Margarita, he's not answering me. Get me the name of the group that disowns children. I'm joining them with you." Alex turned to Danziger. "You are the biggest creep I have ever met in my life." The screen went blank. The lid came down and retracted into Robot Alex.

I meandered back to the living room and sat down. I put the phone to my ear. "Annabelle, are you still there?"

Annabelle said, "You sound so harried, Margarita. Slow down and tell me what's going on."

I cupped my hand over my mouth and whispered, "The robots have returned. In fact, one's sitting in my living room across from me."

Annabelle said, "Oh my!"

"They kidnapped Alex and returned him to Airets to work out some loose ends. It seemed Alex forgot to mention to our progeny the outcome of events surrounding his prior meeting with the Serpent." The big question being, did Alex eat the forbidden fruit or not? I said, "He hasn't told anyone."

After a moment of silence, Annabelle remarked she was curious to know the answer. I asked her what she meant. She said if she was in Alex's position, she didn't think she would eat the forbidden fruit, breaking tenets and faith she held dear. But she'd love a chance for the Serpent to woo her with sweet words, trying to seduce her.

Surprised, I crowed, "Annabelle!" She said most days she followed a sensible line of thought. "Sometimes," she said, "we need a day off to commit an indiscretion, just a small one that defines our being."

I said, "Thank you, Annabelle. You said that so beautifully."

Annabelle said she had practice from hearing Merton's sermons and speeches every day. "I'm his adoring audience and I believe everything he says." I asked if Merton's sermons put her to sleep.

Annabelle answered, "No, never. He floats up the *beemah* to deliver the Shabbat sermon." She said last night Merton practiced delivering a sermon on the Garden of Eden. He compared the Serpent in the Eden story to God's adversary in *Job*. The adversary directly challenged the goodwill God gave to Job, while the Serpent challenged God's goodwill indirectly through Adam and Eve."

I thought, Merton must have overheard Alex with his sensitive hearing. I said, "I heard Alex deliver that sermon in our living room. Alex thinks that since he went to Airets, he's become a biblical scholar. He added the professional designation, B.S., to his resume.

We laughed.

I said, "Joking aside, Alex's speeches are convincing. I loved when he told me that being buried below ground meant I would return sacred air space back to God. When I questioned him about it, he said, 'I learned it firsthand in the Garden of Eden.' He bragged that no one in the entire universe knew more about the Garden of Eden than he."

Annabelle asked if Alex ever described the sacred trees to me. "I imagine them to be rarities: grand, imposing, and dignified."

I hated to burst her bubble. I told her I suspected her image consisted of two trees in the middle of the Garden, in full bloom with boughs of figs or apples lowered by the weight of ripe fruit. "Actually, the two trees were in the middle of a village." I told her what was worse: they were dead. Imposing, but dead. Alex described them as hideous; against a silhouetted full moon, they resembled a backdrop to an Edgar Allen Poe flick. Annabelle said she was shocked. I said not as shocked as I was by the trees in Merton's office. Annabelle groaned. I told her that the sacred trees stood in a common green area where ceremonial activities were held. I said, "They're an eyesore and Alex should encourage the village to take up a collection to replace them."

Annabelle gasped, "They can't. They're sacred. They can't be touched." She said, "M, pruning the sacred trees was forbidden to everyone." She went on, saying how disappointed she felt hearing about the sacred trees.

Annabelle said, "M, call if you need me." I said, "When I find Robot Merton, I'll call." I heard a giggle when she hung up the phone.

Robot Alex said, "You have children. They will have families someday and our robot generation will descend from them. Thank you so much." I looked up at him. Robot Alex did make a point. Our children and their progeny would keep the flame of the robot's future alive. Danziger made Alex believe that his functional hot loins saved humanity. He convinced him that with robots eventually running the universe, the world would be a much-improved place. Danziger said robots don't suffer disease, don't pollute, and don't cause global warming. They don't feed on cow or corn. And they are very religious: no cannibalism.

Alex sided with his future progeny, telling everyone how he felt. He thought his children were basket cases. After returning home from college, Roman and Caroline said they would work on projects that advocated saving the world from disease, pollution, and global warming. They hadn't been informed of their progeny's capabilities. Professors taught Roman and Caroline that humans caused the world's problems. They were strongly encouraged to embark on careers to become scientists working on environmental solutions, or become business magnates able to accumulate wealth, and then make large contributions to various *just causes*. Alex dismissed those liberal ideas as rubbish. He fumed, "I pay money to educate my children and those graybeards dressed in checkered Salvation Army shirts accuse me of being the culprit. They work second jobs as janitors."

I was in attendance when the fireworks continued. According to his children, he was a perpetrator. Alex replied, "Do you want to see your father go to prison?" Alex tried a different approach. He orated, "The windmills to produce electricity cost more to construct and maintain than the current sources of energy. I want to live with what we have, not create more pollution." He was derided. Our kids believed the philosophy that the world's ills could be saved by cutting back on our expensive lifestyles, thereby reducing contamination. They told us that their contribution to saving the planet would be not having children. Instead, they will work with lofty goals that lead toward helping the downtrodden. If need be, they said they'd live in the basement of a house. Alex asked, "It wouldn't be our house by any chance, would it?"

When I heard the *no children* comment, I screamed. Alex pretended to faint. He fell on his knees and pleaded towards heaven, "Save me from myself." He stood and mocked his children. "We build *such* beautiful landfill sites for garbage. I love their *schmeck*. Sideways, they resemble the handy work of a plastic surgeon: a breast implant filled with garbage instead of silicon. Earth's grassy mountain breasts are the icons of our contaminated world. The world which in the next twenty years will need thousands of new sites to contain the mounds of refuse generated. Nothing will stop the process. Please use the powers of your cranium to build more. I know you can do it. Design them so the dumps will be useful, like ski slopes. And name them after past and future governors. Mount Granholm sounds so slithery."

The telephone inside Robot Alex rang. He arose from his slumber and opened the monitor inside his chest. On the screen Alex said, "Margarita, I made it."

"Are you okay? It looks cold. Alex, is that snow in the background?" He said, "Yes, it is. Can't you see my breath? Danziger's great mind decided to kidnap me when it was summertime back home. I was wearing bermudas and a short-sleeved shirt. My ass is frozen. On Airets, trust me, Adam and Eve didn't run around in the nude. They were hairy beasts in disguise."

I said, "Ask Danziger for a coat."

"I did. He said no. He said it cost too much. He's a bigger cheapskate than I am." Alex described how devious Danziger was. "He's starving me so that when I meet the Serpent I'll eat anything. Do you understand what I'm suggesting? The Serpent is about to tempt me into eating human drumsticks." Alex finished, "Sorry, M. I've got to run now. I'm being escorted to the Serpent. Danziger just morphed into a buzzard. How fitting. Talk with you later, my love."

The doorbell rang. I went to answer it and Robot Alex followed me. I hesitated to answer the door. From a side window I saw Frank Stansill. Should I open the door and run out yelling, "I'm a prisoner of a robot?" Or should I invite him in to have lunch with Robot Alex? I thought it best to talk with him by the door and send him away. I opened up and Frank said, "Hi, Margarita. Is Alex home? I saw him pull up the driveway earlier."

I said, "Oh, he didn't say anything when he came in. He probably stopped by to pick something up and run."

Frank said his car was still in the driveway. I muttered to myself, "Oh shit ..." I said to Frank, "Well then, he must be home." I flung the door closed. When I turned around, Robot Alex was gone. I called, "Alex, Frank is here."

The doorbell rang. I opened it and quickly said to Frank, "I'm sorry. He must be out in the garden or on a walk." As I closed the door I let out a quick, "I'm really busy. Good-bye, Frank, and say hello to Georgia for me."

The doorbell rang again. I looked out the side window and saw Frank looking in, bobbing his head side to side. I opened the door and blocked his line of vision. He said, "Margarita, I don't mean to interrupt, but as I was walking up to your front door, I thought I saw Alex through your living room window."

I said, "You did? Alex must be indisposed. Listen, we're really busy. I'll tell him to call you."

Instead of answering, Frank yelled, "I see an intruder! I'll chase him out." He pushed me aside as he rushed into the house. I stood by the door and heard a drawer open in the kitchen and utensils being shuffled. Frank shouted, "Watch it, buddy, I have a knife. M, call the police for backup!"

I was startled when I heard a scuffle, a muffled voice, a door slamming, and a hammer pounding on what sounded like wood. Robot Alex walked into the foyer and headed for the open front door. I stood aside. At the threshold, he transformed into a robin flying skyward like Dracula morphing into a bat.

A couple of neighbors were walking their dogs and saw the bird exiting the front door. They appeared puzzled. I put on a good front, smiled, and waved. "Hi! I'm glad we were able to set it free." I closed the door quickly.

Behind me I heard banging on a door with a loud voice repeating, "Let me out."

I ran into the kitchen. I said, "Frank, where are you?" The pounding came from the utility closet. It was boarded shut. I called, "Frank, are you all right?"

He said, "No! I'm beaten to a pulp and I can't see. There are no lights." This sounded like action in a melodrama. Frank yelled, "Get me out of here. Margarita, call the police."

I didn't want the police. My mind raced. "Frank, hold on a minute." I ran into the garage and found Alex's toolbox. I took the hammer, raced back into the kitchen, and started pulling at the nail heads.

Frank yelled, "Call the police."

I said, "Are you prepared to wait thirty minutes for them? They're on strike."

Frank replied, "I don't remember hearing that." I kept pounding on the boards, nearing the end. Soon enough they broke off.

I said, "Frank, try the door."

Frank opened the door and balanced himself by putting his hands on either side of the threshold. His casual sport shirt and Dockers were torn. His hair was ruffled and his face pale. His eyes were swollen and glassy. I saw on the floor a kitchen knife with the blade bent 180 degrees. He slurred, "What happened?"

I hugged him. "You darling. You saved me from a lurking monstrous intruder. I'm glad you saw him before he could harm me."

Frank said, "Wow. He was strong. His fists felt like lead pipes. He picked me up off the ground and threw me in the closet."

I gently locked my arm in his, helping him walk to the breakfast table. I eased him into a chair. When he sat, I asked, "Are you sure you're okay?"

He looked around the room and said, "What happened?"

I said, "You're shaken up. Why don't you stay seated and rest a while? I'll bring you a hot cup of tea, Earl Grey, your favorite, and a pastry. How does that sound?"

"Call the police!"

"Frank, I don't think that would be a good idea. I might have to answer some questions I'd prefer not to. You'll be fine." In a teasing voice, I said, "Let's keep this as our little secret and not tell Georgia."

Frank gave me a grin, while his head wobbled. "Okay, if you say so."

I gave him a kiss on his forehead. "You're so brave. Thanks."

alexander falls
back to earth

Standing with my arms braced against the kitchen counter, I stared down at the fresh cup of coffee I poured. Why I came downstairs to brew coffee was a mystery. Earlier I threw up and should have just stayed in bed. Did I believe coffee's aroma was a home remedy to prevent vomiting? Last night, Robot Alex and I dined at a Mexican restaurant. I ate a cup of black bean soup and an order of quesadillas. Dumb! On the way home, my stomach gurgled in anticipation of a bout of Montezuma's revenge. Robot Alex gulped down about one hundred jalapeño peppers without any effect. The couple dining at the next table gaped in amazement.

Roman came downstairs to leave for the hospital. I told him about my symptoms. He said I probably suffered from a slight touch of food poisoning. He said to drink plenty of liquids and get plenty of bed rest. "Dad doesn't have to go out and get you a prescription. Take some Pepto-Bismol." He turned to leave and said I'd feel much better later in the day. I smiled devilishly. He didn't suspect that Robot Alex had taken his father's place. I drank a glass of water, as the doctor ordered, and went upstairs to bed. On the way, I passed the living room. Robot Alex sat in a stoic pose on a living room chair. I had no strength to tell him to stand up.

Yesterday after I took Frank Stansill home, I scolded Robot Alex, saying he handled Frank too roughly. I told him he had to learn gentleness in certain situations. I growled that Earth humans weren't toys to be beaten up and then dropped on the floor. I stopped and laughed. I talked to him as if he were the real Alex. After I finished scolding Robot Alex, he replied, "Yes, dear."

I thought, "This *golem* listened to me like my real life *marito*."

Robot Alex said he felt bad that he had caused trouble. He wanted to make it up to me, so he said, "Why don't we go out for dinner? It'll be my treat." I suggested a Chinese restaurant. He insisted upon eating at a Mexican restaurant. "I'm new to Earth life. I want variety." He said he'd already gone to Italian and Chinese places.

I replied, "Welcome to the U.S.A."

I crawled back into bed and propped myself up with a pillow. I anticipated throwing off the covers and racing to the bathroom before another vomiting episode erupted. I wondered if I might be pregnant. My breasts felt sore. I knew I'd started dropping eggs again. I became a first-time phenomenon. I had U-turned from menopause back into fertility. I gave all the credit to Alex's sensational primitive odor. My libido skyrocketed as a result of smelling it. I thought, my Alex, a father again. Then I remembered that when I went to Dr. Green for ART treatments, I found out there were two donors: Alex and Steve Austin. Oh my. I played a game show contestant in my head, on a show called *Name the Father*. I screamed, "Alex, please come home! I need to explain something."

I went nuts whatever I did. I ruminated about the events that happened yesterday, when all the Stansill brouhaha started. What started it? Was it the circumstance of Frank Stansill's being locked in the closet, his fight with Robot Alex, my encounter with his wife, or dining on Mexican food? I decided it wasn't the Mexican food that upset my stomach. It was my encounter with Georgia when I took Frank home; that was the catalyst. The shouting match would have knotted anyone's stomach.

After Frank finished the tea and pastry I served him, his confused mental state improved. Frank appeared relaxed and self-controlled. That was short-lived. Frank transformed from a relatively stable individual to an incoherent mess by the time I drove the four blocks to his house. I restated to Frank on the drive that no explanation to Georgia was necessary.

What had happened was our little secret. Well, not for long. By the time I pulled up to his driveway, Frank had unraveled. He kept repeating, "I was beaten up." After the fifth time, he sounded just like a robotic voice saying, "Please wait to speak to the next available agent."

My *kopp* was spinning. How do I get this idiot to shut up? My anger bubbled over at everyone: Alex, the robots, and Frank. My husband *shmoozed* with idiotic robots on Airets, an idiotic robot lived in my home stirring up trouble, and an idiotic neighbor had become unhinged. By default, I became the designated troubleshooter. Everyone asked me to juggle the balls labeled, "Out to lunch. Keep the world sane until we return." It appeared I had dropped them. I turned to Frank. He looked like old baggage to be dropped off at a homeless shelter. Right then, I could be Joseph Stalin or Mother Theresa. I took the motherly route with Frank.

Once inside the Stansill residence, I walked Frank upstairs, and undressed him for bed. The final indignity was Frank saying, "I need to go to the bathroom." I led him into the bathroom and he asked that I aim his *putz* toward the toilet.

After I'd washed his sidespray from my right hand, I escorted Frank to bed and sat by his side. I dreaded the dire consequences when Georgia came home and saw his condition. I really needed to be at home with Robot Alex in case the real Alex called from Airets. If Georgia called the police, as I knew she would, all hell would break loose. I couldn't face the prospect of explaining to the police the events that caused Frank's breakdown. I dreaded the thought that I might have to tell them about Robot Alex. I sat by Frank's bed, playing Mother Theresa. I whispered softly, "You're home." He continued to babble.

Georgia finally came home from her shopping trip to discover her husband mentally unhinged. She lapsed into a state of shock as I began to reveal the events that led to Frank's collapse. With Frank babbling the color commentary, I explained to Georgia the sequence of events. Her face had the look of horror and outrage. She pulled on her hair, screaming. "Why didn't you report it to the police?"

What was I to say, "I was being threatened by a robot?" I told her about the intruder, but tried to downplay Frank's whipping by Robot Alex. I said, "It didn't matter that an intruder was the catalyst. Frank had a mental breakdown."

By this time Georgia was livid. "You're saying Frank was a time bomb that exploded and the intruder was a casual observer?"

I replied, "I brought him home safe, didn't I?"

"Get out of my house!" I just wanted to go home and hide in a corner. Georgia kept up her tirade. "A lot of help you were. You're nothing more than a manipulating bitch. You drove him home and put him to bed. Aren't you the sweet fairy princess?"

Frank chirped in a falsetto voice, "He was a monster. He ambushed me. I was beat up. My clothes were ripped. He locked me inside a dungeon."

Realizing what Frank had just said, Georgia dashed over to the hamper. His slacks, shirt, and underpants were right on top. After examining them, she said, "His pants are ripped and his underpants soiled!" She picked up the phone and dialed 911. I took that as my cue and ran out the door.

Poor Frank. He was committed to the special ward at Beaumont Hospital for a couple of weeks to work through some "personal matters." With a wife like Georgia, he needed the rest. I didn't relish telling Alex, when he returned home; we would be *persone ingrate* in the Stansill household. Roman, being on the Beaumont Hospital staff, looked in on Frank every day. Before he did, he called the nurse's station in Frank's ward to make sure Georgia wasn't visiting.

As if the Stansills weren't enough trouble, a few days later, I sat at the breakfast room table and unfolded the current edition of the *Birmingham Eccentric*. Even through my tears, I could read the front-page banner headline. It read: MONSTER AT-LARGE RETURNS. The lead story, written by Tyler Rennet, the reporter whom Alex spoke with several months ago when we returned from northern Michigan, stated the monster hadn't been seen recently because it had taken a two-week vacation to Miami Beach. However, it had returned to stalk the neighborhood. I couldn't believe that Tyler would distort a story with so much *shmaltz*. He wrote, "The monster was so tall that if he invaded your house, his head would break through the kitchen ceiling." The article concluded, urging every household in the neighborhood to man a machine gun nest for protection.

After learning about Frank Stansill's altercation with the robot at my house, *The Observer and Eccentric* continued to print articles that sensationalized the incident. Circulation exploded and the newspaper planned to cash in on the story for as long as possible. It didn't seem to matter that a conservative, consistently straightforward publication lowered its standards to tabloid level. One day, a photograph of a fiend, supposedly the one who invaded my house, adorned the front page in different poses. Shaking my head, I wondered what the world was becoming. I stayed home the next few days nursing my aching stomach.

When Frank became more lucid, he obtained permission from the hospital to receive visitors. Through Annabelle, I heard the story he told Merton.

He said, "I saw a human made of metal that looked like the terminator. I took a knife from a kitchen drawer and tried to scare him by thrusting it at him. In an instant, the intruder enlarged into a monster that enveloped the room. I froze and pooped in my pants. He bent the knife, tore my clothing, grabbed me, threw me in a closet, and locked it." On another occasion, Frank told Merton, "I couldn't utter a sound, I was so frightened. My heart pounded so hard I thought it would burst." Merton said that Frank's hair appeared whiter to him since the incident. Poor Frank in more ways than one.

The next morning, the phone rang and woke me. I looked at the clock. It read four o'clock. A firm male voice said, "Is this the residence of Mr. and Mrs. Alexander Haralson?"

I said, "It is."

The voice said, "Am I speaking to Mrs. Margarita Haralson?" "Yes."

The voice said, "Are you Mr. Alexander Haralson's wife?'" "Yes, I am."

"This is Officer Hubbard Tetopsky with the Royal Oak Police Department. We have your husband in custody. We caught him trespassing in the Detroit Zoo. We'd like you to come to our Main Street station."

I muttered to myself, "Welcome home, Alex," and smiled. I felt much better. My stomach pains eased.

Speaking into the phone, I said hurriedly, "Officer, I'll be there right away."

I quickly put on a pair of jeans and blouse and rushed toward the garage. While passing the living room, I told Robot Alex I was leaving to pick up the real Alex. "Get up off my good furniture. And I trust you know where the front door is."

The drive to the police station took about twenty minutes. While driving, I thought ahead to the drive home. I knew Alex would ask what was new. What was I to say? In nine months, you're going to be a full-time father again? The only news I could tell him was that our friendship with the Stansills had ended. There would be no more bridge games, no more dinners at the Red Coat Tavern, no more trips to Stratford to see plays, no more golf dates. Poor Alex would have to find a new best friend. I thought it best he hear from me how Frank got admitted to Beaumont's mental ward. I would have to tell Alex the details about the altercation between his alter ego Robot Alex and Frank. *Oy.*

I arrived at the Royal Oak Police Department. It was a familiar place, where Alex and I had, on occasion, bailed Roman out after he was arrested for disorderly conduct. I walked quickly from the parking lot to the entrance.

I anticipated Alex waiting at the sergeant's desk ready to be taken home to a warm bed. Although I was eager to hear his story about meeting the Serpent, I was too tired. I would say, "Good night. Talk to you in the morning."

I went up to the officer behind the desk, "I'm here to redeem my husband, Alexander Haralson. Sorry, I forgot the claim check."

My attempt at humor failed to amuse him. The Officer returned a cold stare.

He said, "I'm the one who called you. My name is Officer Tetopsky."

He was broad-shouldered with blond hair. "We can't release your husband just yet, Mrs. Haralson. We'll need to interview you to understand some things your husband told us."

"Ay, ay, ay, interview me, what for? I may be pregnant. This is not such a good idea."

"Are you crazy too?"

"Define 'crazy.' I'm Italian."

"We found your husband at the Detroit Zoo, floating on his back in the Rackham Memorial Fountain, spouting water. When we brought him in for processing, he was in a state of euphoria: higher than a kite. We breathalyzed him and found no alcohol in his system. He appeared to be high on some substance, though. When we interrogated him, he babbled about returning home from another planet. We couldn't quite make out what he said exactly, but he said something about being part of a family of robots. We'd like him to volunteer for a psychiatric evaluation."

My mind raced, trying to visualize a setup to get Alex released. I couldn't afford to tell the officer about the robots. The news would get released and spoil the excitement for the Wolf Winslow interview. I remembered that Georgia Stansill called the police after Frank went over the edge. The police had called me at home later. I told them it was a domestic affair and Georgia's husband had made lewd advances. But this time it wouldn't be so easy to lie to the police.

"Officer, what is your first name?"

"Hubbard."

"Hubbard. What a wonderful name." I walked behind the desk and rubbed Officer Tetopsky's shoulders. "Hubbard, would it be possible to release my husband without any fanfare?"

He didn't move. I rubbed his chest and nibbled on his ear. "I love muscular men. Oh, and I see a bulge in your pants. I'll bet you're glad to see me."

He spoke in a singsong manner. "I'm feeling very tingly."

I whispered, "I'll make you tingly all over."

He said, "I'm married."

I laughed, "You're not going to let a silly marriage license get in the way, are you?"

He said, "There's an open interview room."

I said, "At four in the morning, I'm sure there is."

"No, no," he said. "I'll bring your husband there."

I said, "You're so smart. You thought I'd tempt you into breaking your marriage vows. Not me. Please Hubbard, if I spend some time with Alex, you won't eavesdrop, will you? I mean anything visual: spying or snooping."

"We can't allow that. You might give him a weapon."

"Hubbard, we may have a few shortcomings, but to think us old people would shoot our way out of here on a little old trespassing charge is silly." I continued to rub his shoulders and moved my head in front to see him. He remained silent. "Is there a couch in the interview room?" I asked.

"Uh, no. Just a table."

I said, "That'll do *just* fine."

I could read the officer's mind. *How far will I be demoted if anyone finds out I allowed this lunacy?*

He escorted me to an interview room and I heard the shade from the two-way mirror close. The tabletop, rectangular in shape, was the exact size of a twin-bed mattress. I sat in a chair and waited. About five minutes had gone by when the door opened and Alex entered with a big smile on his face. I could see it even with his face covered with mud. His expression beamed, "I'm happy to be home." It didn't matter that his khaki bermuda shorts were wrinkled and stained with every color in the rainbow. His hair was a mess; it probably got wet when he was imitating a whale. He wore the brand-new tennis shoes he bought before he left. They looked wet and grungy. If he hadn't been wearing his Brooks Brothers jersey, I would have taken him for a homeless man.

The liaison was perfect. Alex would be the last man whom I had intimate relations with before announcing my pregnancy. I lowered the shade over a barred window with frosted glass and Alex turned off the lights. I threw my body at him. His clothes were wet and his primitive odor revived my overheated sexual desire. Impetuously, we removed our clothes and engaged in passionate sex on the table. I screamed, "You animal!" so loud and so often that Officer Tetopsky opened the door to check on us. Seeing us engaged, he quickly closed the door and said, "Call me when you're finished."

I yelled, "I don't care if you raise the shade so the whole department sees us."

We had glorious sex. I don't know for how long. After we dressed, I looked at the two-way mirror and saw my reflection. Now I looked a mess too. I took a comb and lipstick from my jeans pocket and groomed myself. I stuck my head out the door. "Officer Tetopsky, we've finished our physical therapy session."

He came in with another man who was dressed in a navy blue business suit. "I'm Austin Avera with the prosecutor's office. Mr. Haralson, we've done some checking and found out you have a clean record with no prior arrests. We learned you were a respected accountant with a good reputation. Why don't you go home with your wife and sleep it off?"

Alex nodded agreement, with a stupid grin.

The prosecutor said, "One more thing. I would like to have a report sent to me from a therapist. If he gives you a clean bill of health, I'll delete the computer file. The robot and planet business you told the officers about concerns us. We have so many nuts running around, I'm losing track. The Beaumont psych ward is filled with them."

I said, "Our son is a physician at Beaumont. He's told me there are patients in that ward who are our friends. It's a good thing you didn't take him there. It could have proved embarrassing."

Alex gave me a look with a quizzical expression.

I said, "In fact, my husband is scheduled to appear on the *Wolf Winslow Show*. He's going to tell all about his trip."

Both men chimed in together, "Really, we had no idea. We never considered that possibility."

Austin Avera said, "Mr. Haralson, it appears you are a celebrity. I'll check the TV listings for the *Wolf Winslow Show*. My wife and I will be sure to watch."

Officer Tetopsky said, "I'm glad we were able to accommodate some alone time for you."

I chimed in with a sweet voice, "Gentlemen, thank you so much. You've been a big help. We'll just be on our way, if that's all right?"

"Oh, yeah, sure it is. Good night."

We left the station and drove home. Alex asked me what I was inferring about the psych ward patients. I told him that Frank and Robot Alex had an altercation. "As a result, Frank had a nervous breakdown." Alex shook his head and said he'd visit him the next day.

I said, "That won't be easy." I told Alex the details about Frank. And also that Georgia and I had an altercation. She'll be coming over to our house regularly. She hasn't finished with me.

The other day, she barged into our house without knocking and hauled off on me. "You Delilah! Frank has become the laughing stock of everyone we know. He was terminated by his company's Board of Directors. He lost all his benefits. We're hoping we'll be successful in court in keeping his pension." Her voice rose to a scream. "He's gone haywire. I'm convinced the intruder broke up your liaison with Frank." I tried to calm her down by putting my arm around her.

She screamed, "Don't touch me, you marriage-wrecker." In a lucid moment, Georgia told me Frank would have divorced her long ago. I asked why he didn't. He just shrugged, said, "A wife is a wife." I was flabbergasted to learn that all of Frank's decisions during their forty years of marriage were made during, or in anticipation of, sex. In the past, when she asked him to do a household chore, she used to wonder why his answer always sounded the same. "Yes dear, I'll do it right away."

Alex groaned, "Oh, my God. What a homecoming." I smiled to myself thinking, "You haven't heard everything." Maybe he'll notice I put on some weight.

chapter

TWENTY

alexander tells about the serpent

The drive home from the Royal Oak Police Department turned into a contest of can you top this stinky smell. The contestants were Alex's body odor, and the animal stench as we passed the Detroit Zoo along Woodward Avenue. His stand-alone odor may have been sensuous inside the police station, but the competing odors wore off the charm.

With Alex having been chemically indisposed on something unidentified, as the police had put it, I was designated driver. I gagged a couple of times, at the start of the drive toward home. Alex's odor was so offensive I lowered the window. The outside air reeked just as badly. I was tired and lost sight of common sense. That's where the police found Alex. To get away from the zoo's odors, I sped up the next mile. The danger zone ended when I could breathe outside air without gagging.

At home, I hurried Alex upstairs, undressed him, opened a bedroom window, and threw his clothes onto the front lawn. Alex's malodors lingered. Showering him would be too hard until he regained his senses. Sleeping next to him was out of the question. I planned to hire a service to fumigate the bedroom. The homecoming turned into a replay of Frank Stansill's, except that Alex urinated without any assistance. I walked him to bed and tucked him under the covers. When he started to snore, I flew downstairs to get fresh air.

I peeked into the living room. No Robot Alex, thank God. The sofa would be my temporary sleeping cot. I smelled coffee brewing in the kitchen. When I walked in, Roman was at the breakfast table reading a medical journal.

I said, "Any coffee left?"

He said he was brewing a fresh pot and asked, "What is that stench?"

I said, "Your father went on a binge."

He replied, "Where was the party, at the zoo?"

I said, "As a matter of fact, yes."

Roman jerked his head towards me. He said Dad seemed fine the past few days, just sitting quietly in the living room.

I went over to him and combed his hair with my fingers. I said his father was doing fine. "He was just letting off some gas."

I said, "I need you to answer a medical question. Could a woman my age become pregnant?"

Roman gave me a startled glance. After a moment, Dr. Haralson said, "You're saying it wasn't a touch of food poisoning."

I said it wasn't food poisoning. It felt as if I was dropping eggs. I needed to be tested and examined by Dr. Green, ASAP. Pregnancy was a possibility.

Roman said, "Does Dad know?"

I said, "No!" I told Roman Dr. Green had administered ART treatments. I commented that Alex kept a suspicious eye on me, trying to notice a change in my waistline. I said the treatment failed because of a mix-up with the donor specimen.

Roman said he'd heard me say pregnancy was a possibility. I replied our sex life was over the top. Roman said he'd heard screaming from our bedroom many times.

I pleaded with Roman, saying a favor would help because of all the necessary details to be finished concerning the Wolf Winslow interview. It was coming soon and I had to get his father on his feet so his time could be spent in preparation. I continued that we had a chance to be together as a family. I wanted Caroline to be in the audience. I said, "I've tried to call your sister and she hasn't returned my calls."

Roman said he'd call her and encourage her to come home for the interview. I said, "*Mio eroe, grazie.*" It would be nice for the family to have a gathering. It hadn't happened in a while and we had a good reason to be together.

Roman stared at me. I said, "And?"

He sighed. "You want to know how things are going with Shirley?"

I said, "Will we be able to call her a member of the family at our gathering?"

He said, "We're still dating."

I said, "If I am pregnant, let's not race to see who finishes first: your wedding or my delivery."

Roman stood and kissed me. "Good-bye, Mother." He poured a cup of coffee and left.

I walked into the living room and lay on the sofa. I imagined Alex would be the big hero after appearing on the *Wolf Winslow Show*. I wondered where my big chance in life to do something extraordinary was hiding. I deserved a chance. So far my life consisted of having children and jousting with contemporary bitches. Should I work in a women's shelter, work on a charity board, or work in a poor country caring for children? No. I'm sick and tired of wiping other people's asses. What about my traveling to Airets to meet Delores, Danziger's wife? We could do lunch. Oh, and that robotic bitch, Roma. I would very much like to meet her. What about *mia bambina*, if I am pregnant? Perfect; take him or her along for a ride to Airets. I would tell them I fulfilled my part of the bargain. I expect a parade in my honor. I smiled to myself. Better yet, have Alex take care of the *bambina*. Have him feed and wipe the baby's *tusch* while I'm gone. I must call Annabelle and see what she thinks.

A few hours later, I was awakened by another foul odor. Alex was stirring. He passed gas as a morning routine. The marshy gas odor he brought home attached to his skin was more sensual. I walked to the foot of the stairs and in a firm voice said, "I'll bring up breakfast to your room, your highness." What I wouldn't do for him. My Alex's favorite breakfast consisted of eggs over-easy, crisp hash browns, rye toast with marmalade, and medium strength coffee sweetened with sugar and cream. I didn't mind. After a rough trip, Alex needed regular food in his system. Danziger starved him.

Besides, eating in bed, breakfast or spaghetti, provided a venue to hear Alex tell me about his latest adventure. Saying something about my familial state might distract him. I said in a loud voice before going to the kitchen, "Alex, you have stunk up the entire house. Could you please take a shower and some anti-gas medicine. I hope by the time I bring up your breakfast, you will be able to smell your food."

I heard him singing in a boisterous voice, "Climb every mountain." He hadn't heard a word I'd said.

I made breakfast and brought it into the bedroom on a tray. He lay in bed. What a spoiled brat. I said, "I'll bet the Neanderthals didn't give you this kind of service."

He said, "I know. That's why I came back home to you. You give the best service." He mouthed kisses.

I growled at him. "I hope you took a cold shower." He sat up and I placed the tray on his lap. I said, "How would you like it if I went to Airets?"

Alex laughed. "What?"

I said I had been busy since he left. With all his biblical mumbo-jumbo about the Garden of Eden, I told him, I played a role to perfection: Lilith. With animated arm gestures, I said, "I was the *meister* of evil, the succubus seducing every man, sleeping with loneliness."

Alex said, "You have been busy."

I took the breakfast tray and put it aside. I crawled into bed. I said, "I slithered into their beds and sat atop them like I'm about to do to you."

Alex commented, "As I recall, Lilith became pregnant many times."

I nibbled Alex's ear. "Whose story sounds more exciting, mine or your story from a children's Bible?"

Alex said, "Yours of course. But I noted you haven't pushed me to tell my story; why Danziger told me he had to bring me back to the Serpent."

I said, "The three Godly senses. Robots have one, missing the senses of smell and taste."

Alex jumped, "How did you find out? Did I tell you?"

"Who cares? I can smell you, you animal. Anyway, trash your book. My story should be published."

Alex said, "You're talking as if you went to Airets."

I giggled. "How does it feel to sleep with a *Shedim*? Adam didn't appreciate me. But you, my dear, will enjoy my holy of holies."

We lay exhausted. Alex finally spoke. "You weren't the Serpent I visited were you?"

With my chin resting on his chest, I said, "I only wish."

Alex told his account. The robots lived without the enjoyment of the sense of taste; taste being essential to the Garden of Eden story. They could transform themselves into anything they pleased; they could have thumbs, critical thinking and the ability to make up stories, but the inability to taste, it seemed to them, denied them humanity. Being so rational and descending from beings who had for thousands of years hacked each other to death over religion, it pained them that they lacked a spiritual definition to their electronic existence. So what were they?

How sympathetic was my response? Talking tin cans they are, so who cares? Alex ignored my bitchiness and told me his returning to Airets didn't necessitate traveling to the sideshow places where animals were tame and humans dangerous. I crossed my arms and listened. He said, "Dan took me straight to the Garden. Thank God, I avoided all the cannibals."

Alex was appointed as Danziger's proxy. Near the Tree of Knowledge, Alex explained to the Serpent that enticing his progeny, such as Danziger, to eat forbidden food would be difficult, so Danziger designated him, Alex the accountant, to be his stand-in. Alex made it clear to the Serpent that Danziger wanted to be tempted and challenged. But Danziger wasn't much of an eater—no tongue, no taste—what can I say.

I interjected, "You spoke to the Serpent like that? Oh this is good."

Alex admitted the Serpent intimidated him. Flush against his skin was a tightly woven garment constructed from various autumn-colored leaves. He flicked his tongue and smiled at Alex. His head duplicated the shape of a wolf's, ready to devour. Alex tried to conceal his shaking, but to no avail, since the Serpent said, "Feeling nervous?"

Alex wasn't about to admit anything. He tried to divert the Serpent, suggesting a substitute test of temptation. "Give Danziger a chance."

The Serpent said if he did that, he wouldn't have the upper hand. And making the robot taste the forbidden fruit would be boring. Fun to him was seeing suffering. Alex told the Serpent, "Not everyone knows you hold the upper hand. I do." Alex sermonized, saying that even the most spiritual persons in the world were defenseless. They would drool and eat the forbidden fruit, after hearing the Serpent's shrewd lure of words, even knowing that eating the fruit symbolized cannibalism. "Humans have learned that evil actions often lead to happy endings."

I said, "Oh, Alex, you are good. Merton would be proud."

Alex said that the Serpent told him he enticed potential sinners with a ripe fruit, displaying its inspiring beauty, bringing it close so they can inhale its aromatic fragrance, and rubbing its firm texture against their cheeks. The great moment came when Alex told the Serpent that he knew the Tree of Life was a mother. It was untouched. And the Tree of Knowledge was a father.

The Serpent applauded. "You have learned your lessons well, Mr. Haralson. Eat heartily. Virginity and naïveté go together. Outside of those parameters, understanding and obeying laws allows you to enter an era of common sense. The curtain of open nudity must come down and a curtain of modesty must be unfurled."

Alex said, "I'm not a virgin and not naïve."

The Serpent went in for the kill, saying, "Good! Now you can bring out the worst in yourself. Why not practice greed and spite for entertainment? The possibilities are endless. Your inner soul contains so many more negative characteristics than ordinary animals' souls do. You're holding back, trying to convince yourself that you don't want to enjoy them. Go to a therapist. He'll relieve your guilt."

Alex retorted, "I've seen that way of life in action. It won't improve mine. I'm content with my life. Sinful activity is like dieting. We need food to eat. What we don't need for nourishment is alcohol, drugs, or a human body part to nosh. I'll pass on your suggestion. My soul will be nourished when I die, floating blissfully free. My eternity will subsist on intellect, without the necessity of a physical prop to commit evil."

The Serpent held out a human arm adorned with a papillote and said, "Bite it."

Stepping back and cringing, Alex said, "No."

The Serpent, its voice alive with seduction, pressed him, "It's all right. All the pilgrims partake. It's the tastiest nosh you'll ever nibble."

Alex said, "The pilgrims I saw returning from here, did they eat human flesh, as opposed to the symbolic fruit?"

The Serpent said, "They delighted in every bite, however small. They preferred mankind to define morality. You want God to do so."

Alex held his ground saying, "Yes."

The Serpent, trying to hold his temper, said, "You are the first person to have refused me, Mr. Haralson. Dishonesty is so natural. Were all those client tax returns you prepared for the IRS during your career kosher? Or might you have cheated insurance companies by claiming losses that were nonexistent? Have you ever shaken someone down for money?"

Alex stood silent, feeling guilty that he had cheated and feeling angry at the Serpent for bringing up the subject. The Serpent had made a direct hit on an exposed nerve. Smarmy and feeling in control, the Serpent pressed home his domination, "Gobble it up now, there's a good little Ukranian paskudnik."

"I will not. Insult me as you please, I will not eat human flesh!"

The crafty Serpent tried another tack, "And what about Margarita? Was she ever lonely while you were at work? Did she ever have an affair?"

Alex lost it. "You scaly son-of-a-bitch! Call my wife a tramp, would you?" He charged the Serpent, who retreated, cowering in fear. The Serpent, shocked at such brazen disregard for his place in rabbinical history, tried mollification, "Now, now ... Just a minute ... please. I didn't mean it in that context."

Alex didn't wait for an interpretation. He landed a kick in the Serpent's fishy-looking groin that doubled him over, pushed him to the ground on his back, took away the human limb the Serpent had been holding, and beat him between the eyes with it.

"Stop, you're hurting me!" The Serpent yelled. "He's gone *meshugga*! I can't stand pain! You passed the test! You passed the test already!"

I threw off the covers and jumped on top of Alex. "You protected my honor and you didn't eat any forbidden fruit. You're a *mensch*!"

Alex, lifting a finger, said to let him finish. Danziger was flying overhead. He saw and heard everything and went nuts. He morphed out of his bird form and jumped with joy. He yelled, "I'm saved."

I tickled Alex's chin and said, "Who cares about that *schmuck*? By the way, how many tax returns *did* you fudge?"

Alex said, "Don't make me answer that question." What mattered was everyone thought the fall of humankind happened with Adam and Eve. The prelapsarian period didn't end with Adam and Eve. They were only a snapshot in time. It's going to end when Danziger takes off into outer space. "Forget the meek. Robots will inherit the earth."

I thought Alex worked hard to find the answer to the missing commandment. He said that cannibalism was and would be the most important issue in the universe.

I asked why a snake was chosen as the enticer. Alex said the Serpent was a phallic symbol, devilish, smart and, most importantly, charming. "M, my dear, you already know that."

I said, "When we make love, I will slither all over you."

Alex continued, "When the commotion finished, the Serpent stripped off his costume. Underneath was cluster of electrons. Then he dressed in a costume that formed the shape of a smiling man. I saw white teeth and a plastic look. I recognized him immediately … it was Rabbi Merton."

I screamed, "It was Merton! Annabelle, you're in luck. I found your robotic soul mate."

Alex said, "Everyone broke out into laughter. Danziger had slipped away and returned wearing a robot costume. He stood next to Chapman who had come out from his hiding place. Alex put his arms around Danziger, Merton and Chapman's shoulders. His body completed a circuit. POW! He got an electric jolt that zapped him and caused his clothes to smolder. His hair stood up like a wheat field. They roared with laughter. Danziger sputtered, "I've never seen anything so funny."

Alex remained standing, fuming that he was the brunt of a joke. Chapman said, "Alex, don't be a stick-in-the-mud. Let's get a drink. Let's celebrate. Let's dig into that bag of evil spirits."

Merton said they could get a drink in his hut. "And the drinks are on the house." Alex dismounted his high horse. He would never pass up a free drink.

Meanwhile, the entire population of the Garden ran outside their huts to see what caused the commotion. The villagers looked at Alex and the robots in dismay. Adam and Eve ran a quiet operation. The robots knew the rules. A devotionally oriented couple, sort of Yiddisher Grant Wood types, stood in front of the crowd and said, "Could you please tone down your excitement?"

Alex said they left for Merton's hut. He, Dan, Chapman, and Merton went shoulder-to-shoulder without any electronic contact and skipped together as if they were off to see the Wizard. The inside of the hut resembled an untidy animal cage. White droppings were on the dirt floor. The hut was constructed of mud braced up on the sides with a few wooden beams. A fire burned in the hearth and smoke went up a small chimney. Light entered from the door, since there were no windows.

Chapman went over to a tall barrel, opened the lid, and dipped a chipped wooden bowl into it, ladling up some thick emulsion. The bowl had dirt embedded in the wood and the liquid inside was a brown swirl with bugs floating on top. Alex said he hoped it wasn't oil. The robots rattled with joviality. Chapman handed Alex the bowl and responded by saying, "Since we can't drink, you can have all our portions."

Danziger slapped Alex's back and said, "Drink up."

Seeing Alex's apprehension, Merton said, "Don't worry, it's kosher. They're locusts."

Alex said, "What, you're a rabbinic supervisor now, as well as being Rabbi Robot?"

Then, saying, "Here's to life!" Alex drank a couple of gulps. When he crunched a couple of locusts, he choked and coughed, spitting them onto the floor. The robots went into hysterics. Chapman fell on the floor.

Danziger said to Chapman, "Alex is having too much fun. We must transform back into humans and be like him." Alex jumped in and said, "Danziger, please don't. It'll be a disaster. Earth and Earthlings are not ready for your kind of fun."

I nuzzled close to Alex. "And now that you're home, Wolf Winslow awaits you." Alex said he was ready. He continued, saying he shed tears saying good-bye to Danziger. And believe it or not, Danziger, Merton, and Chapman were sad to see him leave. Before boarding the spaceship to return home, Alex said, sniffing, "Dan, will you be okay?" Danziger and Chapman began to cry. Danziger babbled like a baby. Who could believe it, a crying computer? Alex thought part of him wanted to stay with Dan and the crew for the rest of his life. Of course, he nixed that idea, knowing he'd be put to work fundraising for Robot Rabbi. The galaxy *Nova Easy Gro* sounded communal and they were family. And the Garden of Eden was Heaven. Alex said he would have sent for me. He continued, saying, "Who was going to miss us back home, our creditors?"

From the past, I knew farewells had always been hard for Alex. They give him a sense of loneliness. When he left with Chapman in the beginning, he was melancholy. Alex missed his dysfunctional family. He didn't know another dysfunctional family existed and he was struggling, loving both. Keeping in contact was going to be tough. Galaxy *Nova Easy Gro* wasn't a short weekend drive to visit. Alex said, "We have a family tree with branches including not just recent ancestors, but our future ones."

Danziger said to Alex, "Will you ever forget us?"

Alex said, "Never!"

Alex hugged Robot Rabbi and said, "I'll see you on the *beemah* next Shabbat." They laughed.

Alex said the robots were the instrument and compass directing him to the primitive places. They took him to the Garden of Eden. They pleaded with Alex to let them make Earth their home. Alex said it wasn't a good idea. "How would I introduce you to people? Meet Danziger, my great-grandchild thousands of generations into the future? And how would you socialize? Put a flowerpot on your heads and exist as furniture? Did you expect to meet and hobnob with the rest of the family?" Alex told them if he was caught talking to the furniture, the responsibility for madness fell on him. On occasion, everyone was caught spouting off to the wall, though not as a steady diet. From the robot's side, a sign reading DO NOT TOUCH would hopefully prevent an accidental bump. If it occurred, an "ouch" from a robot would render any house haunted. Dan, downcast, said he understood.

Alex said he heard our elders lived without all our creature comforts. Alex said, "We need to tell stories to our grandchildren so they pass them on to future generations." Alex said he imagined himself telling the grandchildren that milk was delivered to his house by horse and cart when he was a little boy. Dan doesn't need to hear the stories. He already knows them.

Alex entered *Northern Spy* for the trip home. A bottle of single malt scotch waited. He toasted everyone on the way home: me,

Chapman, Danziger, Roma, Merton, Annabelle, our children, and our parents.

Chapman said he'd drop Alex off at a relative's house so as not to be noticed. Wobbly from the robot scotch, Alex stepped off the spaceship right into the Rackham Fountain. What a bunch of comedians. The cops were not quite the relatives Alex expected to greet him.

alexander versus wolf winslow

Alex and I rode in a stretch limousine along M-14 headed to the University of Michigan television studios. They would host the live broadcast of the *Wolf Winslow Show* with my husband, Alexander Haralson, as Wolf's special guest. For the first time, a space traveler would tell all to a statewide audience about his mysterious adventure and about the robots he met.

Alex had prepared hard with his communication coach, Stanley Whitescarver. He remarked, toward the end of the lessons that there was no way Wolf could back him into a corner and then rough him up. Alex thought of another way to prepare. He arranged a room for private lectures at the Birmingham Community House. He invited close friends and acquaintances, cleverly using them as warm-up audiences. They heard pre-interview parts about the trip. At the sessions, Alex orated beautifully. It was evident to me that Alex had risen to the top. His form was assured, articulate, quick-thinking, and assertive. To his delight, his audiences gave him standing ovations. Alex, in a rough and ready state, anticipated meeting the *grosse k'nocker*, Wolf Winslow, head-on. What could go wrong?

I accompanied Alex to the warm-up sessions. My supporting role was playing the devoted and adoring wife. Alex warned me not to ask him during Q&A to explain the difference between Alex and Robot Alex. He feared he'd get angry and let out I was *schtupping* the robot. Alex suggested I wear nose and ear plugs. That way the possibility of me overheating and causing a scene would be diminished.

My contribution to earned family income consisted of selling chips of rock from our backyard, which I told audiences at the warm-up sessions came from Airets. "Alex brought back only a few samples." Sales were brisk. I also sold bottles of swampy aphrodisiac, which contained skin scrapings I harvested from Alex while he slept. The formula was the derma mixed with olive oil and garlic. To customers I said you apply the concoction to your lover's skin and wait for things to heat up. I even guaranteed results. No one returned a bottle for refund. One eighty-year-old woman told me the results were spectacular. She sent her husband grocery shopping, and as he left, the men of the fire and police departments arrived. Alex considered it tacky selling souvenir rocks and an aphrodisiac. But then, I wasn't the only crackpot in the family.

I felt completely confident of the show's success, doubts in my mind nowhere to be found. I envisioned, after the show, the spotlight of stardom would switch on and highlight Alexander Haralson as its newfound celebrity. As we exited the TV studios, I would look up into the sky and see rose petals fluttering downward. Tomorrow, a clamor nationwide would demand more television interviews with Alex. I envisioned answering a telephone call from Barbara Walters in about two weeks. A book detailing his adventures would soon be released. Worldwide recognition, in time, would be magnetized to Alex. It was big potatoes and I was excited.

I said, "Alex, I'm sure, after your book is published, it will be translated into many foreign languages, including Italian. I would be the perfect candidate to do the Italian translation." He replied that my suggestion reminded him of a Jimmy Durante line, "Everybody wants ta get inta the act!" He said he wasn't convinced it was a good idea. I might translate into Italian a different version of the adventure, not what he actually wrote.

Alex's attitude disgusted me. I said I noticed since his return that he was obnoxious and becoming worse. "Shouldn't you have mellowed and become more sensitive?" I said he had the opportunity to learn a great deal from his travels, having lived and learned about basic life under harsh and primitive conditions. I believed a person's personal qualities should improve when they have such outstanding adventures.

Alex frowned and treated me to another round of his philosophical drivel, saying that was the outcome of conventional wisdom. Authors traveled about on book tours, radiating in melodramatic fashion their essence. They expounded, saying they have been enlightened. They've been exposed to a different viewpoint and they've seen the error of believing in a Dark Age tradition. It changed the course of their lives, and since then, life had become unbelievably marvelous. Or authors used a tear-jerk approach. They've seen the doe-eyed underprivileged and want to improve their lot in life. Authors want them to advance and become like they are, over-privileged. Coming down from his soapbox, Alex said, "I will, my dear, admit I had a marvelous experience. My conclusion: bring back the Neanderthals or bring *forth* the robots."

I said, "Oh, Alex. You said it with such force. I love you."

Alex said, "Keep aggrandizing me. I love it." Alex moved closer to me. In a romantic voice, he said, "Did you really miss me while I was on Airets?"

I replied, "Absolutely, you snake charmer. Even though I am the Tree of Life, you may touch me."

Alex rubbed my thigh. He said, "I mean, were you sex-starved and hot as ever?"

I said, "I was ready and waiting for you to return every minute, so you could have your way with me."

Having to tell the story in front of a camera would be difficult for most people. But I couldn't imagine Alex crumbling under the pressure. Roman and Caroline would not be in the live audience. They told us they were jittery and preferred to watch the TV show at home. No matter how brilliant or foolish Dad appeared, they were embarrassed to admit they were generational links in the chain leading to the robots.

We arrived at the University of Michigan television studios, exited our limousine, and walked, holding hands, toward the studio's entrance. Numerous photographers already poised with cameras as we walked by greeted us with a barrage of blinding flashes. I glowed with cheerfulness. Alex had complimented me before we left home. He said, "You look smashing." His compliment projected a confidence in me to walk steadfastly into the bright lights. So did the satisfaction I had wearing the expensive outfit I purchased at the Linda Dresner shop. Alex wore University of Michigan colors, a navy blue suit with a soft yellow small-checkered tie. There would be no picture of us looking like *schlumps*.

The walkway to the stairs leading to the entrance was lined with ropes manned by security personnel on either side for crowd control, no red carpet treatment provided. What I noticed were the thirty or so placards being pumped up and down by hecklers shouting obscenities. I couldn't understand what was said, as the various groups drowned each other out. The signs said it all: "Down with the Jesus Hater" and "Death to the Mocking Infidel." The one that caught my eye and hurt the most was "Welcome Alien Adam and Nymphomaniac Eve." Even the robots had ta get inta the act! There they stood, waving with bright toothy smiles. I smiled at them and gave them the Italian version of the bird: raised right fist while slapping my bicep with my left hand.

Once inside the studio vestibule, we were greeted by one of Wolf's aides who escorted us to a private room where the interviewees and their families could freshen up and relax. The aide told us that Wolf would be by shortly to welcome us. She handed us a message. It was from Annabelle and Merton, wishing us well.

Wolf, we had learned from Stanley Whitescarver, was a flaming liberal. He was a staunch supporter of ACLU policies and loved to use cheap quotes from *New York Times* editorials on the air, holding them as maxims on the same level as the theory of gravity.

Alex told me that when Wolf called him with the invitation, the conversation between them deteriorated toward the end. Alex said Wolf was a bit too cavalier on the Bible. Wolf referred to the inscriptions on the tablets Moses brought down the mountain as "The Ten C's." Wolf then snickered that most days he followed about four, more or less. Alex called Wolf a pick-and-choose intellectual snob. Alex told him he respected people who were able to articulate and live by well-established principles. Many were businessmen, whom Alex said thought up new adages learned in life from getting their hands dirty. Alex told Wolf that Mickey Cohen, a notorious gangster, was honest by comparison when he was quoted as saying, "I adhere to the Ten Commandments, except when they're bad for business."

The news about Alex's trip to outer space spread like wildfire and media interest ballooned. Wolf's staff probably picked up the story and brought it to his attention. It didn't take much thinking on Wolf's part to arrange for Alex to be his guest. Where would he find a human being in the twenty-first century who traveled to another planet and resided in Michigan less than an hour from the studio?

Wolf visited us before the broadcast. His facial features resembled a wolf, his nose and mouth seemed to be two feet away from me, while the rest of his head stood about five feet away. His Paul Harvey baritone voice projected a warm welcome. He reassured Alex with, "No reason to be nervous." My impression, with his shrugged shoulders and pockmarked face, was he would have made a great Serpent.

An hour later, an aide came to our room to escort Alex to the studio. I sat alone, looking at a row of TV monitors. Each screen would project a different angle of the studio set. When Alex and Wolf had settled into their seats, one monitor had a head and body shot of Wolf, one of Alex, one of the audience, and one of Wolf over Alex's shoulder. The monitor with the red light was the one being broadcast on-air. I assumed someone would constantly switch angles during the show, creating excitement.

Wolf's hair was silvery, professionally combed over to cover his bald spot and lacquered, no pop-up strands. The set had a backdrop with pictures of Fidel Castro, Karl Marx, and Malcolm X. Wolf was seated so the TV picture gave the impression it was a group photograph. A camera zoomed in on Wolf to begin the show, while a background musical interlude played Hoagy Carmichael's "Smoke Gets in Your Eyes." A hip-hop tune came to mind that I thought fit the moment: "Back Stabbers" by the O'Jays. A narrator said, "Welcome to the *Wolf Winslow Show*." I heard applause. The on-air monitor switched to an audience of about twenty-five people applauding. Some men wore beards, the women wore plain or old-fashioned dresses with disheveled hair styles. Although these persons appeared gentle, it dawned on me they were academic sorts. I sensed they were the number two of a planned one-two punch, Wolf being number one. I believed they would ask Alex tough questions to undermine his story or intelligence. My underarms pumped sweat.

The preliminary opening by Wolf was a lead-in explaining Alex's travel to the Garden of Eden.

Then Wolf said, "Alex, robots took you to a planet in outer space. When I heard about it, I was skeptical. I still am, but I'll play along. How did the robots contact you?"

"It's pretty simple, Wolf. They sent one of them to my house and he knocked on the door. I answered and he introduced himself."

"What did he say?"

Alex said the robot told him there's a planet named Airets similar to Earth, which has a Garden of Eden. "He asked if I'd like to visit it, and I said, 'It sounds good to me.'"

Wolf asked, "Why did they contact you?"

"They learned I was a strong believer in the Bible."

"Don't about two billion people believe in the Bible?'

"It was narrowed down by the fact that I was a direct ancestor."

"You're an ancestor of the robots? You say it so straight-faced."

"Why wouldn't I? They said I was on the family tree. The robots said they came from the future to visit me in the present. I believed them."

Wolf gave Alex a significant look. "So they took you to a future Garden of Eden? It sounds loony."

"No, no Wolf. The Garden of Eden I visited on Airets was in the past, fifty thousand years earlier than our present time, one million years into the future."

Wolf squinted at Alex and loosened his tie.

Alex continued, "Since you're a man who expresses universal existence in scientific terms, I should have brought some dirt from the Garden to the studio. Better yet, my wife sells souvenir rocks. Would that have satisfied your curiosity? I'm just reporting what I saw. I'm no cartographer or geologist or intellectual or scientist. Maybe I should have taken a camera and brought my photo album. My purpose was to visit the Garden of Eden, not to explore the planet or make scientific observations. I'll let you and your professorial friends go there and dirty your hands."

"No, that's not necessary. It's just so hard to believe."

"History has always had extraordinary events and phenomena. That includes the past, present, and future."

"Let's take a caller. Paradise, Michigan, you're on the line."

A lady with a sweet tone spoke. "My pastor said the Garden of Eden was Heaven. Was it as beautiful as it's portrayed in the Bible?"

Alex said, "It was beautiful. The grove of trees was a Kodak moment."

Wolf asked, "How many people live there?"

"About one thousand."

"I don't get it. I can understand there would be more people than just Adam and Eve. One thousand sounds huge. Who were these others?"

"Some people were members of the priestly family. Some were pilgrims who decided to make the garden their new home. The bonding was the cultural beliefs and daily religious practices."

"Which were?"

"*Numero uno* was denouncing cannibalism. It was forbidden."

"Well, you don't say. Cannibalism was forbidden ... Blissfield, Michigan, you're on the air."

A man with a raspy voice spoke, "I've read lots about you and your nonsense already. You're living a fairy tale, pal. Even in the best of times, human beings always fight. Why should robots be any different?"

Alex said, "The robots I met saw the devastation of our way of life. If you think the robots were warmongers dropping atomic warheads, suicide bombers blowing up innocent people, or good old-fashioned pickpockets at work, you're wrong. They were down-to-earth people."

Wolf commented, "You said the Garden of Eden was a village. How was it laid out and how did the population expand?"

"The Garden of Eden was the name of the sacred temple grounds. A village surrounded it and in turn wheat fields surrounded the village. The population grew from births and pilgrims who made the Garden a permanent home."

The lessons with Stanley Whitescarver seemed to be paying off. Alex appeared relaxed and his answers fluid. I sensed that Wolf wanted to spice up the show with controversy. He already said that Alex's story was crazy. He couldn't let the viewers think Alex bested him. He had to shake off the ease of Alex's responses. On the monitor was a straight shot of, well, a wolf ready to attack.

I could sense that Alex wasn't enamored of Wolf. Up until now, they seemed to be civil to each other. How long it would last was anyone's guess.

Wolf, with a look of disdain, said, "Let's go back to the robots. How did they come into existence? And from your description, they took over the universe."

"They did, Wolf. That's exactly what happened. A man named Danziger Kantaphel predicted the Earth's devastation and morphed himself and his wife, Delores, into complex electronic androids. Danziger built a spaceship and together they soared into space. I met them. They were smart and gentle. In fact, all the robots I met were friendly with each other. I felt safe. There were no outerspace battle ships shooting laser beams."

Wolf said, "What was left of Earth?"

"Nothing. The robots said people dropped like flies from hunger and disease. Extinction became an acceptable word."

"Hemlock, Michigan, let's hear from you."

A southern drawl spoke, "You mean to say no one was left?"

"Earth was abandoned. I imagine Mother Earth's farewell to us was said with a breath of freshness, 'Hasta la vista, Baby, and good riddance.'"

"Hell, Michigan, go ahead."

A child's voice spoke, "Who ruled Earth?"

Alex said, "I don't know. I do know who didn't rule: humans. The biblical *'Dominion over the fish of the sea and over the fowl of the air, and over the cattle, and over all the earth and over every creeping thing that creeps on the Earth'* ended."

"Luther, Michigan, you're welcome to ask Alex Haralson a question."

An older-sounding lady spoke, "Was there an Armageddon?"

"Sinners and believers perished together without a war."

Wolf said, "Our ideals weren't realized, therefore we turned into robots?"

Alex said, "Oh no. The robots became the hoped-for melting pot. Learning tolerance was very difficult for humans, easy for robots."

"Tell me about the Serpent. Did it have legs?"

"The Serpent still had two arms and two legs when I met him. He hadn't yet been punished."

"Did you talk to him?"

"Oh sure. He tempted me, telling me about all the rotten characteristics I possessed and would have forever. I told him to mind his own business, and kicked the bejesus out of him."

"What? Wasn't he demonic, impossible to harm?"

"Look Wolf, the Serpent was Italian, a lover not a fighter."

"And what about Adam and Eve?"

"On a few occasions, I broke bread with Adam and Eve. They taught me that cannibalism was the quickest way to link humans to knowledge. Otherwise, you went through life as a nerd."

"Like a robot."

"Wolf, I think you've got it!"

Wolf took a question from an audience member. "My name is Foster Fulkerson. I'm a professor of Astrophysics at the University of Wisconsin. What you've described about robots and traveling into the future is nonsense. Transcending into the future is fantasy at best. Secondly, there is no way robots could have taken over the world. Robots have been developed with limited functionality. Robots with brainpower superior to human capacity, with unlimited powers, cannot be created in laboratories. In addition, to think that robots would function independently of human control is dangerous."

A man sitting near the professor stood and shouted, "I beg to differ!"

The monitor panned to the person who had interrupted. I muttered, "I know that person." I stood and leaned toward the on-air monitor to get a closer look. I felt weak. It was Chapman.

He walked over to the professor, grabbed him by the lapels, and lifted him a foot off the ground. The sound of clothes ripping could be heard, while Chapman spoke, "Don't you *ever* contradict what my ancestral grandfather Alex says, you cheese-head."

I sat, thinking, "*Oy vey*, here we go." The hallway soon filled with people screaming and running for the exit. For now, no way could I muster the strength to brush people aside to run to Alex. The guest room door flew open. One of Wolf's terrified aides ran in and dove under the couch and began whimpering.

The professor paled with fright. Chapman chattered his teeth a few times. Screams and the sound of chairs being knocked over enveloped the room. Chapman released Professor Fulkerson, who plunged top-heavy to the floor. On another monitor Alex and Wolf were at close quarters. I thought I heard Alex accuse Wolf loudly, "You're nothing but a Sunday morning bagel and lox Jew." I would see and hear the full exchange later on videotape.

On the audience monitor, I saw Chapman rip off his clothes. Exposed was his metallic nakedness. His body grew larger. Chapman walked toward Wolf, knocking over a standard of studio lights. Bulbs popped and electrical sparks exploded. Chapman opened a compartment in his body. He removed a scoop of dirt and dumped it on Wolf's head with a warning. "I hope this convinces you of the future's existence."

Wolf fell to the floor and cowered in fear. I was sure he was yelling for help. On another monitor, I saw three security guards jump over broken furniture and glass to rescue Wolf. They confronted Chapman, which was not wise. One guard shot a taser. Chapman grabbed the wire and wrapped it around the shooter. He grabbed the other guards, one in each hand, and raised himself taller. He dropped them in the catwalk. Chapman then shrunk to the size of a speck of dust, as the Ann Arbor SWAT unit arrived. Chapman was nowhere to be seen.

We were laying in bed that night, trying to sort out the evening's events. How did we get out of the studio? Who drove us home? We agreed the discussion was for another day.

I said, "Alex, you were fabulous."

"Thank you, my dear. Chapman, even with his eccentricities, opened the eyes of the world. A little overdone in making everyone believe what I experienced. No one is going to bed tonight with any doubt about the future course of humanity."

"What did you and Wolf say off-camera?"

"I told him spending a lifetime casting off former beliefs should be considered with caution. Just make sure any replacement beliefs stay non-judgmental of the past."

"Then what was the bagel and lox Jew part I heard?"

"Wolf changed his identity. He was no different from any other upstart religious dictator, updating past theories or beliefs, like selling an improved laundry detergent. I'm a middle-of-the-road guy who doesn't have to turn left or right to help a needy person. My father always said, "Know your enemies on both sides." That adage was etched in Alex's soul.

I picked up an apple from my nightstand. I said, "I've brought you an apple. Your favorite, a crisp Fuji." I tempted Alex. "Take a bite, sweetheart."

He said, "Is there any symbolism attached to it?"

"No, dear."

Alex bit into the apple and lay his head back onto the pillow.

I said, "Alex! Wipe that stupid grin off your face."

There was also a bowl on my nightstand, which I had brought up from the kitchen. I lay back and placed it on my stomach. Inside was a Topor's Old Fashioned dill pickle, coated with vanilla ice cream and dripping with chocolate syrup. Alex looked at me as I bit down on the pickle. I said, "Now here's plenty of symbolism."

The penny dropped suddenly and your father yelled, "You are! We did it!"

I giggled and fed Daddy a spoonful of ice cream.

Welcome to our world, little Roberta.